ELLA PERRI MYSTERIES BOOK 4

MOMENT
OF
TRUTH

KRISSY BACCARO

First Print and Electronic Edition: November 2024

Book Cover Design and Interior Formatting by 100Covers.
Editing/Proofreading by Megan Basinger

www.krissybaccaro.com

For my cousin, Gary

"The trust of the innocent is the liar's most useful tool."
—Stephen King

"Only when we are brave enough to explore the darkness will we discover the infinite power of our light."
—Brené Brown

Ella Perri's Family Tree

The Russo Connection

Rocco Russo

Maria Russo

Greta Russo

Sienna Russo

Cecelia Russo

Jamie

Gianna Russo

Salvatore Perri

Isabella Perri

Franco (Poppy) Perri

Olivia (Nonna) Perri

Grace Perugapo

Emma Perugapo

Gabriella Perri (Gabby)

Sal Perri

Luca Perri

Ella's father

ELLA PERRI

Lena Perri

Liv Perri

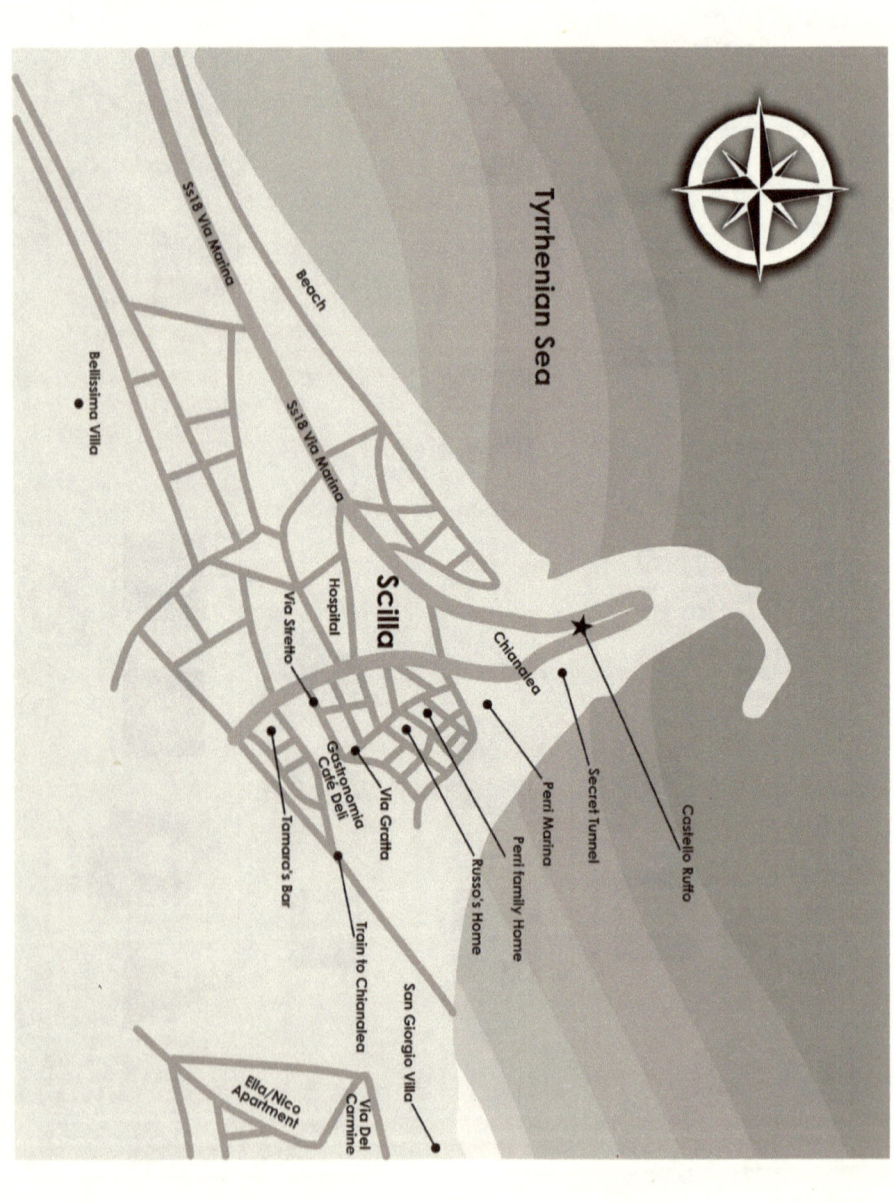

Tyrrhenian Sea

Bellissima Villa

SS18 Via Marina

Beach

SS18 Via Marina

Scilla

Hospital

Via Stretto

Chianalea

Secret Tunnel

Castello Ruffo

Perri Marina

Perri family Home

Russo's Home

Gastronomia
Café Deli

Via Gratta

Tamara's Bar

Train to Chianalea

San Giorgio Villa

Ella/Nico
Apartment

Via Del
Carmine

CHAPTER 1

MONA

His eyes won't let me go.

I'm standing next in line at the café counter when a strange sensation pulses at my temples, my vision fading fast to a narrow, feathery line. What remains are his eyes—penetrating, piercing. His unrelenting eyes won't let me go.

But I escape his gaze. Somehow, in my mind, I've slipped away, and now I'm a young girl again, sitting at my desk at school with friends I haven't seen in years. They fix their expressionless faces and impenetrable stares on a dark hole in the upper right-hand corner of the chalkboard.

Our teacher, Miss Olivia, glides about the classroom, and I'm mesmerized by her singsong voice, flowing through a radiant smile. But she stops fast when she sees me, and she shoots an icy stare as she climbs, cold and rigid, through the rows of desks toward me. As she continues to speak, her voice morphs into deep, dreary tones, forced through a tight grin.

I desperately attempt to make eye contact with my friends to see if they notice what's happening with Miss Olivia. But they concentrate their gaze on that dark hole in the chalkboard. I squint to make out what they're watching so intently. I gasp when I see it: it's me standing in line in the café when the man walks in. He's watching me, waiting for me, but I don't know it yet. Then he's suddenly upon me. I feel my breath escape now as it did then.

I want to know more, but Miss Olivia has finally caught their attention, taken it from that hole in the chalkboard. Taken it from me. They're enchanted by her. Spellbound. Lost.

I wipe my brow and pull at my shirt collar as the room, now devoid of air, leaves me breathless. I'm alone except for Miss Olivia, who approaches me uncomfortably closely. Face to face, peering into my eyes, mere inches apart.

All at once, the doors fly open for recess, and I'm whisked away with my classmates. We spill out onto the playground, releasing a collective sigh of relief. Shoulders and brows relax in the fresh air, and we disperse to our accustomed spots on the playground.

I float from one conversation to another, not adding anything of value and strangely unbothered by it. But as I pay more attention, I hear a difference in the surrounding chatter.

I can't explain the restless nervousness that pervades the conversations among my classmates. They seem to choose their words carefully, as if they are all on the edge of slipping and revealing something they were forbidden to say. Something everyone knows but me. I sense a build-up of emotion about to unravel.

I open my mouth to speak, but I can't form the words. And without warning, the chatter fades and the playground disappears. The day is over.

We burst through the front door as the last bell rings, our pace much quicker than usual. Katarina and Leah lead the way, muttering something I can't understand. Mia and Anna trail slightly behind, whispering to each other. I have to run to keep up with my friends, and the farther we get from the school, the tighter the knot in my stomach becomes.

"Come on," Katarina says, craning her neck toward us.

"Kat, please slow down," I say.

"We're going to miss it," Leah yells.

One small drop of rain falls on my nose. I pull my coat around me to keep the chill from finding its way inside. We're practically running, but then Katarina stops suddenly, perhaps because she forgot something at school. But when Leah stretches an arm around Katarina, and Anna and Mia flank either side of them, I realize it's not that.

"What's wrong?" I say. "Kat, are you okay?"

Others gather behind and around us, and together, we resume a slow, deliberate walk straight ahead. I place my hand against my burning chest as we draw closer to each other and then stop. All eyes except mine fixate on that same direction. A confusing mix of anger, frustration, and dread falls upon me as the close-knit crowd blocks my view.

In a small, open space on the right, I slip away and observe the grim expressions of my classmates, their eyes burdened with something terrible. I need to know what they see, but I'm petrified at the same time. Slowly, I maneuver my way to the front where Katarina stands. Her expression mirrors the sad faces of the crowd. A tear escapes the corner of her eye as she draws her hand to her mouth. As something erupts inside of me, fiery and strong, I reach for her. It presses down on me like a waterlogged blanket and squeezes out every breath. I place both hands on my chest and lift my head to the sky, trying to gulp in the tiny amounts of air available. I desperately search for someone to help me, and that's when I notice Father Anthony.

He's standing at the center where I shouldn't be looking. His outstretched hands come together, folded in prayer. Familiar faces draw close to him and a troubled young couple. I soon realize I know them. They're my parents, only younger. My father stares at the crowd with bloodshot eyes, dazed. His cheeks are wet and shiny. My father wraps his arm around my mother as she pleads for help through broken sobs.

Father Anthony motions for all of us to come closer. He speaks in an unfamiliar language, but everyone nods in agreement. I try to get his attention, but his eyes are on my parents and the space before them. I wave my hand to interrupt his gaze and to ask him one simple question.

His head snaps up. He sees me, and I am jolted by his piercing, unrelenting eyes. Those same dark eyes from the café. That's when I know I must look in the one place I'd been fighting not to look. The place on the ground where they're all staring empathetically. My stomach flips as I cast my eyes on a colorful scattering of my favorite flowers: tulips, roses, and peonies. A few small trinkets lie peppered among the flowers, and a framed photograph that looks like me, taken on my fifteenth birthday.

But I'm not fifteen; I'm twenty-five.

Notes lie among the flowers, some neatly folded, others open wide, exposing words of sorrow and encouragement. Notes all written with the same name at the top.

My name.

Mona.

I cup my hand to my mouth and swallow the scream-filled bile rising. An overwhelming scent of roses saturates the air, and all at once a sharp, painful piercing slices into my chest and then again at my side.

I look down, horrified at my dress, which is now covered in blood, and then I fall to the flowers below me, exposing my truth.

The café. Those eyes.

They all think I'm gone.

But I'm not gone. I'm alive.

I'm very much alive.

CHAPTER 2

ELLA

Fear and guilt are always present now, along with an incessant need to protect my family. Fear's powerful grip paralyzes me, confining me to my bed. My limbs weighed down, my mind swirling clouds of nothing. It dominates my dreams, my thoughts, my life. I am helpless under its spell, always looking over my shoulder, constantly calling to check on my family.

On the days I can get out of bed, dark, persistent thoughts plague my mind: Will Luca be back to exact his revenge today? Will it be tomorrow? Maybe I'll open my front door one day and he'll be on the doorstep waiting for me with a crooked, victorious smile at finding me. Or worse, he'll show up at the wedding. I shudder at the thought, and every thought about Luca, my ex-favorite uncle, wanted for the kidnapping and attempted murder of Gianna, his brother and my Poppy's lover. Wanted for kidnapping and murder of other women. Wanted for ruining our lives.

When fear is at bay, guilt kicks in, and guilt on its own is just as bad. There's no rest, no relief, no respite. Worrisome thoughts, dark and heavy, grab hold and squeeze tight. An active spirit of defeat, rendering my psyche to harm. My mind is trapped in a never-ending loop of thoughts about the past, replaying what I could have done differently. Questions I ask myself, knowing I won't find the answer.

If I hadn't gone to Italy and brought to light the darkness in our family, maybe we would still be whole. Imagine if I never found the storage unit packed with women's clothes and personal items. Had I not forced Luca at gunpoint to dig behind the vineyard for Gianna's body, a body I desperately didn't want to be there, we'd never have known she was alive.

To our surprise, Gianna, a grandmother I never knew existed, wasn't dead in the shallow grave as we had all expected. That was when we also learned about Grace, my mother's twin sister. Because Gianna's mother couldn't accept the idea of her unwed daughter having two babies, she had deliberately separated them at birth. Both Gianna and Grace had been kept from us all this time.

If only I hadn't pushed Luca to confess his sins against our family, shattering us like glass, cutting us deeply, irreparably.

But then I think I *should* bear the burden of these feelings because it's all my fault. I was the one who unraveled the tightly knotted, well-kept secret. What if I hadn't done that?

I'd still have my favorite uncle, and I'd still have my best friend, Jamie. Life would be simple, predictable, normal. We'd be living in blissful ignorance among the lies, protected from the shameful truth threatening to expose our shameful history.

That's when Poppy's voice comes to me, soft, soulful, reassuring, and I know that I did what I had to do. It was for Poppy, my beautiful grandfather; his last request. He needed answers to the parts of his story that were missing, answers he ran out of time to find. He needed me to release the dirty secrets. Rid them from our family, wash them clean so we could be free to live in the truth. He'd trusted only me with his secret. And, of course, I listened, although it was one of the hardest things I've ever done, but I would do anything for Poppy.

I'd struggled with it—the truth. It wounded us in ways I can't explain and damaged us beyond recognition. Exposing our family's secrets brought people I once loved and trusted into a light I never wanted to see. It complicated our relationships so that we are still trying to find our way back to each other.

"Sometimes doing what's right is the hardest thing to do," Poppy would say.

He was so right about that. But exposing the truth isn't the only difficult challenge. When everything was out in the open and we were reeling from the fallout, I quickly learned that the most challenging task ahead was to keep my family safe and pull us all together again. Like the frayed edges of an old, well-loved blanket, we were falling apart.

And I don't care what anyone says—not my mother, not even Nico. It absolutely *is* my job to put us back together. It's up to me to make sure we're safe. I can't wait around any longer. I need to uncover Luca's whereabouts somehow before he hurts us or someone else. There's got to be a way to move forward in our lives and at the same time find out where he is. Poppy would want that. "You can't stop living," he'd say. I do think I've stopped living the way I'm supposed to be living, and I'm trying hard not to do that.

I want to believe we can move on and everything will be okay. That's why Nico and I postponed the wedding. The happiest day of my life—postponed! Nico is one of the good outcomes of this tragedy. Had I never sought the truth, I'd never have found him.

My mother tries to reassure me it's different now. She says this time the police know about Luca, and thanks to Sienna, another good outcome, they're looking for him. He can't continue hiding. He doesn't have Aunt Lena anymore to protect him. Poor Aunt Lena—how devastated she was when she learned her husband had another wife.

Eventually, he'll have to come out of hiding.

But what if they never find him? What if the evidence that Luca left behind isn't enough, or worse, what if the evidence is gone by the time the police get around to finding it? Luca undoubtedly still has reach into the police force, to certain members who can make evidence disappear.

I push myself through the rest of the morning, sipping my coffee, brushing my teeth, running a comb through my hair, anticipating the next few hours ahead. Before I step out the front door, I check all the windows and the back door three times each. Then I give Hercules, my sweet, fluffy, three-year-old lab, a kiss on the head, toss him a treat, and grab my purse.

On my way to the door, I look through the window, and only when I see the empty doorstep do I open the door and step outside. I scan the street and houses and then lock the door behind me, checking it twice before walking away, ignoring the powerful urge to check again.

I slide into my car, close and lock the door, and quickly fire up the engine.

*   *   *

I'm waiting to see Luca appear on the front porch of Grace's beautiful Tuscan home when I arrive. My mother pulls in after me. It reminds me of the first day we finally came here to meet the parts of our family that were kept from us. My true biological grandmother, Gianna, and her sister, Sienna. My mother's lost twin, Grace, and her daughter, Emily. All hidden and unknown because of one man. The extension of love, history, and culture I had missed out on for so long. I embraced it all, at every chance, including Gianna and Grace shopping for wedding dresses with my mother and me. Having dinner together. I made sure to include them in my life at every opportunity I could, because life is short and nothing is guaranteed.

The same fear exists now, just as it did then. Luca must already be here, hiding inside the house, waiting to punish us and take us down together. A perfect opportunity. I glimpse the side of the house and almost see him emerging from the shore, walking on the sand to the deck where my mother and I will gather with our new family members. Our guard will be down, rendering us vulnerable.

I force him from my mind like so many times before. I won't let him take this moment from me. But there is no way to shut him out completely. Someone has to be on guard. Because no matter what I do, I know he can't be far.

Even in the long, arduous hours at the hospital, spending time with my patients, I sense Luca's presence behind the curtain. He's with me in the elevator, follows me to the help desk, and out into the parking lot. And even on the drive to my home with Nico, I sense his car trailing slowly behind me, headlights popping into the night, keeping far enough behind to predict my next turn. Headlights that follow me to my street. I drive past and they follow, turning where I turn, stopping when I stop. And I question myself—the validity of these moments. Am I imagining it? Is it just another car driving a similar path, and my mind is playing tricks again?

I don't think so. The intense fear within me as I pull the key from the ignition and place my hand on the door overwhelms me. I throw it open, jump out, and hug my mother. Then, without words, I pull her along with me up the porch steps because I think I see someone behind the cypress trees, and I can't get into the house fast enough.

CHAPTER 3

ELLA

Grace stands at the door with a peculiar expression on her face as we spill into the entryway. I close the door, lock it fast, and peer through the peephole. Then I spin around, aware of how crazy I must look.

"Ella," Grace says, concerned. She searches my face.

"Why wasn't this door locked?" I say.

"Ella, take it easy," my mother says. "What's going on?"

"I'm sorry, Grace—*Zia* Grace." I'm still getting used to calling her "aunt." "We can't take any chances. Luca is onto us. He knows where we are, but we have no idea where he is. He has the upper hand, and that's dangerous. We have to be more careful." I hear the scolding tone of my voice and I don't like it. I need to get a hold of myself.

"What's got you so upset?" my mother asks. "Did you see something?"

"No, I—not really," I say. "But I sense his presence." I realize how that sounds, but I also know what it's like to feel him around me.

My mother glances at Grace, her twin sister. "She's been right before."

Grace opens her mouth and then closes it, as if she is uncertain about how to respond, but then she adds, "Well, that's why we're all here—to come together and comprehend how to protect ourselves."

Aunt Grace ushers us to a small sitting area off the back of her house. It's right on the beach, similar to Emma's, but much larger. The flowing edges of her sundress bounce behind her as she leads the way. Ocean waves kiss the shoreline as little terns and seagulls push their beaks through the sand, digging for food. The sun is high in the sky, and a warm breeze carries the sweet, salty scent of the Tyrrhenian Sea and suntan oil.

I don't want to spoil our precious memories from the first time my mother and I met these beautiful women in our family. I don't want to shadow our joy at finding each other. But a dark presence who walks among us haunts our joy.

We greet each other, hugging tight and kissing cheeks, love and smiles and happiness bouncing off each other. I pinch myself. This is happening. We are together after all this time.

Positioned on two small sofas facing each other, we gather with a carafe of wine and a *tagliere di salumi*, a cold cut platter of cheeses, meats, and olives on a table at the center. We raise our glasses.

"To us," I say, and then we sip.

Gianna lifts hers higher, "*La famiglia é tutto.* Family is everything."

We sip, and my mother raises her glass. "And a toast to Ella's fellowship as a cardiologist at the hospital under Dr. Girofolog, one of Italy's best cardiologists." She gazes at me with a sense of pride, "I admire you, El. I know Poppy had something to do with your decision, and he is proud of you."

I smile, and we clink our glasses. She's right. Congestive heart failure claimed my Poppy, which created a desire to understand this terrible disease and help others suffering from it.

The marvel in each of our eyes, a spark ignited from our first encounter. The moment we found the missing and broken pieces of ourselves. Long-lost souls finally connected. Awe and wonder, like a mother's first sight of her precious newborn baby.

People use various names to describe the group they belong to: circle, clique, tribe, posse, crew, clan, family. But it's deeper than a simple label. It's a feeling of safety and comfort, like being home. The essence of a kindred group with shared interests, goals, and outlooks on life. It is unconditional love, not exclusive. The right group of people will always embrace others.

This is the way I feel about these women: Gianna, my grandmother; my great aunt, Sienna, Gianna's sister; Aunt Grace, my mother's twin; and Emma, Grace's daughter and my cousin. Most important of all, my mother, Gabby. And there isn't just one word to describe us.

We discuss every topic imaginable, except for Luca. No one wants to talk about him, but we have to. Poppy, in his own way, brought us together to complete our family and uncover the secrets that have haunted us for decades. He must have known that, to bring this story all the way to the end it deserves, we will need each other.

The corners of my mouth fall as anger and fear steal my smile. I take a sip and place my glass on the side table. "Well, I suppose we should get to it," I say, folding my hands in my lap. "Luca doesn't deserve our time and energy, but it's something we have to do."

"Yes, we do, Ella." Gianna's voice is smooth like honey and still catches me. To hear her speak after all this time. She removes the sunglasses from her face and rests them atop her silvery-chestnut wavy hair. "Whatever it takes, however much of our time and energy, we will do it. Because right now, Luca stands in the way of our happiness, and he has for far too long."

"And our safety," Aunt Grace adds, her finger pointed up.

"Especially our freedom."

Gianna, more than any of us, knows about not being free. The emotions she must've experienced when she initially opened her eyes beneath the dirt. The realization that Luca, the man she trusted, had buried her alive after she told him she didn't love him. How terrified she must have been all alone in the middle of the woods, trying to escape without being seen. In hiding for the rest of her life. Always looking over her shoulder, fearing that her new life could be shattered by her old one. Yes, Gianna, above all, understands fear profoundly, and she knows what it feels like to have her freedom taken away.

Gianna places her hand on my knee. "We will no doubt spend a lot of time together catching up on the things we've missed, but you're right—this has to come first."

Sienna's face peeks through the back door. Grace rises to greet her, and we turn to watch. Sienna half smiles as she approaches Grace. She wears a beige, wide-brimmed hat that matches the swirled pattern of her pants suit and high heels.

Something flashes through Gianna's eyes when she sees Sienna, and I can only assume the pain and confusion behind them.

Grace fills a glass of wine, hands it to Sienna, and together they make their way toward the sofas. Sienna smiles, kisses her palm, and waves in one universal hello.

I contemplate the parallel lives these two sisters have led. Years of separation, and the same man always between them. How ironic.

I imagine conflicting thoughts in Gianna's mind—Sienna, her favorite sister, married the very man Gianna had been hiding from, all in a desperate attempt to keep Luca from finding Gianna. When Luca realized that Gianna wasn't in the shallow grave he put her in, he became obsessed with finding her. Sienna believed that if she captured Luca's attention, he might forget about Gianna. What a sacrifice. What a gamble. Sienna and Luca did grow closer, and they fell in love. Sienna convinced Luca to marry her, hoping to end Luca's obsessive pursuit of Gianna. She convinced him that Gianna must not have gotten very far alive because, of all people, Gianna would have disclosed her location to Sienna. And it worked for a while until I exposed Luca for who he really is. At least that's what Sienna says.

Sienna greets Gianna with an awkward hug and a kiss on both cheeks. Gianna scarcely returns the hug, likely questioning Sienna's motive for marrying Luca. It did work, after all—he never found Gianna, even after several attempts over many years.

It's quite remarkable. I couldn't do what Sienna did. She gave up so much of her life. Was it dreadful for her to be with Luca, or did she come to love him? Had she ever witnessed Luca's dark side, or did he keep it concealed, even from her? Maybe she saw it and turned the other way. It's beyond my understanding how she could tolerate Luca, despite being cognizant of the harm he had inflicted upon her sister, Gianna, and the terrifying potential he possessed. Was it her unyielding love for her sister that made her do it, or was there another factor at play?

There's a storm brewing within us, far below the surface. An entire world of words unsaid, denied, hushed. Topics we allow ourselves to talk about and other things we can't. The atmosphere is thick, and Gianna has been quiet since Sienna arrived. Like a spell cast upon us all—a paralyzing, addictive spell.

Aunt Grace drums her fingers on the table. "Let's begin with the last piece of information we're sure about, which is—"

"Sienna," Gianna says, narrowing her eyes, "from what I recall, you were the last to see Luca, correct?"

Heads turn to Sienna.

"Yes, I suppose I was," Sienna says. "But that was a few weeks ago."

"It's still the most recent of any of us," Gianna snaps.

"Keep going," Grace urges Sienna. "Tell us what you know."

Sienna sighs. She removes her hat and runs her fingers through her hair while staring straight ahead. "Luca was acting strange when he came home from work that day." Her eyes pop to Gianna, waiting for her reaction.

"You mentioned this happened a few weeks ago," I say. "Can you be more specific?"

"It was three weeks ago," Sienna says. "We had plans to visit friends on the weekend, and I had to decline when Luca came home upset. He said to pack a bag because we had to leave for a while. He was frantic, manic even." Sienna puts her hand to her chest. "There was a knock at the door. The panic in his eyes—it was terrifying! He was desperate, pacing like a caged animal. I was afraid of how he might react if someone were to come in."

"Did he answer the door?" Emma asks. "Was anyone there?"

Sienna shakes her head. "No. We grabbed what we could and ran out the back door. I don't know how the intruders didn't see or hear us. We weren't that far from them."

"Did you ever see who was there?" I inquire, considering the possibility that it might have been Liv and me at the front door prior to our break-in.

"No," she says, breathless. "I couldn't look. I just wanted to get out of there."

"You must have been so scared." Grace says, shaking her head.

"I was terrified," she says. "Luca has changed over the past several months. It happened over time, so it wasn't obvious at first. I was worried he was involving himself in something unlawful again, or that he had possibly learned something about Gianna." Sienna glances at Gianna.

"But you went back to the house," Grace adds, "to Luca."

"We returned to the house after Luca said it was safe. But a few days later, it happened again—same thing. Luca rushed us out of the house, saying we weren't safe. Instead of going back to that hotel, I stayed with my sister, Maria. She convinced me to seek a private detective, and that's how I learned about Lena in New York and the storage unit. I witnessed it myself."

"You went there?" I say.

Sienna nods. "I contacted the police and brought them to the storage unit. After that, I never went back home. I called my daughter—Cecelia—" Her voice catches, overcome with emotion at the recent death of Luca's and her only daughter.

I clear my throat and explain the part of the story I'm familiar with. "Luca manipulated his daughter, Cecelia, and his granddaughter, Jamie. Sienna did not know the three of them had been colluding with one another all this time. They were the ones who also found my sister, Liv, and me in Luca's old private estate."

"You broke in?" Gianna says.

"Yes, we were looking for any information we could, and we found it. Luca, Cecelia, and Jamie held us captive in one of the private rooms. If it weren't for Nico—"

My mother shakes her head, her eyes blazing. "You and your sister could have gotten killed. It's bad enough what happened to Liv. . . . We almost lost her."

Gianna places a hand on my mother's shoulder, mother to daughter. "Thank God that didn't happen, Gabby. Poppy—Franco—must have been watching over his granddaughters."

My mother's eyes fill with tears. She nods and looks away.

We're all staring at Sienna as she fidgets, likely searching for the right words. "Gianna knows everything now. We talked at length on the phone. I called her right after I called the police . . . after I discovered Luca's storage unit." A catch in her voice, a look of horror on her face. "A while back, Luca's family was tight with the 'Ndrangheta, the mafia, and I feared he was working with them again. My fears were confirmed—Luca's involvement was much deeper than before. Much worse. How had he become so hateful?"

"Seems like you were fooled," Grace adds.

"We were all fooled," my mother replies.

Sienna gulps down the last bit of wine in her glass and pours some more. "We stayed at the hotel for two nights. On the second night, Luca called me, out of breath, desperate. I'd never heard him that way. He made me promise to stay at the hotel no matter what. He wouldn't tell me anything else, and I knew better than to ask. Then he hung up. I was so afraid he'd found Gianna."

"So you stayed at the hotel the whole time?" Grace asks.

"I'm unclear about the reason we're revisiting all of this," Emma says, giving Grace a look.

"It's okay," Sienna says. "It helps to know Luca's last moments. Maybe his next move. Yes, I stayed at the hotel because I was too afraid to leave. Besides my sister, Maria, I had nowhere else to go. I didn't want to get her involved."

"Sienna, wait—I might have been the last to see Luca," I say.

"Why do you say that?" Sienna replies.

"Liv and I broke into your house," I continue. "I initially believed that we might have been the ones at your door that day, but you mentioned that someone knocked multiple times. We definitely did not knock. We knew Luca lived in that house with a woman, but we had no clue it was you. It couldn't have been more than a day or two at most after that first incident you described with the knocking. Liv and I were probably the ones who put Luca in a panic when you saw him, like that at the hotel." I pause. My blood boils as I remember what Luca and his deranged daughter, Cecelia, subjected us to—especially Liv.

Sienna's eyes widen like she's remembering something. "Ella, go back to what you said before about the hallway in my house." She's referring to a conversation we'd had when we first met at the hospital. "The secret hallway. Where did you say it was?"

"A secret hallway?" Gianna says. "This is absurd."

Chills prickle my skin, remembering when I'd first discovered the secret door to a hidden corridor. A corridor of evil. "It was like nothing I'd ever seen before. You go up the stairs and stop at the landing." Sienna nods. "You face the wall that has all that busy, crazy wallpaper."

Sienna nods again. "I always hated that wallpaper."

The wide eyes surrounding me are a mix of astonishment and fear. "Hidden in the design is a lever. You have to know precisely where, otherwise you'll never see it. If you press it a certain way, a door opens to a hallway with four or maybe five rooms."

"A hallway with rooms?" Sienna says. "I don't believe it. I would have known something like that was there."

"I can show you myself. It's real, and it's there," I say, growing uncomfortable. "It is impossible to see just standing in front of it. That was the point. I would never have known if I wasn't told how to find it. The intricacy of detail in the design, created for that exact reason, so no one would ever know it existed."

"How did you know about the secret hallway, Ella?" Sienna asks.

"I found the blueprint to your house in an old abandoned mansion that either belonged to Luca or his father. I tracked down the blueprint's architect in Fiesole. He is a sweet old man named Giovanni. Since he designed yours and Luca's house himself, he showed me how to find the secret hallway and gave me directions to your house."

I recall Giovanni's protective wife, doubtful, reluctant to let me enter her home. Not until I started talking about Poppy's wish to expose a secret which was threatening our lives. How her husband might be the only one who could help us. She allowed only me inside. Nico and Liv had to wait on the porch.

Sienna puts her hand to her mouth and then drops it to her side when I finish talking. "I don't know what to say. Please accept my apology. I truly had no awareness of this. I suppose I shouldn't be surprised about a secret hallway, knowing what I know now about Luca. Nothing should surprise me anymore. I can't imagine the things I don't know. I'm so mad at myself for being so naive. And I can't unsee what was in that storage room."

"Don't be so hard on yourself, Zia Sienna," Grace says. "We're working together now."

I cringe when I recall my emotions upon first discovering the storage unit as well. All those boxes with women's belongings—hair clips, hats, scarves, pieces of jewelry each in its own box, like trophies. I probably opened ten of them before I had to stop.

"Luca is very cunning and wise," I say. "He is skilled at hiding things. He has been in our lives all these years pretending to be the exact opposite of who he is." My stomach curls at the betrayal. "I'm learning that he's just like his father."

Emma, who had been quietly watching the conversation unfold, places her glass on the table and straightens up. She tucks a piece of her shiny, dark hair behind her ear. "I'm not gonna lie—this is a lot to absorb. I can't believe Luca has affected so many of us. I don't know where to begin. How could he possibly entertain the idea of harming my dear Nonna?" Her eyes fill and her face scrunches up. "And marrying her sister?" She turns to Sienna. "You had no idea about the women he abducted?"

Sienna shakes her head. "No, not one."

Emma crosses her arms, her face puzzled. "How could you not have known? How did you not suspect something was off when he'd be gone for long stretches of time? Did you believe he was traveling for work every time?"

I detect small traces of Gianna in Emma's features and gestures.

"Emma." Grace gives her daughter a look.

"I'm trying to understand, Mamá."

Gianna shifts her position on the sofa and crosses one leg over the other. "Did it never cross your mind during all the time you were together—married—that perhaps you should consider getting away from him at some point? Did you think he'd changed? That he was no longer dangerous because he was with you?"

"Yes," Sienna says. "At one point, I thought I should get away. And yes, I believed he had changed. He was different— attentive, calm, present—or so I thought."

Gianna's eyes narrow as she stares at Sienna. "Sienna, I think you're very lucky to be alive. Luca is a ticking time bomb. We've always known that, even when we were kids. I'm sure you meant well at first. At least I can't conceive it any other way. Your beautiful heart must have had pure intentions, I have to believe. I'm attempting to grasp the entirety of it."

Sienna is quiet. She seems deflated and tired. She takes a sip of her wine, glances at the floor, and doesn't reply.

My mother tries to bring some peace and order, as usual. "Right now, there's an overwhelming mix of emotions and questions. So much to process—too much." She runs her fingers through the top of her thick, wavy hair like I've seen her do a million times when she's trying to focus. "This is going to take time. We all know that. Little bits and pieces will surface throughout the next few days, weeks, even years. It's too much right now."

"You're right, Gabriella," Gianna says. "You're absolutely right. Now is not the time to let our emotions get the best of us. Now is the time to pull together. A unified force against the man who has affected each of us. We need to stand strong and bring him to justice."

Gianna rises from the sofa, walks over to Sienna, and hugs her.

When she returns to her spot, she faces me. "Let's start with you, Ella." The way she says my name is sweet, soft, a touch of soul, grandmotherly. "Tell us about the architect and what you found in those secret rooms or anywhere else you've gone where you've uncovered Luca's dirty secrets."

I take a deep breath and begin.

CHAPTER 4

ELLA

As I tell how I first discovered Luca's betrayal, their eyes remain fixed on me. How he'd pretended to be a caring uncle, deeply invested and involved in my life. Inserting himself into my life to become one of my favorite people. Feigning worry about my trip to Italy, calling every day to check on me. He'd even questioned why I would take Poppy's diary with me to Italy, a diary he later stole. And the worst part—how he had orchestrated an elaborate plan to insert Jamie into my life. What a bonus for him when we became best friends. He used her to gain knowledge of what I was doing, what I might know. He used us both.

"Let me get this straight," Emma says, tucking one knee beneath her. "Your best friend, Jamie, is Luca's granddaughter. That makes her your second cousin?"

"Something like that," I say.

Emma squints and tilts her head. "But Jamie was never aware of this."

"Correct. Not until the end."

"But she still continued to help Luca, even after she understood the connection."

21

"Yes," I say.

"And at some point, Luca realized the special bond between you and your Poppy," Gianna says, "which made him extremely uneasy."

Emma props an elbow on the arm of the couch and rests her chin on her fist. "He went to such lengths using his own family—and having a secret family—for his selfish needs."

Grace turns to Sienna, her forehead creased. "Jamie is yours and Luca's grandchild?"

Sienna nods. She wraps her arms around herself and gives a slight rock back and forth. "Yes. Luca and I had Cecelia, God rest her soul." She makes the sign of the cross and continues. "Jamie is Cecelia's daughter. Luca had control over both of them. But Jamie didn't know at first about Luca's true intentions for her friendship with Ella. And I did not know about any of it."

"I'm sorry for your loss," Grace says, then turns to me. "This has got to be one of the hardest things for you, Ella."

I swallow hard. "Yes. Next to losing Jack and Poppy, it is one of the most heartbreaking things I've ever had to deal with. The level of betrayal . . ." I shake my head.

I explain that, after Luca realized I knew he was the one responsible for Gianna's disappearance and attempted murder, he followed me to Italy. He stayed near the villa where I was staying. We revisit the conversation about how we ended up in the woods behind the vineyard—making Luca dig in the spot he claimed to have buried Gianna. How Marco, his nephew on Lena's side, aimed his gun at Luca as Nico and I watched for any sign of Gianna. Then the realization, the genuine shock on Luca's face, when he discovered Gianna's body wasn't there. The depth of that moment. It was the first time I thought Luca seemed so small. From that moment on I no longer saw him as my charismatic, larger-than-life uncle but a weak, despicable man.

Emma's eyes blaze. "So you went to an old, abandoned house of Luca's, found the blueprint of the Montepulciano house, and brought it to the architect. How did he show you the secret rooms if they weren't already on the blueprint?"

"Giovanni revealed it to me with an overlay of the exact layout that included the secret hallway. He marked the map and wrote a few notes in the area I needed to look. I'll show it to you the next time we see each other.

"It's fascinating. Giovanni called it a house within a house. From the road, people could have no knowledge of the secrets inside. But, he said, over time, neighbors and others began to suspect something was off about the house and Luca. Rumors started about Luca's connection to the 'Ndrangheta—the mafia.

"Giovanni also told me that Luca's father gave Luca the abandoned house where we found the blueprint. Both father and son used that house for their separate, private lives. It's disgusting. I can't explain the overwhelming feeling of dread in that house. The basement was just . . . I don't want to think about what went on there."

"It's the same house where Angelina was attacked," my mother says.

Gianna straightens up. "Luca had to be behind that."

"He was watching everything," I say. "Otherwise, he wouldn't have known to go back there. He must have assumed after Angelina was there that I would go there next." The memory of Vinny's phone call telling me what had happened is like a punch in the gut. "Angelina said there were at least two assailants and they were young and strong. Sent by Luca, no doubt. He knew we'd be back, and he made sure he was the one to find us next."

My mother clenches her fists. "That son of a bitch broke into Ella's house when she went back to the states. Stole Poppy's diary. He hid in her attic!"

Everyone gasps.

"He's always one step ahead," she groans.

Gianna rises from her chair and approaches me, open-armed. I stand and we embrace. "Oh, honey, you have gone through so much."

"Never as much as you," I say.

She pulls back and smiles.

"What was it like in the abandoned house . . . in the basement?" Grace asks. "Do you mind talking about it?"

My stomach sickens. "It's hard to put into words," I say. "It was so dark, cold, and depressing . . . and dirty. The smell was heavy, musty, and smoky. There was a small room on the side. You wouldn't know it was there if you looked straight down. It was only when I got close to the room I noticed it was there. It made my skin crawl." I rub the chills in my arms. "There was wallpaper in that little room and it was peeling everywhere. And there was a bed."

"A bed?" Gianna blurts.

I nod.

Heads shake at the horror of it all.

"How did you come to know about this house?" Emma asks.

"I found it in a bunch of pictures when we were packing up some of Poppy's things at the cottage. I showed the picture to Angelina, and she recognized it right away—a house she had been to as a child. She took me to it."

"Angelina is your friend?" Gianna says.

"Yes, I met her on my first trip to Italy and stayed at her villa. We became very close. You'll meet her one day."

"Well, I'll be damned," Grace remarks, amazed.

"We all knew each other up and down that coast," Sienna says. "It wasn't difficult to find someone connected to someone else you knew. But it was hard to keep things private."

"Unless you are Luca."

Then I suggest, "We need a plan to keep Gianna and the rest of us safe, starting with keeping our doors locked, whether or not we're in the house. We need to close and lock our windows when we're not in the room, and especially when we're not home.

We should get security cameras on each of our houses, including the cottage."

"It's like we're prisoners," Grace says.

"We need to be vigilant," my mother replies firmly.

Emma suggests we hire a private investigator, and she mentions a few names from her connections at the university.

Gianna fiddles with her necklace and seems restless. "I like the idea of hiring a private investigator, but the person has to be someone we trust. Do you trust these people you mentioned, Emma?" she says.

"I don't know them, but they have excellent reputations. I'll check into it."

Gianna sighs. "I worry about getting the police involved because of Luca's and his father's connections to many of them in the police force."

"The police around here are good, Nonna," Emma reassures her. "And I respect how you feel about this, especially because of your experiences with Luca. That's why I'm suggesting someone private. Money is not an obstacle. We'll do what we have to, no matter how much it costs."

My mother volunteers to contact a few security companies and get us all scheduled for installment.

I notice Sienna is quiet. "Sienna, are you okay?"

"Oh, yes," she says. "I'm sorry. I'm just listening and processing, but I very much agree with what you are all saying."

"Okay, good," I say. "What do you think about putting a small, inconspicuous camera at your house in Montepulciano? Maybe up in a facing tree or in the planter by the door. If we see Luca, we'll know when he got there. We might see from which direction he came. We can follow him."

Before Sienna can answer, my mother interrupts. "I don't like the sound of that, Ella. Think about what happened the last time you went sneaking around. No, you will not do that again. I can't handle it."

"We'll have the private investigator do it," Emma says. "They can watch the house for a few days, take pictures, and install the cameras. Then, if they see Luca, they can follow him."

My mother nods, the lines around her eyes softening. "I like that much better. The more encounters we can avoid with Luca ourselves, the better. Have someone else do it."

A lively conversation ensues about where to install cameras. Gianna suggests on the house where Luca and Poppy grew up, a few trees near the bench in the vineyard where Luca was last seen with Gianna, at the market, the marina, Angelina and Vinny's villa. My mother suggests we get one installed at the cottage and at Luca's house with Lena.

Everyone's nodding, talking, planning as I fade to the background, thinking of all the reasons it's better that I'm the one who goes to the Montepulciano house. Thinking I should try to get back inside and look for signs that he's been there.

There's a loud rapping at the front door, immediately silencing us.

Grace rises.

"Wait," I whisper as my heart pounds in my chest.

A minute later, the knocking resumes. Everyone stands and freezes with panic-stricken faces.

I whisper again to Grace, "Is there a way to see who's there without being seen?"

Grace nods and treads up the stairs to a window above the door. She comes down seconds later. "It's a florist," she says, puzzled.

"Do you want me to answer it with you?"

She nods and mouths, "Yes."

Grace and I walk together to the front door. My whole body trembles as we near it. Everyone else follows close behind.

"Special delivery for Grace Peragrapo," says a young man holding a beautiful bouquet. "Is that you?" Grace gives a slight nod. "Must be a special occasion," he adds, handing Grace the flowers and showing her where to sign. "This is our most exquisite bouquet."

"My anniversary is coming up," she says. "Maybe it's an early gift?"

I study the wide-eyed, ambitious young man, his dark hair slicked to one side. I notice how the left side of his lip lifts higher than the right, almost like an Elvis Presley grin, but ugly. I look out at the street but don't see his vehicle.

"Where is your car?" I ask.

"Oh, I had to park way down the road today. No spots," he says, waving his hand to show how far down it was.

"What's the name of your company?" I ask.

"It's all on the card with the flowers," he says. "The name of it is Beautiful Flowers." We thank him and watch him proceed in the direction he says he parked before shutting the door.

The flowers are a gorgeous, gigantic blend of whites and pinks, peonies, dahlias, and a few others mixed with lush greenery. We pull off the plastic covering while walking back into the living room. A small card falls from the bouquet. I pick up the card and hand it to Grace. I take the flowers from Grace while she reads the card.

A second later, the card drops to the floor as her hand goes to her mouth.

I retrieve it and read the note aloud:

A lovely bouquet for an equally lovely group of women. Hope you're enjoying every minute. It could be your last.

CHAPTER 5

MONA

I awaken in darkness, chilled by the dampness of the cold floor beneath the tiny carpet square I sit on, the rough wall behind me, and the reality of how I got here. Eerie silence gives way to an unsettling stillness, as if the world has ended. How did I let this happen?

My body is heavy, lethargic, my mind fuzzy with the edges of details I can only grasp at. I pull my legs in as close as possible so only my toes will touch the hard floor. The icy wall at my back is rough, like the bricks my father once made by hand for our fireplace. Ice cold. I slide my hand across the blocks that form the wall and then I pull both hands to my face, but I cannot see them.

I recall, as a child, when my father rebuilt the bricks of our old crumbling hearth and mantle. How he carefully laid one brick down upon the smoothed mortar. The rhythmic movement of my father fascinated me, the repeated pattern of laying a row of bricks, spreading the mortar over and between them, and then adding another layer of bricks. I remember at the time thinking how odd that the lines didn't run evenly down. I had asked him why the lines of mortar that extended between the bricks didn't connect. Why was there a difference in positioning between one row of bricks and the next?

"You stagger the row of bricks to strengthen the wall," he'd said. "And it looks better."

I remember how he glanced over at my mama, who was playing the piano. How I adored listening to her play.

I trace the wall again with my hand, confirming the uneven rows of the sturdy walls around me. I could try to get up and explore my new surroundings, but that might take any energy I have left, which isn't much.

I shift to relieve the numbing in my bottom to find that a dull, surprising pain throbs at my side. The spot feels warm and wet. I brace my arms against it, and a small voice cries out. It's my voice that echoes back. Somewhere between the pain and the echo, thoughts are forming. Dark, frightening thoughts, which I reject.

Thoughts about the man who walked into a hardware store as I crossed the street on my way to the café. When I first spotted him, I paid no attention except to notice that he walked with a slight limp. But when he stepped into the café just as I finished paying for the pastries, I took heed of his presence. He stood uncomfortably close behind me in line. *Some people have no social awareness,* I remember thinking.

I wanted to get a few more baked goods, but I felt an urgency to pay for my pastries and get out of there. The cashier placed the change into my clumsy hands, and the coins fell to the floor. I left them there, took my bag of pastries, and slipped away. It couldn't have been more than a couple of minutes when I sensed a presence behind me, detected the sound of shoes clicking. When I walked faster, the footsteps came faster. When I stopped, they stopped, picking up again when I continued. I knew it was him.

When we were side by side, I was about to ask him why he was following me, and he asked me for a light. I said I didn't have one. He smiled and said, "That's okay, Mona." I remember wondering how he knew my name and questioning if his face seemed familiar.

"Have we met?" I'd asked, feeling embarrassed.

"Yes, of course we've met," he'd said. "It's Lorenzo. You know my wife, Gianna."

I still wasn't connecting. "I don't know anyone named Gianna. Maybe you have me confused with someone else. Or maybe we've met through my father."

"Yes, your father," he repeated. "That must be it."

My father's tailoring business was well-known around town. Everyone he met loved him because he made them feel like family, often inviting customers to our home for dinner. My father's warm personality and his extensive farming and agricultural knowledge attracted people to him. My mother was the same way, catering to everyone she met and anyone who accompanied my father home. I thought that must be why he was so familiar.

"Do you work with my father?"

"I used to," he'd said, adding, "Can I interest you in an espresso before you head home?"

This man distracted me, noting his age seemed closer to my father's than to mine. It was unexpected, considering his age and being married, that he would want to have coffee with me. Maybe he was hoping to make a good impression so I would talk favorably about him. I should have known better.

I don't know why I even considered it.

Perhaps he noticed my hesitation. "Just one," he'd said.

Maybe in my mind I reasoned the need to go back to the café for the pastries I hadn't purchased. "Well, I guess I can squeeze in a quick espresso before I head home."

As we sipped our espressos, I thought how interesting Lorenzo was, how charming, how smart. I would mention his name to my father as soon as I got home.

The espressos went fast, as did the time. I remember feeling anxious about arriving home late for dinner and that I should call my parents to let them know. I told Lorenzo I had to get going. He must have noticed my frequent glances at the clock above the café counter. Maybe he sensed I was rushing when I got up to order the remaining baked goods I wanted. I remember his smile, still pleasant, but not quite reaching his eyes.

He offered me a ride home, and I'd agreed. He seemed like a perfect gentleman, offering to hold both bags of pastries, insisting on holding the café door for me, and even opening the passenger car door for me before getting in on the driver's side.

With the pastries in the back seat and the sun setting behind us, we drove off down the road, and I couldn't wait to get out of the tight shoes I'd been wearing all day working at the tailor shop.

"Next street on the right," I'd reminded him as we neared my neighborhood.

It wasn't until we passed the second intersection and he apologized again for missing it that I started to worry. Lorenzo insisted I meet his wife. He mentioned our uncanny resemblance and suggested that it would be a small world if we discovered we were related in some way. He mentioned having something for my father that he wanted to grab while we were there.

It was just around the corner.

I'm unsure if the dark, menacing house that stood before us was a bad dream or if the house was real and I was in denial. It was pointy and withered, leaning into the shadow of a tree, like an old man leaning on a cane. Paint chipped in various places. Darkness in all the windows. The porch with its missing spindles reminded me of an unsavory, shifty grin.

"You live here?" I'd asked.

"Yes," he said matter-of-factly, but his offended eyes revealed his true emotions. "It might take a minute to find what I need, so you might as well come inside."

My entire being warned me against going. But I ignored the feeling in my stomach and the warnings in my head. Against my better judgment, I followed him inside the house.

"Please sit down." He pointed to one of four chairs around a table and waited until I sat. The house was dark and murky and smelled like mildew. Any warmth or love that this house may have once emitted was absent. It was chilling to the bone to think anyone could ever live here. I watched him shuffle around, looking under papers piled on the counter, picking them up and moving them to the other side, opening drawers, looking for the important item he insisted I give to my father.

"Would you like something to drink while you wait?" he'd asked.

"Drink?" I said, annoyed. "No. I need to get home." The tone in my voice likely mirrored my expression. I felt my cheeks grow hot and my eyes burn, my eyebrows squished together. I spoke through clenched teeth. Yet, regardless of my obvious opposition, he filled a glass of water for me and another for himself. And then he sat down across from me at his dirty kitchen table.

And when I stood, he stood. When I stepped back, he stepped forward so close that our noses were almost touching. I pulled away, but his arms caught my back. And then he kissed me fast and hard. Not good at all. He smeared his lips onto mine and pressed against me. I pressed my arms against his chest, pulled back fast, and pushed him away.

"What are you doing?" I said as he yanked open a kitchen drawer, clearly offended. "What's wrong with you?"

Metal objects collided with each other as he rummaged through the drawer. Then I heard metal sliding out of something. Like a sword from its sheath.

With his right hand, he gripped the black handle of a large, shiny butcher knife and held it in the air. A crazed look formed in his eyes. He stepped forward again, but not as close. Did he want me to see what he was about to do?

"You're all the same," he spat furiously.

I panicked, rapidly thinking of what I could say or do to change his mind, change the trajectory of this moment. "That's not true—we're not all the same," I yelled, not really knowing where to go next. "I'm not like other women. I—I actually care."

"Oh, do you?" he chided. Still holding the knife, a line from his face fell, and something shifted in his expression.

"Yes, you just caught me off guard," I said. "I wasn't expecting you to kiss me. I don't even know you."

"I like the element of surprise." His eyes darkened. "And I like you."

No.

"But what about your wife? What about the item you want me to give my father?" I tried to redirect his attention back to the reason we had come here in the first place, but at that point, I doubted it was the true reason.

The knife stayed securely in his grasp, but his expression grew sullen and melancholy. And I knew there wasn't anything for my father. He probably didn't know my father. Did he even have a wife?

"We can be friends," I blurted, desperate, my heart beating wildly in my chest.

"I don't need a friend."

"We could start slowly, go on a date, get to know each other. Come to dinner tonight." I spat the words out, saying anything to get us out of the house.

He drew near, feigning interest, the knife still at his side. He pulled me closely, gently. Was he giving thought to my desperate plea? He studied me, his eyes racing over my hair, my eyes, my lips, and back to my eyes. And then something flashed through his dark stare, as if a war raged within him. As if the true reason for his fury was right in front of him.

But why me?

And that's when it happened. Pressure and pain that took my breath away. It grew deeper, agonizing, frightening. And when he pulled the blood-stained knife from my waist, he held his cold, hard gaze on me. My breath caught as I pressed my hand against my side.

The room spun around me. I closed my eyes to make it stop.

The next time I opened them, I was here in this dank space. Thoughts of my parents, my family and my friends, undoubtedly sick with worry, flashed through my mind.

I cannot die here.

CHAPTER 6

ELLA

My mother and I return to a sleeping San Giorgio Villa. Angelina and Vinny's street exudes an irresistible charm, with silence broken only by the sweet melodies of crickets. Dimmed streetlights poke through fog, casting a smoky mist against a black backdrop.

Where the dark one hides.

We rush inside, close and lock the door, and head to our rooms, but we're stopped by Angelina standing at the foot of the stairs in her bathrobe, hair pulled to one side. She had read my text, warning her that Luca or someone connected to him might come her way.

She hugs both of us for a very long time before letting go. "I have a terrible feeling about this," she says.

We follow her to the kitchen, and she pours each of us a glass of water.

I explain that, after receiving the note and the flowers, I called all the florists in the area to see if any deliveries went to Grace's house, but none had. And no local florist called "Beautiful Flowers" exists. They had to have come from Luca. How easy it was for him to find us, send us something. What will he send next time? He's toying with us. Being in control is what he loves most. He thrives on it.

Before that knock on the door at Grace's, I was confident in our plan. Other than some tension between Gianna and Sienna, it is clear that we want the same thing: to catch Luca, to be free from his tyranny. To be out of his watchful eye. To feel safe again. To get justice. And it's evident that we can't waste any time.

My phone buzzes, and I jump. A text from Emma: *"I was hoping we could meet somewhere and talk without the rest of the family."*

I reply: *Where and when?*

Another text follows. It's Emma again, inviting Nico and I to dinner at Rocco's Ristoranté after my shift tomorrow night. No doubt it's something to do with what happened tonight.

I'm glad she's including Nico. I can't keep hiding things from him. We talk at the kitchen table like old times, long into the night. I recall earlier conversations about my confusion and guilt over my developing feelings for Nico and the difficulties of letting Jack go. All the discoveries and memories while staying at this villa. What would I have done without Angelina's and Vinny's guidance? Where would we be today?

I tell my mom and Angelina I noticed something off about Sienna. My mother believes it's my lack of trust because of what Aunt Lena did, hiding Luca all this time. The way she turned a blind eye to what he might or might not be doing. She's right. Sienna couldn't have been completely naïve about what Luca was doing. At some point, she must have questioned something. But the idea of Sienna marrying Luca for the sake of keeping him from Gianna doesn't sit right with me. The ultimate sacrifice or the ultimate betrayal? Were her intentions honest and genuine at the start?

Of course, Gianna was a little standoffish today. I expected her to have mixed feelings about her sister Sienna's involvement with Luca. Sienna was her favorite sister and her only confidant. It was Sienna whom Gianna sought after she escaped from her shallow grave behind the vineyard, where Luca put her. And then Sienna married Luca, the very person Gianna was running from.

"I don't know, El," my mother says. "As his wife, she's had plenty of opportunities to tell Luca that Gianna was alive and where she was living, but she never did, because he never found her. Maybe Sienna has always wanted Luca."

She has some valid points, but something is not right. "Of all the people Luca has manipulated and controlled over the years, how do we know this isn't another extension of that manipulation and control?" The more I hear myself say it, the more I believe it. "Sienna could still be with Luca. He could have easily orchestrated this whole thing: Sienna pretending to be frightened and concerned, and appearing to be on our side wanting justice, while gathering information for him—private information about how we plan to find him. She could be with him right now." I can't sit still any longer and begin pacing back and forth, my head stormed by thousands of thoughts like this.

Poppy's soulful and wise words ring in my head, again breaking my reckless thoughts. "Watch who you trust," he'd said. Maybe I'll share a few thoughts with my mother, sprinkle a few with Emma and Nico, and maybe I should keep the rest to myself.

My mother and I follow Angelina's suggestion to change into comfortable clothes, because we're not finished sorting through everything. I pull on a sweatshirt and yoga pants and grab a cup of tea. I take my journal and a pen and return to the kitchen table, ready to record our thoughts and a few notes from our family meeting this evening.

As I do, a chill sweeps across the back of my neck. Like someone is watching me. A feeling. A warning.

My eyes sweep the dark corners of the kitchen, the house, the windows. I'm suddenly cold. Exposed. My skin crawls and I can't sit still. I dim the light and go to the window, peek from the side of the curtain at the blanket of darkness covering the grounds of the villa.

As my eyes adjust to the glint of the moon's light through the trees, I think I see something—someone. My heart squeezes tight, realizing someone was out there and now they're gone, obscured within the trees. Just like that time at the cottage.

It's him. It's got to be him. Or it could be her—Jamie.

And now I'm frozen, fearing that they saw me.

Is it my imagination? I have to be sure. I have to know. I slide to the living room window that shares the same wall, but with a better vantage point to where I spotted him. My eyes water, straining through the darkness. I glide again, light and fast, to the window on the other side, and then to the back, to the large window facing the veranda where I'd spent so much time on my first stay here. Panic steals my breath as I'm sure I see the shadowy figure hiding within the olive trees at the edge of the veranda.

The shadow boldly steps from the trees into the open space. I reach for my phone in my pocket and realize it's not there but on the kitchen table next to my journal. I feed myself reassuring thoughts. He's stepping out into the open, so he must not have seen me. But now he's moving slowly and approaching the veranda. Will he climb the steps to the veranda and come all the way to the window?

My hands are clammy and shaky, and I'm freaking out because, if I leave this spot to get my phone and call for help, I might lose sight of him or, even worse, he might see me. And if I yell for Angelina or my mother, could he hear me? No, I cannot—will not—take my eyes off of him. I will not lose him.

I see him now stepping onto the veranda with the stealth of a black cat. He's wearing a dark hoodie that generously covers his face and dark pants, dark shoes so he can blend into the night.

I watch as he observes the furniture, saunters between the sofa and the table, caresses the fluffy pillows as he passes, like he's claiming each piece. Trespassing, violating by his very presence.

And then he snaps his head at the window, and my heart stops. The window which overlooks the beautiful veranda, the lemon and olive trees, and the sea. How different it seems now, through this terrifying view. The shadow figure comes closer, and now we stand opposite one another, separated by glass and an opaque linen curtain. I still can't see his face, but I know he's there. It has to be him. Luca.

I bring my hands to my face, as if that would hide me. Then I step back. We're inches apart. A tiny scream inside me fails to break free. Fearing my silhouette might give me away, I get to the wall that shares the window and press my body up against it. I want to disappear right into it, fade into the paint. My hand feels for the light switch to the veranda. I hope I don't regret what I'm about to do, but I can't let him think he can get away with this. I have to know if it's him. Nothing else matters.

I flip on the light switch.

CHAPTER 7

ELLA

The black-clad figure on the veranda jumps back, leaning into his legs like a warrior. He hesitates for a moment, calculating his next move, but then he pivots slightly as if he's changed his mind.

As he turns, his hood slackens and reveals the one thing I want to see: his eyes. And I know those eyes.

Adrenaline pulses through my temples and through my veins. I unlatch the lock, throw open the door, and step into the doorway of the veranda as he runs toward the olive trees.

"Luca!" I scream, as an unexpected, bolder version of me emerges. I want him to know I saw him. I might have imagined it, but I swear his body stiffened at hearing his name. The thick olive trees on the left might obscure him, but I know there's only one way out of the yard, and that's toward the public access to the beach.

Unless he's standing by, waiting for our guards to fall, ready to approach again.

Common sense pulls me back inside. I lock the door, check that the windows are covered, and turn on all the lights on the lower level. Vinny and Angelina round the corner from their bedroom, and my mother is right behind them.

Vinny shields his sleepy eyes from the brightness. "What's going on?" Angelina stands beside him in her robe, a look of worry on her face.

My mother comes up close. "What happened? Are you okay?"

"It was him," I say, trembling. "Luca. He was right there." I point to the door.

"Inside the house?" she says, frightened.

"On the veranda," I say. "I heard a noise, and when I looked out . . . he was there."

"Oh my God. Did he see you?" she says. "You're sure it was him?"

"Where is he?" Angelina says.

"He ran off," I say, panicking. "I don't think he expected me to turn on the lights and open the door."

"You did what?" My mother's eyes blaze.

"I yelled his name when he ran off." I instantly regret admitting this.

"Ella, no." My mother covers her mouth with her hand. "Why?"

I tell her I want him to know we're on to him. I want him to know that he doesn't have complete control. But as long as we don't know how to find him, she says, he is in control. I explain how I saw him approaching from the olive trees and his peculiar behavior on the veranda. I told them how he came right up to the window.

"I was afraid he might try to break in and wanted him to know he'd been caught. I hoped to scare him off," I say. "Don't we want him to know we're not afraid of him?"

"But we are," Angelina says.

"And he likes that," I say.

"I know what you're saying, El," my mother says, bending an arm around me, "but—"

"If I hadn't turned on that light, he would have tried to break in. And then what? What would he have done? Scare us? Kill us?"

"She's right, she's right," Angelina mumbles as she paces the floor.

I pick up my phone from the table. "I'm calling the police."

"What about his connections?" Angelina says.

"We have to report this."

All three of them stare at me, wide-eyed, mouths open.

"At the very least, it's an attempted break-in, trespassing. We have the right and I'm doing it."

"Yes, yes, call," my mother says.

* * *

Two officers arrive almost thirty minutes later. I explain what happened from the moment I heard a noise and saw something suspicious outside. I tell them his name, Luca Perri, my great-uncle who has been harassing us for years. While I'm at it, I explain his connection to an unsolved missing person in this area decades ago. I show them a picture of Luca on my phone and describe what he was wearing tonight.

The officers listen with frequent glances at each other; are they silently communicating? Do they know him? They jot down a few notes and tell us they will write up a report. They also promise to park a patrol car in front of the villa overnight.

I hope Luca's watching. I want him to see a police presence. To know we're not too afraid to report him. I just hope they're on our side and not his.

I also ask the officers to check on a report filed by Sienna Perri three weeks ago about a storage unit filled with women's personal items, which belonged to her husband, Luca. I even explain the location of the unit. I say that I know Luca has kidnapped and harmed other women for years, and if we don't find him now, he will continue to do it.

"He confessed to a kidnapping and attempted murder of a woman over fifty years ago," I say.

The officer furrows his brow. "Confessed to whom? You?"

"Yes," I lie. Maybe he didn't confess with his words, but he did in every other way. I'll never forget that day. The earthy forest and the smell of pine. How we stood watching in horror—Nico, Angelina, and me—as Luca's shovel cut into the fresh earth. Humidity, dirt, and fear clinging to our skin. A look of surprise and horror on Luca's face at not finding Gianna's body where he'd put it.

"*Signorina*," the officer says, "did you hear what I asked about the storage unit? Would you be able to take us to it?"

"Yes," I say. "There might be more than one, but I'll take you to the one I found."

We agree to meet at the police station tomorrow, and I will take them to the storage unit. I watch as they return to their cars and review their notes. One of them points at something, and they head in opposite directions, guns in hands, until they're no longer in sight. I close and lock the door and move to the front window.

Lights flash and aim in one direction to a path behind the trees. My mother, Angelina, and Vinny are by my side, watching the commotion. In the distance, we can hear faint shouting and a siren approaching from over the hill. Lights bounce through the trees and on the ground.

Is this it? Have they caught him?

A knock at the door startles us. It's one of the officers.

"We saw someone hiding in those trees," he says, pointing across the road. "You were right. But it wasn't the man in the picture. He's a bit younger."

"What?" *Who was it, then?* "Did you get him?" I say.

"Not yet," he says, and it's like a punch to the gut.

"He got away?" I say, and he nods. I turn to the desperate, anxious eyes of my family and repeat, "He got away."

"We've got officers out in all directions. It's just a matter of time. We'll find him," he says. "I'll be here through the night. We've got the area covered. He has nowhere else to go."

"You don't know him like we do," I say. "And now we've made him angry."

CHAPTER 8

ELLA

Night blends to morning, and there has been no activity since the near miss of Luca—or the person I thought was Luca. From the living room window, I see the unmarked police car at the end of the road. I leave a note for my mother telling her I've gone to Nico's, and when I've conjured up enough courage, I exit the villa. Then I pull up to the unmarked car to let the officer know I'm leaving.

Nico is beyond thrilled when I get to his apartment and tell him that, with everything that's happening, I won't be going home to New York anytime soon. My sister, Liv, has agreed to stay at the cottage in Skaneateles while I'm gone. But his mood changes when I tell him about last night.

"That son of a bitch," he says. "I'm sick of this, Ella. Let me take care of this. . . . I know people."

"Nico!" He's never said that before, never alluded to any connections.

"I don't care. He's ruining our lives. I love you, Ella. I want to be with you, but this has to stop."

"You *are* with me," I say.

"It doesn't feel like it sometimes. You're distracted half the time, and why wouldn't you be? We're not living while this is unresolved."

"They don't think it's him," I say. "I showed them a picture."

"They're wrong. Or they're lying. It was dark, El. How could they be sure? Who else would it be?" His voice is sharp. "I'm going with you to the police station today. I can take a half day."

I explain I won't be able to go today because Dr. Girofolo rearranged a few observations at the hospital and I'll be there instead. "But tomorrow I'm going first thing," I say. "I want to make sure they filed the report and to see if there are any recent developments." I look into his dark chocolate eyes and resist the urge to omit the part about going to the storage unit. And I know not telling him will only backfire. "I'm also bringing them to the storage unit."

"What? Then I'm definitely coming with you."

* * *

After a quick shower, I brew a cup of coffee and head out to the mailbox with towel-dried hair. It's part of my morning ritual, thumbing through the mail while I drink my first cup before work. It makes me feel organized, prepared, normal.

Most of the mail is junk, as usual, and then I see a half-folded piece of paper. At first, I think it's strange that it's not in an envelope and assume it's another invitation to a neighborhood barbecue or a party.

But as I unfold the paper, I realize this is nothing of the sort. It's typed, and it reads:

> *I'm watching you. I know what you're doing. Don't think you can outsmart me. If you continue to pursue this, I will stop you no matter what it takes. This is the only warning you will get.*

My whole body trembles.

Nico comes into the room and sees the paper in my shaky hands. He rushes to me and takes the paper and reads it. As he heads to the front door, I follow behind. Swinging it open, he stomps out into the front yard and, with a hard stare, scans the street, the houses, everything. He's showing the author of the note that we are not afraid . . . even though we are. Nico turns back toward the house and comes inside, giving one last blazing look through the doorway before slamming it closed.

"That's it," he says. "We're calling in sick, and I'm going with you to the police today. We have to go *now*." His jaw clenches and a vein flexes in his neck.

"I—I can't go now. I have to be at the hospital."

"They'll understand."

"Nico, it's not like that. They won't understand. It's not as simple as not showing up. It took a lot to get this fellowship and then I had to ask if I could start it early since I wasn't going home. I can't call the shots on this one."

"I know," he says, his voice heavy, his expression softening. "I'm just pissed off." He shoves a chair into the table. "I feel helpless. We're sitting ducks. He sees us, but we can't see him. I'm sick of it. If you can't go to the police today, I'll go myself. This can't wait."

I open my mouth to object but stop. He's right. The note is a threat. "You're right. Go. Show them the note. It has to be taken care of now, especially after what happened with the florist and last night. I will try to stop at the station to check on the report after I leave the hospital. Maybe we'll go to the storage unit then. You can meet me there if you want."

"I can check on the report while I'm there today."

"Sure, if you want, but I don't know if they'll share information with you since you didn't report the incident at the villa, and you weren't the one to see the storage unit. They might have questions they'll need to ask me, though—questions only I know the answers to."

I can tell by the way he's standing with his arms crossed, not saying anything, that he doesn't like my reply.

After a brief staredown, Nico sighs and comes closer to me. He tucks a piece of hair behind my ear and gently places both hands on my arms. "Are you okay?"

"Yes," I say, even though I am far from it. "Just a little shaken up." I know he's not referring to this moment, but I leave it at that. I pull back. "I have to finish getting ready."

He kisses my forehead, hugs me tight, and lets me go.

CHAPTER 9

ELLA

I am overjoyed that the prestigious Arcispedale Santa Maria Nuova has accepted me for a fellowship, offering me the rare opportunity to learn under the world-renowned Dr. Girofolo. Studying under Dr. Girofolo is incredible. It's not just the experience I'm gaining as his student in this program, but it's his intense personality and his intelligence, and expertise in his field. It's his charming and welcoming nature. He draws me in and makes me feel like what I'm contributing is important. His high demands expect to be met with integrity.

Not a minute in the day passes without Dr. Girofolo immersing us in a teachable moment. What he exposes us to we must absorb efficiently. We must regurgitate what he does, says, and believes back to him. I am both exhilarated and exhausted when I leave every day, but it is worth every bit of effort.

I am thankful for the long drive to and from the hospital. It's a gift that allows me time to clear my mind, switch gears, and prepare for my personal life. The sheer intensity of my professional and personal life is consuming me. I need to leave one behind before embracing the other.

Not having to live in an off-campus setting means I can live with Nico, and sometimes I stay at the villa with Angelina and Vinny. If I had accepted the fellowships in Florence or Tuscany, I would have been closer to my new family there. Although I would have loved being closer to my grandmother, Gianna, so we could make up for lost time, right now it's better to be near Scilla rather than Tuscany.

The only disadvantage of not living on campus with the other fellows is that I won't interact with them as much. I'll miss out on building relationships, the connecting and the bonding that happens when people coexist outside of their work environment. What they'll learn about each other, both good and bad. And maybe for that reason alone, it's better that I don't live on campus. I'm not ready to let anyone into my life or into my family's business. I'm having a hard time trusting at the moment.

The heat of the sun burns the top of my head on the short walk from the parking lot to the building. *It's going to be a scorcher today,* I think, chuckling about that phrase often used by Poppy.

As soon as I walk into the hospital, I can tell it's busier than usual. People waiting to be treated and waiting to be informed about their loved ones congest the halls. I wonder what has happened today to make it so busy.

Straight ahead, I see the other five fellows checking in at the desk. I join them in getting my ID badge and clipboard and then we head off for our meeting in Dr. Girofolo's office. We walk down the corridors in twos. Chase Peters and Anastasia Patrova at the front, followed by Miles Henry and Jacques Martin, and Jonella Silva and me. Each of us from different countries except for Miles and myself, the only two from the United States.

We keep to ourselves other than cordial smiles and faint hellos on the way to our meeting. Jonelle, I've learned, can be hot-headed and competitive. She often boasts in a loud, obnoxious voice about the work she is involved in. Her expressions, her voice, and her behaviors are all dramatic. Even her tight, wild-patterned clothing is loud. She craves attention and seeks it at any cost. We begin our conversation with polite, brief small talk, which then turns to the research we're both working on and what we will accomplish today. I surmise by her pursed lips and pointed brow that Jonelle is in a foul mood, and I'm keeping my fingers crossed we won't be assigned as partners.

Dr. Girofolo greets us at the door in his white lab coat and stroking his neatly trimmed beard. He seems distracted, serious. He offers a brief smile and ushers us in, telling us where to sit at the dark mahogany table. At the center, swirling steam escapes from the spouts of several small stainless steel carafes of cappuccino. Platters of pastries sit beside white coffee mugs and pitchers of water. I've learned that many Italians prefer to drink water before having their coffee to cleanse their palate and enhance the coffee flavors. After we prepare our coffee to our liking and choose our pastries, Dr. Girofolo clears his throat and addresses us.

He informs us that today he will have to reschedule our planned time together in order to perform an emergency surgery on a young woman. She has been shot in the chest, and the bullet has lodged near her heart. He clears his throat and swallows hard. It must be difficult to do his job sometimes. But then he tells us that this woman was shot as she narrowly escaped being abducted. She got away, but her sister wasn't so lucky.

His voice cracks, "I received information that the assailant set the house on fire with her sister still inside. They don't know if she got out or if he took her or . . ."

A heavy silence settles in the room.

"When did this happen?" someone asks.

"Early this morning," he says. "They extinguished the fire, and the rescue team is still searching the house for her sister, but if they don't find her soon, I fear it'll be too late."

It feels like the air has been sucked out of the room as we sit frozen in thought. No words can bring sense to such a horrible tragedy. Dr. Girofolo breaks the silence, informing us that in his absence he has assigned us to work on our research in pairs. But he may choose one or two of us to assist him in the surgery.

The sullen mood in the room is like being smothered with a pillow. We struggle at first to connect, deep in thought about the poor woman almost kidnapped and her sister left to burn to death. How can we allow ourselves to go about our day while this woman suffers such a horrific tragedy? The note I found this morning pales in comparison to her suffering.

Miles Henry, one of the fellows I have not yet worked with, is assigned as my partner. We are to bring our notes and research to work in Conference Room A.

Jonelle saunters through the room in my direction with a strange look on her face, no longer an angry glower but a crazed, wide-eyed expression. As I turn around, I realize I am the intended receiver of the silent death stare. I squint, assessing her, questioning the situation. Have I missed something?

With a steadfast gaze, she brushes past me without saying a word. Before entering Conference Room B, she stops at the door and shakes her head at me in complete annoyance, then stomps inside.

Miles and I exchange confused glances. "What the hell was that?" he asks.

"I have no idea," I say. "We started off—*she* started off—in a pissy mood as soon as I got here, like I offended her or something."

"Hard not to."

"Is she always like that? I don't know her very well," I say. "Maybe she's just having a bad day."

"Jonelle often has bad days," he says, "and it's usually with other women. I try to stay out of her way." He gives an uneasy laugh. I know there's more to it than that.

We work through the entire morning, taking only a thirty-minute lunch. We break once more just before four o'clock. The doors to the other conference rooms open, and the conversations overshadow each other as we compare notes and talk about our day. Desk drawers close, and people shuffle about. Some will leave for the day, while others will stay as late as it takes to complete their assignments.

Jonelle stands in the doorway of Conference Room B. She adjusts her skirt and fluffs her hair before exiting. She saunters toward Miles as if she's about to ask him something, but then she faces me with another cold, hard stare. Jake, another fellow, emerges from the same conference room as Jonelle and strides quickly to catch up to her. When she sees him, her hateful face blossoms into a pleasant, wide grin. Her face and eyebrows relax, and she places her arm through Jake's like a giddy child.

"A few of us are going out for drinks," Jake says. "You guys should come."

The corners of Jonelle's mouth fall as Jake's invitation includes Miles and me.

I glance at my watch. "Maybe some other time," I say. "I'm going to do some work in the library while it's still open. Thanks for the invite, though."

Jake looks at Miles. "You too?"

"Thanks, man, I appreciate the invite," Miles says. "El and I are working together. Just want to put a dent in it."

"No worries," Jake says. "Next time."

"Sounds good," Miles says. "See you tomorrow."

Jake shifts his attention to Jonelle. "You're coming, right?"

Jonelle's smile returns. She clutches her clipboard to her chest. "Yes, I'd love to."

Jake turns toward the doors, and she follows him out.

"Jonelle," I say, and she whips her head back. "Could I talk to you for a minute?"

Her eyes dart around the room as if gathering excuses from the air. "Why? Can't you see I'm on my way out?"

"I'll be quick. I just want to ask you something."

She gives a heavy sigh and comes back to where Miles and I are standing. "Be quick. I don't want to lose the others."

Miles steps back.

I step closer. "Is everything okay?" I ask Jonelle. "Have I offended you?"

She puts her hand to her chest and looks flabbergasted. "What? I don't know what you mean."

"I think you do. Every time you look at me, you have an angry, raging expression on your face. Just a minute ago, you huffed past me, glaring. What was that about?"

She laughs it off. "Don't you think you're overreacting a bit? Maybe being a bit sensitive?"

With my blood boiling, I firmly say, "I don't think so. I know what I saw, and I'm reacting to what I saw—you glared at me." I wait. "Is there something you need to say to me?"

Jonelle's face reddens, and beads of sweat form at her brow. She glances at Miles, then me, and leans in close. "I hope you won't cause any trouble while you're here. You wouldn't want to do something you'll regret."

I step back, shocked. "Was that a threat?"

"I'm just making sure you understand, Ella," she says.

"What's that supposed to mean?"

"Whatever it is you think you know, you don't," she says.

"I think you're confusing me with someone else," I say. "I hardly know you. Why would you say that when we don't even know each other?"

The corner of her mouth rises to a partial grin. "Don't draw any unnecessary attention to yourself." Then she turns on her heel and catches up with the other fellows.

Miles approaches me as Jonelle glides out the door. He says something, but I tune him out, processing what just happened as if I'm lost in a tunnel with no end in sight.

Miles taps my shoulder and points to the TV monitor on the wall. A news report about the attempted kidnapping. The volume is off, but the words stream across the bottom:

"Home invasion house fire claims no victims. One woman in critical condition. Police are searching for her sister."

The woman Dr. Girofolo is operating on.

"Police are searching for her sister," I say to myself. What happened to her sister? Why wouldn't they have found her by now?

"That's not good," Miles says, after reading the caption on the screen.

"I agree, it's not," I say, "and if she's hurt or if someone has taken her, every minute is crucial for her survival. I hope they find her soon."

I check my phone several times for Nico's reply to my text about having to work later than expected, but there's nothing. Miles and I work until sundown and, as the library closes, I leave feeling satisfied about all we have accomplished.

As Miles walks me to my car, I try to hide my fear of what might be lurking in the dark. At my car door he says, "You are brilliant at what you do, El. I'm impressed with how much you know already, and you've just started. You're surpassing me, and I've been here a lot longer."

"Thank you," I say, dipping into the car and keeping the door open. "I'm passionate about it. I want to be the best cardiologist I can be."

Miles closes my door, his hands resting at the top. He's staring as I start my car, lingering a little longer than I'd like. I shift into drive and he steps back. I smile and give a half wave.

"Drive safe. See you tomorrow," he says, and stays in my rearview mirror until I turn at the traffic light.

I take a deep breath, preparing to process what happened with Jonelle, concerned about Nico's silence today, fearful of the dark roads ahead.

I call Nico, and he picks up right away. He tells me he worked all day, and he waited to go to the station together. He says he wasn't near his phone most of the day, and by the time he saw my text about being late, he figured we would talk like usual on my drive home. But after we hang up I am left with an uncomfortable, undefined feeling.

CHAPTER 10

ELLA

An officer at the police station takes us to a back room after waiting for about an hour. He's young, late thirties or early forties, short brown hair, and olive tanned skin. With a wide grin, he introduces himself as Officer Paulie Bello and requests that we refer to him as Officer Paulie. Nico and I introduce ourselves and explain our reasons for being there. We hand him the note we got in the mail yesterday. He holds it in his thick, calloused hands and reads it to himself.

He asks us a series of questions. What time did I go to the mailbox? Had I retrieved the mail the day before? Was I sure this was from today's mail? He asks if I have any idea who might have put it there. Do I have any enemies? I would never have thought I'd have an enemy, especially not my uncle, who I once admired. But he is now my enemy.

"Yes," I say. "I think it's my uncle, Luca Perri."

"Luca Perri," he repeats. He asks me to spell it as he writes it on a piece of paper. He asks for descriptive details—how old he is and what he looks like, and any distinctive traits.

I show him a picture of Luca on my phone and explain that he looks far younger than his age. Even with the picture in front of Officer Paulie, I describe his short, wavy, salt-and-pepper hair and well-trimmed white beard with a few black hairs scattered throughout. I explain that Luca often wears suit jackets and dark jeans, and he walks with a slight limp. He looks quite ordinary. I tell him he has a home in Skaneateles, New York, one in Montepulciano, and one outside of Tropea, in Scilla.

The officer nods and puts the tip of his pen on his lip. "Is your uncle on your mother's or father's side of the family?"

"My mother's."

"Why would he threaten you like this?"

It takes a while, but I explain everything from the beginning. Trying to condense it is next to impossible. Everything that happened to Gianna, how I came to know about her, and where she is now. How she's been hiding from Luca for decades. I tell him about Luca's double life and then I mention the storage room.

His fat fingers push the pen across his notepad as I ramble off the details of my life. How Luca broke into my home in New York, how he'd held Liv and me captive in his Montepulciano mansion with the secret rooms.

At times, Officer Paulie pauses, squints, or furrows his brow.

"Sounds like a great guy," he chuckles. When we don't laugh, he clears his throat and straightens up. "And now he wants revenge on you and your family for exposing his secrets."

"Yes."

"Go back to the storage unit for a minute," he says. "You said you told the police. Where was this? Which police?"

"Here in Tropea."

"Do you remember who you spoke with?"

"I have it documented, but I don't recall at the moment."

"And what was the result of that report?"

"At that time—about two years ago now—I obtained a warrant to dig in the woods behind the vineyard because I had proof that my grandmother was buried there."

"What proof?"

"I found part of the necklace she was wearing when she went missing."

"Astonishing that it would still be there after all this time."

"I almost didn't see it."

"And you said your uncle was digging in that area. She wasn't there?"

"Correct." Nico puts his arm around my shoulders.

"And you held him at gunpoint as he took you to the storage unit?"

"Well, yes," I say, realizing how that sounds. "I don't know if the police followed up on that. We never heard. But you should have a recent report from Sienna Perri, one of Luca's wives. She called about the storage unit right after she discovered it. And she brought the police to the storage unit, which was locked, and I'm not sure if they ever got into it. Do you have that report?" I glance at Nico. "About three weeks ago, right?" He nods.

Officer Paulie is typing something on the keyboard. As he reads the screen, puzzlement crosses his face. After a few minutes, he looks at us. "I see nothing like that. No report."

"What? No statements or anything from Sienna Perri?" I say. "I don't understand."

"There is nothing about Sienna or Luca Perri," he says.

My face flushes and sweat trickles down my back. I look at Nico. "How can this be?"

"Can you tell me more about this storage unit?" Officer Paulie seems like he wants to help us. "Where is it? Tell me again, with details about what's inside."

I explain the organized boxes filled with women's personal items. An earring, a watch, hats, purses, a shirt. I recall a sheer scarf folded into a perfect square, the faint smell of perfume rising to the air as I unfolded it. And Gianna's hat, the one in Poppy's painting. It was, without a doubt, her hat.

I explain where the storage unit is and how to get there. I tell him it's number 109 and offer to go with him now. He says we can't go now, but he'll send a deputy to verify my information.

"So, what do we do now?" Nico asks.

"You let us do our job and, in the meantime, you will be more cautious and careful. If you receive any more threatening notes, phone calls—anything—you let us know." He hands me his business card. "Is there any other evidence you have against your uncle, aside from this note?"

I shake my head. Other than a hunch and a sick feeling in my stomach, I have nothing else to give them. "But there will be DNA from the storage unit," I say, although I have nothing of Luca's confirming it's his DNA.

Officer Paulie looks at the screen on the monitor again. "I see your report about an attempted break-in at Villa Georgio a couple of nights ago. They almost apprehended him. An under-cover officer is still there now."

"Yes, we think it was Luca, but the officer at the villa, who also saw him, didn't think he was the same man from the picture I showed you."

"This man is dangerous," Nico adds. He has likely stayed quiet and subdued out of respect for me, as he knows I want to handle this myself.

Officer Paulie gives Nico a look. "We will do everything we can to help you, but some things are out of our control. You have an officer at the villa and my card."

Nico clenches his jaw. "We're gonna need more than that."

Officer Paulie prints the report and hands it to me to sign. We leave the station with more questions and no answers. And on the silent and tense drive home, I'm racking my brain for ways to get Luca's DNA.

CHAPTER 11

ELLA

Nico sleeps soundly as a sharp wind howls and lashes at the walls of our apartment. The wind from the Tyrrhenian Sea can be beastly in a storm. The windows shake and rattle with the force of an earthquake, and I expect the glass to shatter at any moment. I wish I could fall asleep, but I won't be sleeping through this.

My head swarms with thoughts about Luca and a small, nagging worry about Nico's growing impatience with me. I roll over and spoon against Nico's warm body. His wavy black locks bend at his cheekbone and lie against his neck. I kiss his cheek, but by the sound of his breathing he is long gone. Once he's asleep, there's no waking him.

I listen to the rhythmic pattern of his breath, hoping it will lull me to sleep, but no luck. Between the wind and my anxious curiosity, I will not be sleeping anytime soon.

I check my phone and notice a text from Angelina that I had missed this morning. It's a message about an old house and an estate sale in an old neighborhood, but nothing more than that. Sometimes she purposely leaves out information like she wants me to guess. I glimpse the clock and it's almost midnight.

Angelina is usually up later than that and always sleeps with her phone on the nightstand by her bed. I text her back:

> *"I'm awake. Are you? Text me back if you're up and can talk."*

Not a minute later, she responds: *"I'm up! Call me!"*

I study Nico for a moment, confirming that he's still asleep. Then I slip from the bed and pull on a sweatshirt and sweatpants and quietly head to the kitchen, closing the bedroom door behind me.

When Angelina answers her phone, her voice is like a warm hug, which I need right now. She talks as if it's been years instead of hours since she saw me. She and I have had very little time to talk lately. She is overjoyed with the news she wants to share.

"Listen," she says. "I have something to tell you. I've been dying to tell you this all day, but with everything that's happened, it didn't seem as important at the time. But now I think it's urgent."

"What is it?"

"I found out that a builder is coming into some of the old neighborhoods in the south. I think it may be near where your Poppy and his family lived when he was a boy. Near that fishing village that starts with a C."

"In Scilla? Chianlalea?"

"Yes, that's it! They're coming and re-doing ... fixing up ... what's the word when they take an old house and make it beautiful to sell right after they're done?"

"Flipping?"

"Yes! Flipping! I hear they're flipping houses all along that part of the coast. I think it's terrible! All those beautiful, old houses, all those memories. They should leave it alone. We have to put a stop to it."

I analyze not just what she's saying but how and why. What is she getting at? "Angelina, I don't think there is anything we can do about it."

"We need to stop them. Get a petition going in those neighborhoods. I'll bet all the neighbors will sign it. Not to mention . . . you know . . ."

"What? I know what?"

"You said you've always wanted to go inside that house. Well, this could be your opportunity. Maybe they'll let you in. You could pretend to be an interested buyer. Maybe you can even buy it yourself. Wouldn't that be something? We should make a visit."

I check over my shoulder to make sure I'm still alone in the kitchen, and in a quieter voice I say, "How can you be sure it's the same neighborhood?"

"Well, I've done some digging."

"Of course you have."

"And your grandparents' old neighborhood is, in fact, among the others being renovated."

"Why didn't you just lead with that?" I feel myself smile because I know where she's headed and I like it.

"I don't know," she says. "Maybe I'm just hoping you'll want to go and you'll take me with you so we can discover it together."

Going back to Poppy's old neighborhood in Scilla is something I would absolutely love, but it will require me to take a couple days off from work—one for travel and another to visit the house.

"I would love to, Angelina, but without prior planning for my fellowship, I don't know if I can do that. I also have a presentation to give on my research at the hospital, and those presentation dates are firm. Do you know how long this rebuilding process has been going on or how much they've already completed?"

"No, but I can find out. Let me work on that and I'll get back to you. See what you can do with Dr. Girofolo and your fellowship and let me know," she says. "I really want to get into that house. I might even take a ride down there just to see."

"Angelina, promise me you won't go without me," I say. "You shouldn't go alone."

"I don't know if I can promise that, *cara*, dear."

"Well, make sure you take Vinny with you, or at least make sure he knows you're going."

The last time Angelina went somewhere without telling anyone, it was to explore one of Luca's old houses because she insisted she'd been there as a child. She was right, of course. She had been there as a child, but when she went inside, someone attacked her. We later found that it was someone connected to Luca. Thankfully, after they left, Nico found her and brought her to the hospital.

"Don't worry, I will."

After we hang up, I use Google to locate Poppy's old neighborhood on Via Gratta. I zoom in with the little Pegman until it reaches the road, and now it's me walking on the cobblestone road. I recall the first time I went to Italy to follow Poppy's diary entries. How excited I was when my feet first hit the Italian countryside. How thrilled to be walking on the same streets where Poppy grew up.

I was unsure of Poppy's exact address, but there was this one house in particular that I believed was his. Only photographs led me to this conclusion. Other than that, I had no actual way of knowing.

But now, Gianna and Sienna can confirm which street Poppy and his family lived on. Their houses were side by side. Since house numbers were not used in that area, I need to determine which house belonged to him.

I'm exhilarated by the possibilities that a visit back to Poppy's neighborhood presents, and I imagine standing in front of both Poppy's and Gianna's houses before going inside. Step onto the porch where Luca abandoned my mother, Gabriella, in her baby carriage only hours after thinking he'd killed and buried *her* mother, Gianna, in the woods of the vineyard.

I imagine what it will be like when it's time to go inside the house, entering over the same threshold that Poppy's and Luca's mother had upon discovering the carriage. What his mother must have thought when she discovered the baby there.

The comforting smells of an old home and the lives that were lived there undoubtedly remain etched in the grains of the wooden floors, doors, and walls. What those walls must have known of the living area and kitchen and, of course, the bedrooms upstairs.

Then a thought occurs to me. What are the chances that Luca is aware of the reconstruction of his old neighborhood? I'm sure if he knew he would immediately put a stop to it. Or maybe he would want it all to disappear. Maybe there are still secrets none of us know about.

If he learns about the demise of his neighborhood, will he want to come back and see it one last time?

I shiver at the thought of running into Luca while we're in the neighborhood or at his old house. Although I don't think anyone would search for him in the southernmost region of Calabria, Luca is cunning. He'll keep a low profile and his affairs private. But what if he lets his guard down? And then I think, *Maybe I can trap him and inform the police about his whereabouts. They will finally catch him.*

There will be no sleeping tonight.

CHAPTER 12

ELLA

Nico finds me on the patio sofa, staring at the dusky trees backlit by a golden sunrise. He hands me a cup of coffee and places his own on an end table across from me. Steam rises between us from our mugs. He says nothing, and he doesn't have to, because his eyes reveal his troubled thoughts.

He moves next to me on the sofa and tucks a strand of hair behind my ear. He takes my hand in his and squeezes gently. His eyes have warmed a bit and smile at me. A grin forms on his lips.

I love his smile and everything about him. Something about him anchors me; even when we were oceans apart I felt tethered to him. A timeless, natural bond, an unspoken understanding. A sense of home. It feels like years, not weeks, since I left Skaneateles. The cottage. Home. And a lifetime ago since I said goodbye to Poppy. Since the box. Luca.

Nico says something about Nonna, which makes me jump.

"Oh my gosh! Nonna. What time is it?" I'd almost forgotten that Nonna arrives today, and we are picking her up at the airport.

"It's fine," Nico says. "You have plenty of time. It's early yet."

I relax for a moment, but forgetting that today is the day she is coming only proves that I am not present and haven't been for a while. My mind easily floats in several directions. Today I will see my Nonna for the first time in months. I cannot wait to see that beautiful smile on her little face and kiss her pudgy cheeks. In just a few hours I will hug her and tell her how much I love her and how much I have missed her. I want to show her everything I know and love about Chianalea and Scilla, Poppy's old stomping ground. Share with her the incredible beauty and peace I've found here in Italy when Luca's not around. I'm curious about where she grew up and how and where she first met Poppy. I want to see the places she saw as a child and learn everything about her life.

Her voice was bursting with excitement before the words came out of her mouth telling me she was coming. Its joyful sound still rings in my head. We cried on the phone and then we laughed at ourselves for crying. But I'd noticed, as she spoke, her tone changed. It lowered an octave and sounded less genuine, like there was something else she wanted to say. Like her authentic voice was hiding behind this newer one.

I had hoped she might have tried to time her trip with my mother's visit, because I knew she would never come all the way out here alone, and I wouldn't want her to. But to my surprise she suddenly blurted, "Lena is coming with me!"

I couldn't find the words to reply. My throat was dry. I cleared it and said, "She is?"

"Oh, Ella. I had a feeling you'd react that way," she'd said. "But don't worry, dear. Lena is like a sister to me. We've been close since forever—long before any of those things happened." *Those things.* Nonna refuses to engage in conversations that have to do with Luca's betrayal, so she uses generic terms such as "those things" whenever he's brought up.

"I know you and Aunt Lena are close, Nonna. I'm just not convinced—"

"No—don't say it." Her voice is sharper, higher. "She doesn't know a thing. Trust me. I know."

"But Aunt Lena has lied to us before."

"Yes, I know that, dear, but it's different now. She knows about Luca's double life. She didn't know before. Trust me—she wants him caught as much as we do. Her days of hiding him and pretending are over. I know her."

That was not a battle I would win. Nonna has held a grudge or two in her day, but she's different with Lena. After Luca disappeared, Aunt Lena lied to us every time we saw her. She pretended she didn't know where Luca was, yet she was hiding him all along. And she continued to protect him even after learning about his double life being married to Sienna.

I can't imagine how hurt Lena was to learn that her husband was married to someone else. How do you forgive that? But none of that seems to matter with Nonna. She makes excuses for Lena, often overlooking the obvious red flags that the rest of us have warned her about. I didn't want Nonna to travel from New York to Italy all by herself. I just wanted anyone but Lena to come with her.

"Did you hear what I said?" Nico says. "Where did you go just now?"

"I'm sorry. I guess I'm a little distracted thinking about Nonna."

"You have a glazed look in your eyes. Like you're staring at something that's not there. Or maybe you're seeing something I can't see," he says, waving his hands.

I chuckle. "It's that obvious, huh?"

His eyes are wide, confirming.

"It's Aunt Lena I'm thinking about," I say. "I know it sounds bad, but I don't want her around Nonna. I don't trust her."

"But Nonna does," Nico says.

"Yes, she does," I say.

"Do you think Lena is still in contact with Luca after everything that's happened?"

"Yes, I think it's possible."

"Even after knowing about Luca's other family? A house, a wife, and a child with another woman?" He says.

"It sounds ridiculous when you say it like that, but, yes, I think Aunt Lena would protect Luca. She has before; why wouldn't she continue? I've had a hard time trusting Aunt Lena. She took Luca back and hid him even after we found out what he'd done to Gianna and all those other women. I mean . . . how do you do that?"

"So you're telling me that if *I* did that you wouldn't take me back?" He can barely keep his smile straight.

I hit his arm. "Don't even joke about that. And no."

"She must love him a lot," Nico says.

"I don't think it's love anymore," I say. "Desperate, lonely people will do anything to not be alone. For Aunt Lena to do something like that, she must have very little self-worth and no self-love. I'm sad for her—I really am—but I don't trust her motives or her decisions. And I don't trust her around Nonna."

"Don't underestimate Nonna. She can definitely hold her own," he reminds me.

"Yes, she can, but Lena's presence impairs Nonna's judgment," I say. Nonna will downplay the truth, even if it's bad. She'll look the other way and minimize anything bad we say about Lena, even if those things are facts.

"What does your mom think about Lena coming?" he says.

"She feels the same," I say, glancing at my watch. "The one thing I feel good about is that they will stay with my mom at Angelina and Vinny's villa. They'll be safe there, and Angelina will keep an eye on them."

"That, or she'll have evil eyes and Italian horns hanging all through the house." Nico knows how to lighten the mood. We both start laughing because we know it's true about Angelina and her superstitions.

"Sweet Angelina," I say. "Ready to ward off evil in an instant." I fondly recall the time when Angelina performed the *malocchio* using oil and water. To our surprise, when the drop of oil hit the water, the circle widened to the edge of the bowl, signifying an evil eye—negative energy, or, as Angelina referred to it, "evil forces." She was determined to rid me and our family of those forces, and she did. After that, I no longer doubted any Italian superstition Angelina ever talked about.

CHAPTER 13

ELLA

Blue sky peeks behind thick, heavy clouds, which look as if they have exploded and expanded over the hour-long drive to Lamezia Terme International Airport. Where blue isn't visible, wide plumes of white and gray knit closely together appear as a white blanket above us.

Nico pulls to the curb, and we wait for Nonna and Lena to walk through the doors.

Ten minutes later, I check my phone for any flight delays, but the flight status shows that it's on time.

"I hope they didn't get lost," Nico says, smiling. "You've always said those two have no sense of direction."

"Nonna would have texted me if she was lost," I say, tapping my toe on the floor. "They probably stopped in the bathroom, or they could be waiting for their luggage. That takes forever sometimes."

Nico looks at his watch. "If they don't come out in the next few minutes, I'll go in and see if I can find them."

My phone vibrates. I answer fast. "Nonna?"

"Ella?"

I look at Nico.

"It's Nonna. Can you hear me, *cara*, dear?"

"Nonna? Yes, I can hear you. Is everything okay?"

"Well, not really." Her voice is small and confused. "I can't find Lena anywhere."

I put the phone on speaker. "What do you mean, you can't find Lena? Did she go somewhere?"

"We got our suitcases," she says, "and then we both had to use the ladies' room, so we waited in line. I went in first and told Lena I'd wait for her outside the door. So, when I was done, I came out and waited for Lena, but she never came out."

"You're sure you didn't miss her? You're sure she heard you? Did she answer you when you told her you would wait for her?"

"I didn't wait for her to answer," Nonna says. "I just said it and left. I thought she'd be out right after me. I waited a few minutes and then I went back in to see what was taking her so long—see if she was okay. I called her name, but she didn't answer."

"You said you brought your suitcases into the bathroom, right?"

"Yes," she says, "but I didn't see her suitcase when I went back in. I'm really worried. That's not like her. Someone must have taken her."

"Nonna, I'm sure no one took Lena," I say, feeling confused.

Nonna pants. "What if someone robbed her—took her and her things?" she says. "What are we going to do?"

Nico scratches his scruffy chin. "Nonna, it's Nico."

"Oh, Nico, what are we going to do? I can't believe this has happened."

"Listen, Nonna," he says calmly. "Everything is going to be okay. This is all just a big misunderstanding. Lena is probably looking for you right now. I'm going to find a security guard and see if he can help. Maybe they'll page her."

I give Nico an appreciative but uncertain smile. "Nonna, where are you now?" I say.

"Right in front of the bathroom," she says, and I can hear tiny whispers of prayer beneath her breath. "I'm not leaving this spot until I see her."

"Good," I say, glancing at her location on the GPS. "Stay right where you are. Don't go anywhere unless it's with me or Nico. Stay with me on the phone. It will be okay. We'll find Lena."

"I hope so," Nonna says, her voice quivering and frail.

While I mute my phone momentarily, I shift my focus towards Nico. "Nico, my thoughts are all over the place. I should have added a GPS on Aunt Lena's phone, too. Do you think she's okay?"

Nico opens the car door, steps outside, and waves over the guard.

Not a minute later, Nonna is calling me again. "She's here. Thank God she's here!"

"What happened?" I ask.

"It was a big misunderstanding, like you said. We'll be right out."

I tell Nonna where to find us and then I get out of the car to find Nico. When I see him talking with a security guard, I wave for him to come back. Nico reaches the car as Nonna and Aunt Lena emerge from the airport's automatic doors, suitcases trailing behind them.

Both women are sporting cute, trendy clothes: denim ankle pants, black short wedge sandals, and flowy tops. Even as they've aged, they've never stopped trying to look their best. I giggle at Nonna's expression, revealing her unhappiness that the wind is messing up her hair. We hug, and it's all the comforts of home. I breathe in her scent, a scent that transcends time. It makes me smile, and I am that little girl again.

Nonna cups her hands on my cheeks and smiles. "Ella," she says in her crackly voice.

"Nonna, I missed you so much," I say. "We're happy that you and Aunt Lena are here." I face Aunt Lena and we hug—a short, tight hug, different from our former hugs. We're different since Luca betrayed us. It's changed the way I think about people and my trust in them.

Aunt Lena turns toward Nico and me. "I haven't been to Italy in such a long time. Thank you both for having us."

"It's our pleasure," I say, helping Nico place the luggage into the trunk. Once we're all inside the car, I turn to Aunt Lena in the back seat. "So, what happened in the airport? How did you two get separated?"

"Oh, that," Aunt Lena says, waving her hand like it was no big deal. "I, uh . . . I noticed the new bakery, and I was so thirsty I thought I'd see if I could get a bottled water or something to drink."

"Why didn't you just wait for Nonna?" I say.

"Well, the line had finally dwindled, so I thought I'd be able to get a quick drink and get back before she came out. You know how long she can take," she laughs. "But, it turns out I was wrong about both. There wasn't a line *outside* of the bakery, but there was still a line *inside* the bakery. By the time I left, well, you know the rest—Olivia called you because she couldn't find me."

I can't help but feel like there is more to Aunt Lena's story. "Yes, she was worried," I say, "but I'm glad everything turned out fine. You two need to stick together from now on. No more separating."

Neither one comments.

The ride home began with two old ladies whispering and cackling in the back seat and ends with their soft snores. And as much as I don't want to overthink anything, I can't ignore the nagging thought about how strange it was that Aunt Lena hadn't waited for Nonna. How strange for Aunt Lena to leave Nonna in the bathroom without saying a word, knowing how Nonna worries about everything and would be legitimately upset at not finding Aunt Lena.

It is like déjà vu of my first trip to Italy with Jamie. When we were on tour through Tropea, and our tour guide let us all out to spend time at the beach, Jamie had wandered off and eventually came back with a vague explanation of where she had been. I was frantic, like Nonna, along with being in a new country, and with the heavy burden and fear that I'd find something dark about my family. The time Jamie was gone felt like an eternity. Of course, now we know her real motive: acting as a spy on my Uncle Luca's behalf.

Maybe that's just triggering me, bringing me back to that moment with Jamie. Perhaps it's just a feeling and I should let it go.

Or maybe it's a small red flag waving. Maybe I shouldn't let it go just yet. Maybe I should pick up that red flag and stop it from waving.

CHAPTER 14

ELLA

I should be overjoyed having Nonna finally with me in Italy. It's something we always talked about. But uneasiness clings to me, dark and heavy, like an awkward acquaintance who doesn't know their boundaries. I want to shrug it off, step away, and get some space, but I can't. Its sweaty hand clenches mine, it climbs my back and covers my head and my eyes. This feels familiar, and I know what it means.

Someone knows where I am and where I'm going, yet I know nothing of their whereabouts. No idea if they're behind me or ahead of me. I don't know if it's one person or more than one.

But I know one thing: I'm being followed—stalked.

An unknown number frequently called me over the last few days. I tried to convince myself it was spam or an honest mistake. The calls only stopped when I finally picked up. There was no answer, of course, and now I realize that, when I answered that call, it confirmed it was me to whomever was on the other end. And who knows what my stalker will do with that knowledge?

Can people see the monster on my back? Maybe they know something I don't know. It makes me question my actions, the people I encounter, and our conversations. If these people are trustworthy. I've even questioned Nico. *Nico.*

Nico enters the kitchen where I'm having my coffee and wants to know where I'm going, how long I'll be gone, and what I'm doing later. Normal, simple, common courtesy questions you ask your partner because you tell each other everything. It makes me uncomfortable.

"What's going on with you?" he asks. "You seem upset with me."

"Why would you say that? I'm not upset."

"You are. I can tell." He rolls his eyes as if to say, "Here we go again."

I sigh.

"I know you want to handle all of this on your own, but why can't you just be transparent about your plans to find Luca? Don't you trust me?"

"I do trust you, Nico, more than anyone," I say. "But you want me to handle things in a way that isn't me. You know what? Full transparency: I'm not waiting around for law enforcement to do their job. I'm not questioning whether they were doing their job; I just want it done faster.."

"Ella, I want it to happen faster than it's happening, too. But you're not above the law, and you could get hurt."

He's right, and I know this, but I can't stop myself. I put my hand on his arm and swallow the painful knot in my throat as I lift my eyes to his. "Nico, for my family's sake, and my sanity, and for the integrity of our relationship, I think we should wait—"

He pulls his arm away. "Wait for what?"

"I have absolutely no doubt that we are soul mates and we will be married soon . . ." My stomach turns as I fight the rest of my words.

"What are you saying?"

The hurt and devastation in his eyes sicken me, knowing I put it there.

"I'm saying if we know that we will get married, then it doesn't matter when we do it, right?"

"You want to postpone our wedding because of your uncle?"

"Don't you want to get married without all of this drama and danger around us? When we can be genuinely happy and at peace?"

"I am happy and at peace with you, El, regardless of what's happening around us." He stands and clenches his fists. "Life is difficult," he says, pacing. "There will never be a perfect time. Live *now*, in this moment. You don't have faith in us. You don't think I can protect us. I don't know what to say anymore."

I try to convince him I want to marry him more than anything else in the world.

But he tells me, "Not more than anything else; otherwise, this obsession with Luca would not be dictating our lives."

He's right. My obsession with Luca dictates our daily decisions, haunts our conversations, and decides our next moves. He's been so patient, but he's growing tired of it.

"If you knew me, you would understand why this is so important. Poppy trusted me with this secret, and its exposure created all this chaos, so I'll say it: I need to be the one to finish it. Luca needs to be caught and put away for good, otherwise our lives will never be the same. And we're close, Nico—we're so close."

"Stop, El."

"Every time we get together with our family, go somewhere, or celebrate something, he will be watching and he might show up. He might try to hurt us or, worse, kill us because he thinks we ruined his life."

"Maybe you don't trust me. Is that it?"

"Of course I trust you, Nico. I love you."

"This is so unhealthy."

"Luca is a narcissistic psychopath. To him, it's not about his lies or the lives he's ruined. It's about him. Now, his life has become compromised. His truth is out in the open, and he can no longer live it. It is no longer possible for Luca, who comfortably lived two separate lives in beautiful homes with two adoring wives, to exist in the world. The man who called the shots and blackmailed people in all positions of authority and blindsided his family can no longer exist. I know for a fact that Luca cannot accept this, and he *will* not accept it."

Nico, of all people, should know this. He's been with me since the beginning. We met because I was uncovering Luca's lies and secrets. He stood by me the whole way.

"That's just it," he says. "This has been our lives since we came together. What if Luca never gets caught? Does that mean we'll never marry? Never have a family? Will you ever be able to live with the idea that he may never get caught? Are you willing to give up everything you have until then? And for how long? When does it end, El?"

The sadness in his voice—deflated, defeated—crushes my heart into a million pieces. I want to say, "Hold on, Nico. Just give me some time," but he's right. How much time? I can't bear the thought of what this is doing to him. I assumed he wanted Luca caught as much as I did, that he'd seen him as a constant threat taking away our happiness. But he sees it differently—that I'm the one taking away our happiness because, in his mind, I can make a choice. I can choose to look the other way and let it go.

But, in my mind, I shouldn't have to choose, because one relates to the other. I'm overwhelmed by such sadness by what I must admit. "You're right," I say, feeling my eyes fill. "I don't know if I can choose to live in the moment with Luca out there. But, Nico, please believe that you are the most important person in my life." I reach for his hand, and when he doesn't extend his, I almost throw up.

He glances away and then back. "Do what you think is best, El. I love you more than anything, but . . ."

I anxiously wait for him to finish.

"Maybe . . . we should take a break."

I never thought I'd hear those words.

"No, Nico," I say. "How can that be good for us?"

"El, what's happening now isn't good for us, and I don't mean a breakup, just some space. We need it. I need it."

Nico's words don't match the message his body communicates. His awkward, unnatural stance, slouched, unconfident. His worried face and clenched jaw. The way he swallows hard. I hate myself for making him feel so bad, so neglected and worried, and so unimportant that it drove him to say what he said. How can I do this to him? I'm so confused, and I don't know if he's overreacting or if I am.

I approach Nico, who continues to stare at me through hurt-filled eyes. I want to tell him that everything will be okay. That I will stop obsessing about Luca and let the police take care of it. That I will trust and believe that the police are protecting us and that we are safe now. I can do this.

I touch his cheek with my hand, but he is as still as a statue. With a gentle kiss on his frozen lips, I murmur, "I'll collect my things later." Then I brush past him, grab my purse, and leave his apartment.

As I take the steps from our apartment to my car parked a block down the street, I remind myself to think straight, and it's a good thing, because otherwise I wouldn't have heard the footsteps a short distance behind me.

Someone is following me.

I pick up the pace to a brisk walk, and, unless I'm imagining it, the footsteps are faster, too.

Now I can't remember where I parked. Was it this block or the next? My heart races because I can't remember anything. I can't even picture myself parking the car. I press the unlock button on my key fob until I hear a faint chirp. It's this block, close to where I am. The lights of my car flash on the other side of the road as I press the fob again.

A mix of relief and dread fills me and, as I sprint across the street, a car swerves to avoid me. I speed-click the unlock button on my fob and open the door just enough to slide in and close and lock it. My heart races so fast I feel it in my throat. I start the car and, with trembling hands, I pull onto the road, not looking, not caring, just flying out of there.

My hands are clammy and tight against the wheel, and the more distance I put between me and our neighborhood the better I feel, if only for the moment.

Hot tears pour down my cheeks as I realize Nico was right. I am obsessed with Luca, and it's not okay.

My phone vibrates, and I jump. It's my mom. I enable voice command to hear her message: "The camera at the Montepulciano house caught something."

I turn sharply toward the villa where my mom is still staying. There's nowhere else to go anyway.

CHAPTER 15

ELLA

I arrive at the villa and let myself in. Angelina, Vinny, and my mother sit at the kitchen table sipping wine. I must be quite the sight, because their expressions show surprise and worry. No one says a word, but Angelina rises to get another wine glass from the cupboard and sets it in front of me. She doesn't ask but pours a generous amount into my glass.

"Did you see my text?" my mother asks. "Are you okay?"

"Yes," I say. "I was already in my car, so I came right here." I sip my wine and it warms me as it goes down.

"Do you want to call Nico and tell him to come?" Angelina says.

"He's got plans tonight," I say.

"El, you don't look good," my mother says. "What's wrong?"

"I'm a little shaken," I say. "Someone followed me to my car."

"Did you see them?" my mother says.

"Not exactly, but I heard footsteps behind me."

"Are you sure?"

"I know someone followed me."

"It's Luca or one of his people," she says.

Although I can't stop thinking about Jonella's hatred towards me, she's probably right about it being Luca.

They're staring at me. Like they know there's more to my shaky presence.

"You said the cameras caught something at the Montepulciano house?" I ask.

"Yes," she says. "It's not completely clear, but I'll show you." She pulls her laptop from the desk in the kitchen, positions it toward me, and pushes play.

I can make out the front walkway and the steps leading to the porch through the grainy picture. The camera has wide coverage, showing ample space around the front door and between the two pillars.

"Keep watching," my mother says, and I see it. A hooded figure emerges from the trees to the left of the house. An average-sized person with dark pants, dark shoes, and a dark hooded sweatshirt with a hood big enough to obscure any glimpse of the person's face. The hooded figure climbs the steps, reaches the porch, and removes something from the sweatshirt pocket. It looks like a piece of paper being wedged in the door's crack so it sticks out a bit. Then the hooded figure gives a quick glance back, and with its head low, exits the camera's view, becoming lost among the trees. I replay it three more times, stopping and zooming in, trying to catch anything remarkable in the face, but it's impossible.

"It's a note," I say.

"It's a trap," Angelina says.

Vinny shoots her a look.

"It's okay, Vinny," I say. "You two are family to me. You can weigh in anytime you'd like. I don't think it's a trap. Let's go get it," I say. "What have we got to lose?"

They stare at me wide-eyed.

"Oh, no, no," Vinny says, shaking his finger. "None of you are going. You bring this tape to the police and let them take it from here. Let them go get the note. You're not going yourself. It's not safe." He glances at Angelina. "Understand, Angie?"

I look at Vinny with so much adoration. I love him for wanting to protect us. It's what loving family members do for one another.

"Vinny, it's okay. I'm not bringing anyone with me. I'll go myself. It will be fine."

"I don't think so," Angelina says, putting her hands on her hips. "You are not going by yourself.

"I'll go too," my mother says.

My mother is normally against taking risks like this. She gets her cautious nature from Nonna. I'm shocked at her willingness to go. "You will?"

Vinny turns to my mother. "Gabby, you shouldn't go either." When neither of us replies, he says, "Well, I can't tell you girls what to do, but I can tell *you*, Ange, especially after what happened to you."

Angelina warmly reminds him, "I promised you I would never put my life in danger like that again, and I meant it." She turns to my mother and me. "I understand the urgency in all of this. I understand you can't wait, and it's justified. We wouldn't want the wind to blow the note away waiting for the police to arrive. Then we'll never know what it said. It's getting late, and it will take at least two to three hours to get there. You should go now."

My mother's eyes lock with mine. It's now or never.

Angelina unclasps her necklace with the Italian horn and a cross in the middle and hands it to my mother. "Keep your necklace on, Ella," she says. The Italian horn: protector of evil.

My mother puts on the necklace, and we're ready to go. Vinny and Angelina walk us to the door and hug us goodbye.

"Be careful," they warn.

We promise to text them when we arrive and again when we're on our way back. We give them access to the camera so they can watch us when we get there.

* * *

We weave through winding roads, passing beautiful houses perched on the hillside as we near Luca and Sienna's house in just under three hours. At the end of the road, we emerge into the gated and poorly lit community of Via del Macellino. Oddly, many residents haven't turned on their outside lights.

It's strange that the gate to Luca's property is wide open. I remember when Liv and I stood behind the ironclad bars for the first time as we gazed at Luca's best-kept secret. My skin prickles, recalling that moment when Luca realized who we were.

Cautiously, we drive through the entrance and follow the lengthy tree-lined driveway until it ends at a small turnaround in front of the house. Whoever left this note could be here. They could easily hide anywhere, watching, waiting for us to get out of the car and take the note. It could be a trap, but there is no way I won't take that chance.

"I'm afraid to get out of the car," my mother says.

"You stay in the car. I'll get out and run to the door and back. As soon as I get back in the car, we drive away. It'll be okay, Mom." My insides are flipping, and I'm paralyzed with fear, recalling the last time I was here, and that wasn't good at all.

My mother looks at my hands and then my eyes. "You're shaking."

"It's adrenaline kicking in. I'm okay. It'll be over before we know it and then we'll get out of here." I peer through the car window at the darkness surrounding us, making sure no one is there.

"I'll keep the car running," she says. "As soon as you open this door, you better jump in, because I'm stepping on the gas."

I nod.

"And El—go straight to the door and back. Nothing else. Got it?"

"Of course," I say. What else would I do? "On the count of three. One, two—"

It happens all at once. I don't know what direction it comes from when it hits the windshield. We scream and slouch down in our seats.

"What's happening? Was that a gunshot?" my mother yells.

I'm so scared I can't speak. I don't want to look, but I do. By slightly adjusting my position, I stay low while having a view through the partially broken windshield. It's a big circle with spindly legs spreading across the glass like the rays of a crystal sun. Something larger than a bullet hit the windshield. I fumble around in my crossbody bag for my knife, but I can't find it.

My mother and I are face-to-face. She has a wild look in her eyes and is trembling. I am too.

"I'm so sorry, Mom. It was a mistake to let you come with me."

"No. I wanted to come. But we need to get out of here. Forget the note. Whoever did this is close enough to hit our car. They want to hurt us."

We didn't come all this way to do nothing but turn around and go back. I open my door. "Get ready, Mom." I bolt from the car to the door without looking back. My rubbery legs somehow get me to the door, and when I get there I almost collapse from fear. The paper we saw on camera is actually an envelope. I quickly grab it and hurry back to the car. The cracked windshield and dented hood catch my attention, along with a boulder-sized rock next to the front tire.

I jump into the car and close the door and then we fly down the driveway and out of the neighborhood, hearts pumping fast, breathless, speechless. It's not until we've been driving for at least fifteen minutes before I tear open the envelope and read it aloud.

Its bold-faced message reads:

You're wasting your time here. There is nothing that will help you in this house. Go to the old neighborhood. It has more secrets, and we know how you like secrets, Ella.

My mother grips the steering wheel with such intensity that I can see the muscles flexing in her arms. Her eyes remain fixed on parts of the road she can see through the broken windshield. "We shouldn't have come," she says, her voice desperate.

I apologize again for bringing her with me and putting her in danger, and I tell her that even if she hadn't come it wouldn't have stopped me from going.

"That's even worse," she says. "How would you have done this by yourself? We should have sent the police, Ella. What are we thinking? We can't keep putting ourselves in danger."

If I reply right now, it will only cause an argument. Instead, I focus on the note. "Do you think whoever wrote the note also threw the boulder? I mean, it's been three hours since the note was left," I say. "Why would someone go to the trouble of writing a note, practically telling us where to go and what to do, and then try to hurt us?"

"People are sick," she says. "They want to get you when your guard is down. They're purposely trying to confuse us. Or trying to draw us here."

"I guess."

It's possible that the person who wrote the note wanted to confuse us. They know who I am and why I'm here. Did they plant the note and then watch from a distance? When we drove in and parked the car, were they ready to attack us? Or was the attack more of a warning?—a scare tactic? If someone wanted to physically harm us or kill us, they would have done it right away. So why didn't they?

There might have been two people at the house tonight. The person we saw on camera affixing the note to the door might have left after completing their task. A second person might have waited until the person with the note left. Then, when we arrived, they threw the boulder, hoping to scare or hurt us. Perhaps it's two unconnected people, or maybe they're working together. Maybe the purpose of the note is to discourage us from going inside the house because there is definitely something they want to keep hidden from us.

I share these thoughts with my mother, who is still very shaken and angry. With her hands still clenched on the wheel and sweat dripping down the sides of her face she says, "Two people . . . one person . . . none of it matters. Someone wants us to stop looking and mind our business, and that's what we need to do."

A text comes in from an unknown number, but not the number that's been calling me: *You were close to finding the truth a few days ago.*

And then another: *Someone may be in danger there.*

I text back: *Who is this?* But it fails to send. I call the number, but it disconnects immediately.

"We need to go to the police, Ella." My mother's voice is shaky. "Now."

CHAPTER 16

ELLA

Instead of driving us to the police station, my mother goes to the villa.

Angelina sits in her chair in the living room, illuminated by her table light. While crocheting a blanket, she arches her eyebrow slightly and quickly glances up from her work. She throws her work aside, leaps from her chair, and yells, "Holy *Mingia*! I thought you were both going to be killed!"

I didn't think she knew what had happened. Our text messages simply mentioned when we arrived and when we left. When Angelina crochets something, she's engrossed in her work and oblivious to things around her. But she's swearing in Italian, which means she's very upset, so maybe she did see something on the security camera feed.

We stare at her blankly. "Did you see what happened?" I say. We sit down on the sofa across from her.

"Yes, I watched it all on the computer," she says, her voice quivering. "It was horrible not being able to yell into the speaker and warn you. I thought about making a noise to scare him away, but I was afraid it would put you in more danger. The only thing that calmed me down was seeing you get in that car and drive away. Ella, what were you thinking going up to the door after he threw that enormous boulder at your car?" Her words fly out of her mouth in one babbling stream. She stops and sips some water before continuing. "When I saw it hit your windshield I was sure it went through. Just as I was about to call the police, I—"

"Wait," I say. "You said *him*. Did you see who threw it?"

Angelina's chin quivers as her trembling hands refresh the computer screen and rewind the video footage. We go back to where we see our car driving up. Nothing happens for a while and then we see the boulder crashing onto the windshield. My mother's hand flies to her mouth. Seeing it terrifies me all over again. I replay the moments in the car right after, my mother and I fearing for our lives. I watch myself bolt to the door, snatch the note, and race back, but still don't see anyone else as we drive off.

I glance at Angelina, and she nods at the computer screen, encouraging us to continue watching. About three minutes after our tail lights disappear, a figure emerges from the trees. Stocky, muscular, shorter than the hooded figure who left the note. This figure wears a dark hooded sweatshirt which almost obscures the face. I glimpse part of the lower jaw and chin, a light complexion. The figure walks to where the boulder rests, probably wishing they had chosen a bigger, heavier one that might have smashed through the glass.

The hooded figure searches for something and then goes to the door, possibly wondering what I'd taken from there. As the figure turns, part of the hood pulls away, revealing a nose and cheekbone. I notice the odd gait of this person. Familiar. Chills run through me as I watch him walk away toward the trees. I can't see where he's going, but I see him remove his hood and wipe his brow, likely assuming he's out of the camera's view. And I see enough of this person to know who it is.

I pause the video and look at Angelina and my mother, who both stare back with the same realization. It's obvious to me. This is a man who has always easily passed for being twenty years younger than his actual age. Except for that right foot he favors, he's always been fit and healthy. That gait we all know well.

"It's Luca," I say.

Silence follows, but it's written in their eyes. Luca was the one who hurled that boulder at us, and we all know it. It's the confirmation we needed: Luca is back, and he *has* been following me. And he wants to harm us, or at least harm me. In all our admissions of fear, anger, and the danger we've put ourselves in, we agree that what has happened tonight is a good thing. A step in the right direction, finally.

As far as we know, Luca hasn't noticed the small, powerful, highly technical, and well hidden camera we've camouflaged in the trees. He has no idea it's there, watching everything he does. And if we hire someone to install a few additional cameras along the driveway or other vantage points in the yard, we might discover what Luca is doing and where he's going.

I suggest a stakeout type of setup, where we hide and wait for him to arrive. If he goes inside the house, we can attach a GPS tracker to his car and follow him.

Neither my mother nor Angelina are okay with this idea. But they are interested in having the private investigator Emma hired to do it.

"It has to happen as soon as possible—like tomorrow, first thing," my mother says.

"And what did that note say about the old neighborhood?" Angelina asks. "It said we should go there, didn't it?"

"It's perfect for a private investigator," my mother says, looking at me. "Maybe he or she can examine the items from the storage room and the other things you found. It's their job to prove a connection to Luca, not yours."

"Not as simple as it sounds, but, yes, you're right," I say. "Can we play that video again?"

Angelina drags the video back to start, and we watch quietly.

I pause the video just as Luca is about to exit the camera's view. "He's going that way," I say, pointing to the left. "That's toward the back of the house. Did we put cameras in the back?"

"No, only in the front," my mother says. "But we'll add them to the back."

"How about on all sides of the house?" I suggest.

On the way to the sink to get a glass of water, I stumble, feeling the effects of no sleep and too much stress on my body. In a few hours I'll be back at the hospital, preparing to present my findings on the latest cardiac procedures. I feel unprepared and unfit for it. My temples throb, and I hear Nico's voice reminding me I'm taking on more than I can handle. I'm feeling dizzy as I blink back tears.

My mother notices my unsteadiness and puts her hand on mine. "You need to go to bed," she says.

We say goodnight and scatter to our rooms.

I barely make it past the door and throw myself on the bed. I remove my clothes and drag my body under the covers. I take a quick look at my phone to confirm my alarm and notice that I have received no texts or calls from Nico all day. As sad as that makes me feel, I can no longer fight to stay awake.

CHAPTER 17

MONA

The first place I'm held captive is his house. It's right after the stabbing. With an old dishcloth, he blots the bloodstains on my dress, in the two areas where he cut me, one at my side and one near my chest. I'm in so much shock and pain that I don't even cry. He tells me that the stab wounds were only to warn me, not to kill me. He blindfolds me and leads me to the attic. With my hands bound by a rope, he holds onto them and I follow. He says he has a gun and his finger is on the trigger, ready to shoot if I scream or try to get away.

When we first start climbing the stairs, I think he is bringing me to his bedroom. I'm pretty sure we walk into a bedroom, but then I hear the creaking noise that a door makes on rusty hinges. The next thing I know, we're crouching low and he's shoving my head through a small opening, but then I'm able to stand again. We go up another set of stairs, and when we stop, we're met with a warm gust of stale attic air. I smell sawdust and the cardboard from boxes of items long forgotten.

The thick air makes me cough. When we stop, he shoves me, and I fall onto a stool or a chair. He takes the rope from my hands and uses it to tie them to a pole of some sort. He's being very meticulous and taking a long time, and I assume it's because he's making sure that his knots are indestructible.

I weigh my options and try to decide if his mood is slightly calmer so I can ask him a question. When I think the time is right, I ask him one simple question: "Why are you doing this to me?"

He answers me by placing a piece of thick, heavy tape across my mouth. After that, he's so quiet that I question if he's still in the room. I only know he was when I hear the door close after a few minutes.

Each of the three times he returns today, he tortures me with his silence. He doesn't say or do anything, he just stays there. Sometimes I hear his footsteps approach me and then walk away. It's disturbing and unnerving. Maybe he's contemplating his next move, or perhaps regret is getting the better of him. Or maybe he enjoys watching me squirm.

Before he leaves for the last time today, he says, "To your left you'll find a bucket in case you have to—you know…"

I hear his footsteps approaching and stop. I can feel his hot breath on my face.

"I'm going to take the tape off your mouth so you can eat. But if you scream, it goes back on even tighter, and there won't be another chance. Nod if you understand."

I nod. A drink of water is the most exciting thing I can imagine.

He spoon-feeds me oatmeal, which is so thick it makes me gag, and then he holds a container of water at my lips. I want to gulp it down fast, but I can only take small sips.

I'm unsure if it's two or three days before he returns, and I'm starving. I jump as soon as the creaky hinges scream open. A flood of cool air enters with him.

"It stinks in here," he says. "I'm going to change your bandages, so I'll need to remove your dress."

I get a sinking, sick feeling in my stomach, fearing what he might do when I'm undressed, but to my surprise, he does exactly as he says.

He's eerily calm and gentle as he removes the bandages, carefully pressing a warm, wet cloth against my damaged skin. He tenderly pats it dry and smooths on an ointment. Then he wraps my waist and chest in new bandages. Very surprising.

But perhaps most surprising is that, instead of putting back on my dirty, bloodstained, smelly dress, he unties me and helps me into a sweatshirt and sweatpants, which are soft and warm. He re-ties my hands together, but not to the pole. His compassion confuses me.

I wonder about the damage on my insides and why I haven't had an infection by now. Thankfully, he hasn't been violent like that since. He's had temper tantrums and foul moods and times when I think he might hit me, but he hasn't. I need to get out of here before an infection sets in or before he decides to get rid of me. Three times I've sensed light through my blindfold and felt it on my face, which I assume is coming from a window, making my stay in this place around three days.

The door closes, and shortly after, a distant sound of another door closes and his footsteps retreat, becoming faint as the distance increases between us.

* * *

It's the end of day five and I'm so weak. All I do is sleep. Although I'm not confined to one spot, I still don't have my sight, and it is making me feel crazed. The tightness of the blindfold digs into my skin. If I use my hands to move it, I might cut my eyes or my face.

Without warning, he charges through the door, grabs me from the floor, and forces me to stand. I'm surprised he's here at night. Is this the end? Or is he letting me go? He pulls the rope attached to my hands and I follow him back down the way we came up. The fresh air hits me hard and I gulp it in.

He scoops me into his arms and places me in a small compartment. Something slams and jostles the compartment, and I hear the revving engine of a car and realize I'm in the trunk. *This is where I die,* I say to myself. He's going to kill me and bury me somewhere, and no one will ever find me.

But that's not what happens.

I don't know how long we have driven because I slept most of the way. The car stops, and he pulls me from the trunk. Once again, he's moving fast, dragging me behind him. My feet are cushioned by soft grass and then pierced by small gravel. I follow him up cement steps as I try to catch my breath. We stop for nothing, not even when I stub my toe and fall. Eventually the stairs end, and at the top I hear him fumbling through his keys until he finds the right one. It slides into the lock and clicks.

When we enter the building or house, he doesn't take me upstairs like before. Instead, we descend down the longest flight of stairs I've ever experienced. We are so far down I feel the air change. The farther we descend, the colder it gets. The first chill of dampness enters through the soles of my feet as they touch the hard cement floor. An earthy smell emanates from the room, moldy, like death.

He shoves me through a door, and, when he unties my hands, the skin at my wrists cry in relief.

The smell of his cologne and dirty sweat makes the bile in my stomach rise to my throat. I am sitting in a chair with my unbound hands resting in my lap and my feet resting on the cold floor. He stands behind me, unties my blindfold, and lets it fall to the ground.

The cold air hits my eyes, and at first I cannot open them. I pull my hands to my face and gently massage my eyelids. I wipe away tears with my arm and blink a few times. Soon my blurred vision clears, and I see him standing directly in front of me.

He looks me square in the eyes. I hold back my scream, fearing what he might do next. He cups my chin and leans closer. His hot breath smells like sulfur.

"It doesn't matter how much you scream," he says. "This room is soundproof. No one will hear you. No one knows about this place except for me. Do you understand what I'm saying?"

I nod.

My mouth is so dry that I have to swallow a few times to give some moisture to it. I'm afraid to ask him why he's moved me and why he didn't just let me go, although I think it's pretty obvious.

I want to make a deal with him.

I clear my throat. "Please," I say. My weak voice cracks. "Let me go. I promise not to tell a soul about any of this. It can be our—"

"Enough," he says. "You know it's too late for that."

"But it's not too late," I say. "I want to live. I don't care what you've done. I just want to go home."

"I said enough," his voice bellows with a low, rumbling, animalistic growl.

It makes my insides curl, and I question if he's even human. My eyes strain through the dim shadows of the new room. He comes closer. I examine the creased, thick skin around his bloodshot eyes. Anger rages through them, but also a bit of pain. I note his thick, unkempt eyebrows, the sweat beading around his unshaven face and neck, his short, frizzy, salt-and-pepper hair.

I imagine him as a younger man, probably at one time very handsome. But now he is old, and the ugliness that has grown inside him now appears on his face.

I fear how he looks at me, as if he can't decide if he wants to play with me, torture me, or kill me.

An idea comes to me, and I play it out. I reach my hands toward his face. "I don't think I've really given you a chance," I say. "I feel bad about that. We could pretend like this didn't happen—start over. We could go on a date. Why should it have to be this way? I—"

"Silence!" he says, and the force of his breath moves my hair. Flecks of spit settle on my cheek. "Or I'll silence you myself." He's a wolf and I'm his prey. He glances at his watch and becomes jumpy. "I'll be right back, I promise."

I'm sickened by the hopefulness in his voice. I'd rather he didn't come back ever.

He tosses me a thin flannel blanket. "In case you get cold. When I get back, I'll bring you some water and maybe a reward for good behavior." His voice is sweet and giddy, and it turns my stomach. His face shows no sign of the anger and rage I saw moments ago. I hear a heavy thud and the clicking of locks as the door closes behind him.

With my hands in front of me, I cautiously step into the darkness in the direction he went and stop when I feel the wall. I run my hands along the wall until I discover the shape of the door. My hands rest on the firm door handle.

I squat to the floor and lean against the door. I'm cold and tired but not yet defeated. A plan is developing in my mind—a plan to break free from here, even if it means I have to commit murder.

CHAPTER 18

ELLA

My mind is everywhere I don't want it to be. A floating sensation carries me from my car to the hospital, and I barely notice the ground I've covered. Exhaustion possesses my entire body, dulling my fear of being followed. I pay only the slightest attention to the people and commotion around me because my primary focus is to get inside, pull it together, and do what I have to do to nail this presentation. Today I'm presenting my research on stem cells and gene transfer to treat cardiovascular disease to Dr. Girofolo and the fellows in my program.

Keep your eyes on the door. That's what I keep telling myself. I rummage through the front zipper of my crossbody for my ID badge, but it's not there. Luckily, someone else is walking in ahead of me so I can slip inside when they swipe their badge at the door.

The moment the doors slide open, something hits me like a thick wall of hot smoke. A warning shoots through me, urging me to turn around, exit the building, and get back in my car, but I don't. The curiosity of what's happening inside this hospital is stronger than the need to flee it.

They're eyeing me up and down in judgment. Two nurses standing by the information desk, a few fellows near the coffee station, and two others pause on the top stair and look in my direction. All eyes are staring intently at me as if I've done something wrong.

I swipe my hands on my hair, in case I have something in it, and look down at my shirt, confirming I haven't forgotten to put it on this morning. What are they starting at? Are they about to shame me? Maybe I'm overreacting and it's my nerves talking. Or lack of sleep has gotten the better of my judgment.

Still, I need to know what's going on, so I walk straight ahead and climb the stairs, passing by the two fellows on the stairway. Their eyes follow me as I ascend the staircase, watching until I'm out of sight.

Standing directly in front of my locker are two people with grim faces, who cause a rush of nervousness to surge through me: Dr. Girofolo and a security guard.

Dr. Girofolo says, "We'd like to speak with you, Ella," and he waves his arm in the direction he would like me to follow.

We enter a private office space, one I've never been in, and he motions for me to sit down in one of two chairs across from a desk. Then he sits in the desk chair as the security guard stands in the doorway.

Dr. Girofolo is saying something in a soft, low, monotonous voice. Words are coming out of his mouth, but they're not making sense. He is serious, almost stern, and he looks at me as if he's scolding a child.

"In this establishment, we take our fellowship program seriously. What I'm about to say to you is difficult."

My hearing gets fuzzy, fading in and out with waves of anxiety, and his lips keep moving but nothing's coming out. Something about a threat and protecting the other fellows. . . .

What is happening?

He pulls something from his desk drawer—a plastic bag—and places it on the table between us. I see the shape of a knife inside the bag, a knife similar to the one I carry. Next, he places a handful of papers folded in half on the desk. He faces them toward me and opens them one by one, as if waiting for confirmation that they belong to me.

I'd thought keeping the anonymous threatening notes in my locker at the hospital was safer than keeping them at the villa. Inside a small tin I had purchased, I kept the notes tucked at the back of the top shelf, concealed between extra sets of scrubs. I'm particularly concerned about two of the notes in front of me because I had given both of those notes to the police. My knife is usually in one of two places: in a pocket of my crossbody bag or snugly tucked in a specially fitted ankle holster hidden by my pant leg. And I'm praying it's in my bag, because it's definitely not on me.

I search Dr. Girofolo's eyes and face and examine his posture for signs of what he wants me to say, what he expects from me. The items belong to me, but why does he have them, and how did he get them?

When I work up the nerve to ask him, my voice comes out squeaky. I clear my throat. "What is all this? Where did you get these?"

He looks at me, cross. "So, you admit they're yours," he says matter -of-factly.

"I didn't say that."

"I was hoping you would tell me the truth." He removes the knife from the bag and holds up the notes. "Are you saying these don't belong to you?"

I ignore him, fearing that the answer he wants will not help me. "Over the last couple of weeks, I've been receiving anonymous, threatening notes. I pick up the two notes I had given to the police. "Why do you have *these*?" I ask. "I gave these notes to the police. How did *you* get them?"

Dr. Girofolo sits back. "You're saying *you* received these notes?"

"Yes."

"That's strange." He pauses, watching me.

"What do you mean?"

"Jonella's found the notes and the knife . . . and this," he lifts up something else, and dangling from his hand is my ID badge.

My hand instinctively flies to the spot below my chest where my ID badge should hang, and it's not there. That's why I couldn't find it on my way in. My heart sinks. It must have fallen off at some point.

I shake my head. "No. No way. It's not what you think."

The walls close in around me, making me dizzy. It's all unfolding before I can make sense of it. I hadn't paid close enough attention and missed something significant. Nico was right. This is out of control. It's become too much for me.

Dr. Girofolo stares at me with disgust. He's made up his mind. "Tell me how the notes, your badge, and your knife were left behind in the conference room where you and Miles work. What were you planning to do with the knife? Jonella is terrified that you want to hurt her. She told me about the encounters between the two of you and how you tried to provoke her."

"I never said that was my knife," I say. "And I've never tried to provoke her or anyone else. It was the other way around. I didn't write those notes to Jonella; those notes were written to *me*."

"How did they get there?"

"Someone else put them there. I am being framed by . . . someone in this hospital. Maybe it's Jonella."

My chest is so tight I can hardly breathe, and I'm on the edge of a full-blown panic attack. It has to be Jonella. That would explain her odd and hostile behavior towards me.

I know I've been distracted, but I wouldn't have been so careless as to leave those things behind in the conference room. But now I'm questioning myself. How could Jonella, or anyone for that matter, get her hands on the notes, especially the ones I gave to the police? How did they get my knife or my badge?

"The cameras . . . Have you checked the cameras?" I say.

The look that flashes across Dr. Girofolo's face reveals he might not have thought of that. "The cameras in the hallway are being reviewed as we speak. I don't know how much of the locker area they'll capture. As you know, there are limited cameras in the locker room."

"Good," I say, "because then it will be obvious that it wasn't me. You will not see me anywhere near those lockers."

"Why would someone want to frame you? What would they have against you?" he says.

"*Scusa*, Dr. Girofolo," I say. "I know it's early in my fellowship program, and you don't know me as well as the others, but I would hope you might know something about my character. Maybe you should ask why I would do that to someone. What would I have to gain by playing this game? I've always tried to portray the highest professionalism. Have I given you reason to doubt me?"

He's quiet, like he's thinking over what I've said. "You're right—you came highly recommended to us. And, yes, you have always shown professionalism, dedication, and a determination to keep up to speed with the others." The accusatory lines near his eyes fall slightly. "Unfortunately, now that this has been brought to my attention, and some of these items belong to you, we will have to conduct our own investigation. At the moment, we will handle the investigation ourselves at the building level, without involving the police. We'll wait for news on the cameras. In the meantime, I'm afraid I have no choice. . . ."

I tell him I don't understand what he's trying to say, and he tells me they have to suspend me for the next few days, temporarily, while they investigate. I ask him to share who brought this to his attention, and he says he is not allowed to give a name, but, of course, I know it's Jonella. She was the one who found it in her locker.

"Does this investigation include speaking with Jonella again?"

"Most definitely," he says.

I'm sick to my stomach. This can't be happening. I'll miss five days of my fellowship. Five days. Now I can't present my research in a couple of hours as I'd planned. I won't finish in the timeframe I had planned.

Dr. Girofolo stands and I stand, devastated, fighting back tears. He nods to the guard, who steps toward me. I give him a look to say I don't need him to take my arm like a prisoner or even come near me. I understand what's happening. I will follow him without resisting. Dr. Girofolo extends a hand and thanks me for my time. I might have heard a shred of sympathy, but I could be making that up in my head.

By the time we leave, no one is in the corridor or near the information desk. Everyone is in their offices preparing for their presentations. I follow the guard down the stairs with a heavy knot in my stomach. The clerk at the information desk glances up briefly as we pass. We exit through the sliding doors and away from the hospital, all the way to my car. As I start my car, the guard remains fixed to the pavement, his eyes never leaving me as I pull away from the parking lot. He remains there until I no longer see him in the rearview mirror.

CHAPTER 19

ELLA

I make my last turn on Via del Carmine, which leads to the villa. As I enter the traffic circle, I catch a glimmer of shiny silver as the sun beats down on the car in the driveway parked next to Angelina's car.

It's a Maserati. Nico's Maserati.

Why is he at the villa?

I pull in next to his car and examine it. An Italian horn necklace hangs from the rearview mirror. I toss my crossbody over my shoulder and, as I near the front door, the smell of garlic briefly comforts me. In the doorway, I hear faint conversation coming from the kitchen. Through the opening, I see them sitting at the table. They don't detect my presence, and, for a moment, I listen. Nico sits on one side of the table, his head hung low like he's frustrated or upset about something. My mother and Angelina are sitting across from him, looking on with reassurance. Nonna and Aunt Lena are at opposite ends, their hands folded in front of them on the table.

Angelina's voice is soothing. "Don't worry. She's a smart, independent woman. There's no doubt she knows what she's doing." Angelina mumbles something I don't understand, while

Nico nods. "She's also stubborn, like me. Once we have something in our minds, there's no stopping us. You'd think we are related. "

"She gets her determination and stubbornness from my side," my mother says. "I'm that way too."

"What way?" I interrupt, walking into the kitchen.

Heads turn fast towards me. Nico's face flushes, like a child caught misbehaving.

"Ella," my mother says, surprised. "Why are you home so early? Is your presentation done already?"

I scan their faces, finding Nico's last. "What are you all doing at the villa? Nico, I thought you were working."

His mouth opens. He appears to be searching for the right words.

"He stopped by to say hello and talk with us," Angelina blurts.

"Talk about me?" I say.

"Yes, El, about you," my mother says, "and what's been happening to all of us. Nico is just concerned."

"His concern is between Nico and me. If I wanted everyone to know about our private lives, I would have told you myself. Nico and I will work things out between us. It's no one's business."

"Work things out," Nonna repeats, shaking her head.

"El, what's going on? Why are you back so soon?" my mother says.

"I don't want to talk about it," I say. "Especially after you've all been talking about me."

"Ella, please sit down," my mother says. "We weren't saying anything bad about you. We're just worried, that's all. You're right, though—we should have waited and talked with you. Come sit."

I hesitate because I'm angry, and I feel a little betrayed at the moment, but I'm also lost and have nowhere else to go. No one else to talk to about what just happened. And if I don't talk, I'm going to explode. I sit at the table and recount what happened at the hospital. How everyone stared at me when I entered. How my conversation with Dr. Girofolo made me feel like a criminal.

Then I explain what happened between Jonella and me a few days earlier.

"It's the *malocchio*," Nonna says, making the sign of the cross. "Get me some oil and water."

"No, Nonna, that's unnecessary," I say. "I'm fine. It's not that."

"This girl—Jonella—she's jealous of you," Nonna says. "If you know what has made her jealous, you might be able to fix it."

"It's too late for that," I say. "She thinks I'm some sort of threat to her and that I put those things in her locker. But I think she's involved, or someone else is messing with us."

"But if she has the notes we gave to the police, then someone on the inside is crooked," Nico says.

Nonna leans to my mother. "What notes is she talking about, Gabby?" My mother whispers something back, to which Nonna replies, "Oh dear."

Aunt Lena's face remains frozen in a state of bewilderment and confusion. She purses her lips like she's about to engage in the conversation, but she's unsure if she should. I've seen this look many times during old family dinner conversations.

Nico stands, comes over, and wraps his arms around me. His woodsy pine and minty scent instantly comforts me. "I'm sorry, El," he says. "I can't imagine what it must have been like in that office and then being escorted out of there. It's not right."

I gaze into his eyes and he kisses my forehead. He takes my hand and we join the table with everyone else.

"I can't believe it, " I say. "Five days away from the hospital. And now I'm afraid I won't be able to share my presentation. It might be too late by then. What if I lose this opportunity and they suspend me permanently?"

They try to reassure me it won't come to that. The investigation will prove that I'm innocent and they will accept me back at the hospital.

I contemplate telling them what Angelina learned about Poppy's old neighborhood in Scilla. But, for the sake of honesty, and trust in my new family, I decide it's the right thing to do.

"I'm going to do something useful while I'm away from the hospital."

Nico's face is serious as he waits for me to continue.

I look at Angelina. "Have you mentioned anything about Scilla?"

"Until now, I didn't think it was possible," Angelina says, and then she explains about the reconstruction of Poppy's neighborhood in Scilla.

"So, that's that," I say. "We are going to Scilla first thing tomorrow."

The hurt in Nico's eyes kills me. Or is it disgust?

Aunt Lena cocks her head and straightens her shoulders. "You said marina? What marina?"

"You didn't know your husband grew up around a family-owned marina?" I say, trying to soften my edgy tone. "He mentioned nothing about it? Ever?"

"No, not one thing," she says.

Nonna's eyes flash at Lena's, and it makes me wonder if she doesn't believe her either.

"Ella, for the love of God, let the police do what they need to about the note and the threats. Let them take care of this. Stay out of it now."

"What note, Gabby?" Nonna says.

"Yes," Aunt Lena says, "what note are you referring to?"

The two of them look petrified. None of us stop to explain about the note that was left at the Montepulciano house. The one clearly meant for me. The one that points to Poppy's old neighborhood.

I can't bear looking at Nico. "I agree. The police should know about the note. And they should investigate. But I'm not willing to negotiate my involvement. My investigation. I'm only telling you out of respect and because we promised each other we would always be truthful. But I've decided—"

"This is insane," Nico says, clenching down hard on his jaw. "Are you all going to stand by and let her do this? Can't any of you see that she's obsessed with Luca and has been since the beginning? You don't see what this is doing to her?"

"Nico—" I interject.

"No, El," he says, a look of disgust on his face. "You are going to get hurt, or worse, and I can't stand by and let it happen. So, you need to choose."

I search his face for signs that, although he's upset, he still believes in me—in us. But his body language speaks volumes: his fisted hands on top of the table, leaning forward, legs apart. The veins in his forehead bulge beneath the sweaty strands of his hair. He's dead serious. And he's giving me an ultimatum.

"Don't say it, Nico," I pleadingly warn him. I feel the eyes of my mother, Nonna, Aunt Lena, and Angelina boring into me, silently watching us fall. "Please don't."

"El, I don't know what else to do." He doesn't budge an inch. "I can't get through to you. Your thinking is not rational. Your lack of awareness prevents you from seeing the danger you're in. It doesn't have to be you at the front all the time. I understand that you feel a sense of urgency in protecting your family. You feel it's your duty, but it's not your job to keep everyone safe."

His sad, defeated eyes stab me in the heart. I'm speechless, afraid to respond the wrong way, afraid to break the ultra-thin rope holding us together. He is right about everything. I can't let it go because there are a million fragmented pieces and reasons not to,. the number one being Poppy. I have to see this through for Poppy. It's unclear even to me why I'm determined to be the person driving this. But ever since the day Poppy confided in me about this terrible secret, right before he slipped away in our arms, I have felt compelled to see it through. My feelings haven't changed; I still feel that way. It's impossible for me to release it. I just can't.

"I'm sorry, El." His shoulders slouch. "If you continue this—if you go back to the old neighborhood without bringing the police with you, if you continue to investigate this on your own—I think it might be the end for us. I hope and pray that our relationship, our future, means more to you than this." He puts a hand to his head and wipes his brow.

"Nico." I say his name and it feels so final. It hovers in the air above us, it floats in the room as we're frozen in our last position. No one speaks.

Nico pushes out his hand. "Don't tell me now," he says. "I can't bear to hear it. Give us the courtesy of at least thinking about it. Can you do that?—think about us for a change?"

"Of course."

"That's all I ask," he says, stepping away from the table. I walk toward him, but he puts up his hands. "I'll see myself out."

"Go after him," Nonna says.

My mother whispers something to her and she quietly shakes her head.

I follow Nico out of the kitchen, through the living room, and stop at the threshold of the entryway. He doesn't turn around when he opens the door. My heart breaks as it closes behind him.

*   *   *

I return to a quiet, sullen kitchen. Everyone but Angelina remains at the table. Angelina bounces around the kitchen, pulling out meats and vegetables from the refrigerator, some pasta from the cupboard, determined to comfort us with food.

My mother reaches for my hand and pulls me in for a hug. I tell her I don't know what to do. I don't know how it's gotten to this point for us. I ask her if she agrees with what Nico said about me. She says she agrees with the parts about me taking on too much and not being careful, but she doesn't agree with everything he said. She understands where Nico is coming from. He loves me and probably feels somewhat neglected and lost because so much of my time has been spent finding Luca.

But she also understands where I'm coming from. I have honest intentions, and I'm doing all of this for Poppy. That's not being selfish. She knows I began this journey on his behalf and that I need to see it through to the end.

She tucks a strand of my hair behind my ear.

"But, Ella, Poppy is already proud of you. You have already solved what he couldn't. You have seen it through far beyond what Poppy ever expected. I know this because he's my father and I know that about him. I don't think he would want you to be in this dangerous predicament, and I know he wouldn't want this to come between you and Nico. And, by the way, he would have loved Nico."

I can't stop the tears from falling. It's too much. Everything is just too much right now. Maybe I need these five days to read-just my thinking.

Angelina, who had been dancing through the kitchen between two mixing bowls, dropping ingredients into each, sud-denly stops. Concern is etched on her face. Her eyes are glued to the large television in the living room, easily viewable from the kitchen.

An urgent message scrolls at the bottom of the screen. Placing the potatoes on the counter, she wipes her hands on her apron and walks into the living room. She grabs the remote and turns up the volume. The news reporter stands in front of a small café, her face drawn into a scowl, her eyebrows knitted together.

"They're reporting on that missing woman," Angelina explains as we all gather around. The reporter shares new infor-mation that the young missing woman, named Bria Gallo, was last seen at this café a few days ago. She was planning to return home to have dinner with her family but never arrived. No one has seen her since then. Witnesses claim to have seen her with an older man, but authorities have not confirmed those tips.

The reporter asks anyone with information that could lead to Bria's whereabouts to call the police immediately. They are offering a reward of ten thousand euros for information leading to her discovery.

Angelina rewinds to the beginning, where the woman is first standing at the café. She walks up to the television, her eyes racing all over the screen. "I think . . . wait a minute . . ." She fast-forwards a few seconds, pauses again, then rewinds to the beginning. She turns to me. "Look at that café. Doesn't it look like the one we've walked by in your Poppy's old neighborhood? I know it's been a while, but I remember you remarked how cute it was and said you wanted to go inside. It was closed at the time. I swear it's the same one."

I examine the café, the road in front, and the area just outside. "It does look like it. Do you think it is? Did they say where this happened?"

"I don't know," she says. "I'll try to go back to the beginning."

I do an online search and find it right away. "It's the one," I say. I skim the article and read the important parts out loud. "It's a café and deli," I say. "Poppy's deli. The one he often went to for his mamá and his family. The one he wrote about in his diary when he found Gianna after several years apart." They later expanded it to include a little seating area with a few tables and chairs to accommodate more visitors—the exact café the reporter was standing in front of.

I hear excitement rising in my voice. Poppy's deli. How surreal seeing it on TV. How peculiar.

An eerie feeling invades, spreading goosebumps across my arms. A feeling I can't dismiss. By the look on Angelina's face, she feels it too. The note, stuck between the door and the frame at the Montepulciano home, stated that we couldn't find what we needed to know at that house. That we needed to go back to where we were before. A long time before. Back to the old neighborhood, where secrets never die.

Angelina stares at me with one raised eyebrow, and I know she's thinking the same as me. It goes against everything Nico said. Everything my family believes and expects of me. They don't want me meddling in areas where the police should be. Maybe if they did their job, or if they weren't on Luca's payroll, I wouldn't have to.

I give a slight nod to Angelina, undetectable by the others, and she winks on her return to the kitchen. We follow her to the table where she finishes her recipes.

My mother looks at Nonna and Lena. "Well, now, I'm sure the police will be all around that café interviewing people and checking for Bria's presence on those cameras."

"If they have cameras," Angelina says. "It's an old neighborhood."

"I hope they find that poor girl," Nonna says to Lena. "Don't you, Lena?"

Aunt Lena finishes tapping something on her phone, tucks it into her purse's back pocket, and looks up at Nonna, distracted. "What? Oh, yes. I hope they find her too."

CHAPTER 20

ELLA

We sit side by side on the train to Chianlalea, the small fishing village in Poppy's old neighborhood of Scilla. We're like old souls from the past. Insulated by people sitting close together, leaning into the aisle hoping to catch a good piece of gossip. Angelina angles her head to my shoulder and says she's getting a bad feeling or a bad vibe. It makes me uneasy knowing that her intuition isn't something to question. I hope it's just nerves and goes away.

We're sneaking off on a secret mission that only the two of us know about. We're rebellious teenagers, fleeing through our bedroom windows to meet up with our friends. Only now, I'm not looking to push the limits. I just want the evil in my family to be gone.

Angelina rests her head on my shoulder and closes her eyes, pretending not to listen to the surrounding chatter. I'm filled with gratitude to know this beautiful woman, a soulmate of sorts who, in such a short time, knows me as well as if not better than most. It's like she can see into my heart, a protector of my soul. Upon entering her charming villa two years ago, I immediately felt a special connection forming between us, as if our souls were being woven together tightly. I was meant to be there at that moment. Our paths connected. She is a determined, strong-willed woman who fiercely loves her family. A spunky, older version of me.

But it's the other things about her as well: her warm, smiling eyes and soothing voice; the softness of her skin; how she makes you feel like you're the only person in the room, the most important guest in her villa. Her special warmth is solely for you. It's the pleasure she takes in decorating her home, just like Nonna—cute, meaningful knick-knacks placed purposely just so.

Her joyful quirkiness, her Italian superstitions, and her love of food and family remind me so much of Poppy that it is simply impossible for me not to love her. I instantly realized that we had formed a lifelong connection. She calls it divine intervention. I call it fate. Even with the two years and thousands of miles we spent apart when I returned to New York , our bond never wavered. We simply picked up where we had left off like no time had passed. As I get older, I've realized that those kinds of bonds are rare.

I tilt my head toward her. "You told Vinny you were doing this, right?"

"Yes, of course I did," she smiles. "Does Nico know?"

I shake my head and glance away. Nico would be upset and disappointed if he knew what I was doing. It wouldn't have mattered that I didn't go alone, or that I was staying at a beautiful inn in a safe neighborhood. The only thing that would matter was that I wasn't going without police protection.

Angelina puts her hand on my lap. "Everything will be okay."

As Nico has said, I have to live in the moment, so I have to change my focus to now and the plans we have for this journey.

"With any luck, we'll find Poppy's home and spend most of the day there and visit some of the local shops in the neighborhood. I'd also like to see the marina."

"Oh, yes, the marina," she says, peeking into my bag as I rummage through it for my glasses.

"Is that what I think it is?" Angelina says of Poppy's diary tucked in a side pocket.

"Of course it is. It would be a sin not to bring it." I'm anxious to view the house through Poppy's eyes, recalling some comments he made while he was in his house, eating dinner, studying, reflecting on life. He probably wrote most of his entries in private at his bedroom desk, reflecting on the previous day.

She gives me a strange look.

"Why did you look at me like that?"

She puts her hand to her chest. "Like what?" she says. "If I didn't know better, I'd say there's more to that diary than you're letting on."

I smirk but don't reply.

We arrive at Bellissima Villa slightly ahead of schedule. It's a beautiful, light-turquoise building with white shutters and white trim, about three stories high and almost as wide. Workers brush the last strokes of white paint on the wooden fence surrounding the property. Freshly trimmed bushes and recently pruned citrus trees reveal pride and attention to detail in this little villa.

But there's something else among the shiny, bright colors, the bursts of citrus, and the cheerful smile of the desk attendant—something I can't quite put my finger on—and it makes me uneasy.

We settle into our rooms to unpack and shower. Before going to bed, I knock on the adjoining door to Angelina's room.

She yells, "Door's open!"

I step inside and see Angelina sitting at a table with a bowl of water and a jar of oil in front of her. "Are you doing the *malocchio*?" I say.

"It's just a precaution," she says, waving her arm.

I hand her an old photograph of Poppy and Luca when they were about seven and nine years old, sitting on the porch in front of their house. I point them out to Angelina, identifying which is Poppy and which is Luca. "Sienna gave this to me," I say.

Angelina takes the photograph and her eyes beam. "*Che Bello*, how beautiful."

I point to the right side of the photo, where a small portion of another house peeks. "This is Sienna, Gianna, and Maria's house. They lived right next door."

Angelina inspects it. "Oh, how I wish I could see more."

"Sienna said Luca kept this photo in a frame on his dresser. When they had to leave their house without warning, it was one of the first things she grabbed."

"Very good," she says. "It might help us determine which house is your Poppy's when we get to his neighborhood. Unless, of course, they've changed the house over the years."

"I hope it helps, because an estate sale will bring several people from the area, which means it will be a busy scene."

She glances at me and smiles. "I'm sure you'll remember a lot about the neighborhood from the first time you went to Scilla. This time the diary will help you in a different way."

✳ ✳ ✳

I couldn't have slept for very long, because it feels like I only just closed my eyes. A glint of sun reaches through the sheer curtains, rendering me awake. I feel a rush of excitement at the thought of going into Poppy's childhood home.

Angelina insists we take the back roads to Scilla so we can get the full Calabrian experience. As I plug in the neighborhood's name, Angelina puts her hand on my arm. "No, dear, GPS won't help us on these roads." Then she whips out an old map of Calabria and opens it. "Here's where we are. To get there, we'll follow the SS18, or Via Marina, all the way. We must drive slowly because some roads are terribly narrow."

As we depart the mountainous countryside of Tropea and enter Scilla, we emerge into another world. I roll down my windows and breathe in the salty air drifting off the Tyrrhenian Sea.

Scilla is a smaller, charming version of Tropea, where the mountains give way to narrow roads and a simple life. A floating sense of nostalgia comforts me.

The roads become crowded as we approach the quaint fishing village of Chianlalea, the heart of the town. The people of Chianlalea are kind and gentle, welcoming and generous, and, most importantly, they are proud of their community. Most families have lived here for generations. I remember the first time I visited and asked the locals if they remembered Gianna. Many recalled knowing of the missing woman decades ago who was last seen in the vineyard. I wonder how they would react to knowing that Gianna is actually alive.

We draw nearer to the sea. I see it. Protruding from the blue waves at the edge of the cliff is Castello Ruffolo. I marvel now as I did when I first set eyes on the castle and how it split the fishing village on one side of the cliff and the beach on the other.

"Did I ever tell you that there's a tunnel that connects those two sides? The fishing village from the beach? I don't know if it's still usable, but many years ago it was."

We slow to a stop at the end of a road and park in one of few parking options left. We step from the car into the bright sun. I shield my eyes and I see bits of blue bobbing in the water. Those tiny fishing boats, from a distance, confirm that we're close to the enchanting streets of Chianlalea. I can hardly stand it.

Bustling streets are filled with weekend shoppers. Compact cars whisk through the narrow roads with hardly a warning. Up ahead, a few feet to the left, yellow tape stretches between two construction cones, blocking a tiny, peculiar staircase rising between two buildings. Several signs warn trespassers to stay out.

I overhear the low voices of two men talking, their expressions serious. They face the blocked stairway when one of them mentions an attack from the night before, but that's all I can hear. I glimpse Angelina, who stops and studies the men closely. We slow down once we're near the stairs, keeping some distance from the men. I try to see where the staircase ends, but they're perfectly positioned to block my view.

Once we're far enough away from the men, I repeat what they talked about. Thankfully I'm more fluent in Italian than I was two years ago, so I know what they were saying.

"Oh dear," Angelina says. "Please don't tell me that. What do you think happened?"

"I don't know."

Now that we're through the back roads, I'm able to use my phone's GPS for the directions needed to walk through town to Poppy's neighborhood. I see a sign that says *Gastronomia*, a deli, and my heart nearly stops. "Oh, my gosh."

"What happened?" Angelina says, looking around.

I point to the deli. "That's the deli where Poppy used to go. It's where he saw Gianna for the first time after years apart. He wrote about the deli several times in his diary."

"You're sure it's the one? Aren't there lots of delis?"

"I'm more than sure," I say as we cross the street.

We stand in front of the small, family-owned deli, and it appears that someone has taken good care of it despite the worn structure. The closed sign hangs on the door as we peek through the window. A simple deli counter at the back and two small tables in front. Small display cases presenting breads and pastries through windows. Judging by its size, there's probably not much more to this little store.

"Now I'm sure we're almost there," I say, recalling Poppy's mention in his diary about the deli at the end of the last street before Poppy's street.

Angelina smiles wide.

Signs announce "Estate Sale: 10:00 am" with an arrow pointing toward the sale.

"Now some of this looks familiar," I say. "At the end of this street we'll turn left, and that should be it."

"This is so exciting." Angelina's eyes twinkle.

I check the time. Not quite ten o'clock. "Should we wait a bit?" I say.

"I don't think so." Angelina gestures towards a young couple walking ahead of us in the same direction. We follow them and turn left onto Poppy's street.

Several people, young and old, gather at the edge of the property. We face the house that I assume belonged to Poppy's family, and I can't take my eyes off it. When I do, briefly, it's only to confirm that I'm more confused than ever.

People join from all directions, rummaging through tables displaying household items. Dishes, tools, clocks, lamps placed on tables and chairs, with every piece of furniture or kitchen item you can imagine extending all around the property.

Angelina links her arm through mine. "You coming?"

I'm absorbed in the scene surrounding Poppy's neighborhood and the beauty of this village.

"Come on, El. Haven't you been to this street before? When you first visited?"

I nod. "I was in and out of these streets a couple of years ago. I knew I was close to Poppy's neighborhood but never knew the exact address or which house was his. The diary entries don't say specifically where he lived, but it mentions places around it, like the deli."

When I first came here, my primary focus was to walk in Poppy's footsteps, using his diary entries to expose the criminal in our family. Now I'm here to catch him.

We walk along the cobbled roads beneath terracotta rooftops. Clothes strung across clotheslines dry in the sun; the brilliant blue Tyrhennian Sea peeks between houses. It's magical. I hold the photo out in front of me and study each house. The black-and-white photo could be any of these houses. It's hard to decipher the smaller, unclear details.

Something about the estate sale house catches my eye. I don't know why I'm drawn to it. It could be the one, but it seems different from the photograph.

But then I see one shutter on the side of the house, slightly hanging off the window. It's still like that after all these years. I follow the edge of the house below the shutter to where it ends on the ground behind a small metal gate.

I slide my finger from the right side of the photograph to the left, matching and confirming its place on the houses in front of me. I raise the photo a little higher and I know right away.

"That's the one." I point to the house on the left of the estate sale. "That is Poppy's house . . . which means the estate sale is at Gianna's house." My heart flips. I can hardly stand it. "That is Poppy's house," I say, my eyes watering.

Angelina hugs me tightly. "I'm sorry, Ella."

"Sorry for what?"

"Well, if Poppy's house was the one with the estate sale, we could go inside. Now that we know it's the other one, we probably won't be able to do that."

But I have an idea.

I take Angelina's hand and lead her to the estate sale at Gianna's house. Standing in front of the door is an older woman with long gray hair pulled to the side in a twist. Slight wrinkles in her olive skin fan her eyes and cheeks, and I'm guessing she probably looks older than she really is.

She moves aside as we approach, providing space for us to go inside. "Today is the first day of the sale," she says, with a partial grin. "Friday is the last."

"Thank you," I say, stepping inside. "Do you know anything about the house next door?" I gesture toward Poppy's house.

"I know it has been abandoned for a while," she says, "and that someone recently bought it."

"Someone bought it?" Angelina says. "When?"

"Recently," she says. "I don't know who. The original owners lived there for a very long time. And then it was vacant for a while. They left everything when they left—furniture, dishes . . . everything." She fiddles with the ends of her hair like she's thinking. "But then a lovely young family moved in during the eighties. They kept everything."

"I'm sure it was helpful not having to buy anything with a young family," I say.

"Yes, that's true," she continues. "They stayed several years, raised their family, then moved away. It sat vacant again until now."

"Was there an estate sale before the current owners moved in?" I ask.

"No, not that I'm aware. From what I hear, the new owner wanted to keep everything in the house the way it was, although I'm not sure who would want all that old furniture."

I would give anything to go inside Poppy's old house to see it the way it was.

"Is it locked?" Angelina asks.

"Of course," says the woman. "You can't just walk in there. It's not for sale anymore."

"How do you know so much about that house?" I ask.

"I grew up around here," she says. "I am acquainted with most of the people in this town. It's easy getting to know people here because it's a small town and everyone is so friendly."

"My grandfather grew up in that house," I say. "He and his brother." I show her the picture, hoping she'll tell us we can go in or at least be willing to look the other way.

The woman takes the photo and compares it against the house. "Well, look at that," she says. "But how can you really be sure? That picture could be any of these houses, even this one."

"No, that's the one," I say, taking back the photo. I know what I know. I look at the woman. "If you're from around here, maybe you know them—the Perri family. Franco and Luca were the two boys who lived with their parents, Sal and Isabella."

Her eyes bulge as if she suddenly woke up from a deep sleep, filled with fear. She swallows nervously. "Everyone knew the Perris. But I thought they lived down the street, near the end."

This, I knew, was untrue. When Poppy referred to his home in Chianlalea, he always said it was right at the center where you could look to the end of the street and see the top of Castello Ruffo peeking out. I know she is wrong, but I don't push it.

"What did you know about them?" Angelina asks. "The Perris?"

"Not that much," she says, glancing around. "But I do remember the young wife. She was always so kind and gentle, but her husband was an angry, unpredictable, dangerous man. Everyone knew that." She glances behind her as if the mere mention of him might materialize him. "I know little about the boys. I don't mean to be rude, but I should get back to my customers."

"Of course," I say. "We'll let you go." I look at Angelina. "Should we see if the door is open? I just want to take a peek inside."

"I wouldn't do that if I were you," the woman says. "You're better off asking the owner when he comes back. I'm sure he won't be long," she says.

"He?"

"He and his wife—an older couple," she says. "Now that I think of it, they moved out a couple of boxes from the house, but not much. I'm pretty sure they'll be back today."

Something near the road catches her attention. We turn around and see a small truck parked on the road in front of us. Four men exit the truck and push a couple of dollies up Poppy's driveway.

"I guess they're still moving things out," Angelina says.

"I really have to go. It was nice to meet you."

"Thank you for your time," I say to the woman.

"You're welcome," she says. "But I wouldn't go in there without the owners' permission."

Just then, a young woman makes her way toward the older woman and begins to engage her in conversation.

Angelina and I slip away and walk the short path from Gianna's old house to Poppy's.

CHAPTER 21

ELLA

Two men stay behind in the truck while the other two roll the dollies through the wide-open front door. Angelina and I act inconspicuously as we cut across the small space from the Russos' house to Poppy's. I stop when my feet touch the first porch step. In my mind, I'm transported back in time, envisioning my mother's baby carriage parked at the front door. It's hard to fathom my great-grandmother Isabella's expression when she first laid eyes on the baby girl left behind. Her new life began right where Luca abandoned her, along with his secret. My mother would not see her biological mother until decades later.

We follow the men inside, and when they glance over their shoulder, we smile and wave as if we're old friends. I prepare to tell them we're related to the owners, but, thankfully, they don't ask.

Angelina snoops through the living room, poking her nose into everything, even going as far as shoving her hand in between the couch cushions, scavenging for secrets, while I'm glued to the same wooden planks where Poppy first learned to walk and play. When Angelina seems satisfied with the living room, she moves to the kitchen, and I follow her, stopping at the kitchen table.

Poppy's intense diary entries blare loudly in my head. He often vented about his father, Sal, belittling him and humiliating his family. How the lies passed through his father's lips at the kitchen table. Made-up stories of where he'd been and why he was home so late. Work often took the blame for the lies he told. Poppy always knew there was more his father wasn't saying. His father probably believed that lies of omission didn't count.

And those diary entries had a profoundly negative effect on his favorite son, Luca. He exposed him to such terrible things. The thoughts he put in his head. The monster he created.

One mover brushes past me through the kitchen with a small table balanced on his hip. It looks like an old, worn end table. He stares at me with a peculiar expression as I move to the stove. I stare back at him as he passes, unsure of what else to do. At the stove, I imagine my great-grandmother cooking dinner and setting food on the table. I gaze through the window above the sink as she must have done every day.

The window overlooks an expansive backyard. It appears to be about two plots of land, which is an unusual amount of space for the homes in this area. I'm sure it was because of my great-grandfather Sal's influence in this town.

I recall a few of Poppy's diary entries mentioning a small farm out back, and I think I can make out the remnants of an old chicken coop next to a small fenced-in area where they would have kept a few goats. I also observe the remnants of what I assume to be an abandoned plantation. Poppy's diary mentions his father owned a prosperous bergamot plantation. After conducting some research, I discovered bergamot had various uses, including medicines, teas, and even baked goods.

"This is a good-sized house for being in a fishing village," Angelina says. "Not bad."

"I agree," I say. "Let's go upstairs."

At the foot of the stairs, there lies a modest-sized bench with an old phone covered in dust. I blow off a layer of dust and sit on the bench. I lift the receiver to my ear and imagine Poppy's voice on the other end. This is where he and his family would sit and talk. It's the only place in the house that has a phone.

"This is so surreal," I say.

Angelina flips her head toward the stairs. "Shall we?"

"Absolutely," I say, and we climb the rickety, creaky stairs all the way up.

At the top is a long hallway with three bedrooms extending from it. We peek into the first room and notice the two movers inside, quietly sizing up the furniture. Perhaps they're considering how to move the heavy-looking dresser safely. We decide to move on and check that room last.

We continue down the shadowy hallway. I note the cracks and dents in the timeworn walls and the chipped paint crumbs on the floor beneath the molding. On the left-hand side of the hallway is another bedroom. It has one bed, one chest of drawers, and a small side table. Very simple and neat. I assume by the small size of the bed that it must have belonged to either Poppy or Luca. I pull open the drawers one by one, and they are empty.

At the end of the hall, straight ahead, is the largest bedroom, which has a bed slightly bigger than the others, a small chest of drawers next to a taller chest of drawers, and a side table. There is a small door on one wall, and I'm guessing it leads to an attic or some kind of storage area. The only window in the bedroom overlooks the backyard, and I can see an old clothesline and an old shed. Something about the backyard gives me the creeps.

"This had to be your great-grandparents' room," Angelina says.

"Yes, I think so," I say.

"Strange that it's at the back," she says. "Normally, the parents' bedroom is the first off of the stairs. The idea was to keep the children at the back of the house to protect them from falling down the stairs or from something bad happening." The way she says it with such authority makes me laugh inside. "I see you smirking," she continues, "but I'm not being superstitious this time. It's true," she chuckles.

"My great-grandfather always did things his way, usually keeping his reasons hidden."

Angelina peers through the window that faces the backyard. "This window gave your great-grandfather a perfect view of his property. That's probably why he had his house built the way he did."

I stand beside her in the window to see what he might have seen, and she's right. It is a perfect view. A view that includes everything from the rickety old shed to the back of the bergamot plantation. I remember in Poppy's diary he mentioned something about a path behind the plantation that could get them to the beach near their marina. I have a hard time picturing it, and it makes me want to find it.

A noise in the hallway pauses our conversation. We listen intently and then step into the hall for a look. The noise is coming from the first bedroom near the stairs. We cautiously proceed toward the bedroom as one worker backs out through the doorway, holding the top end of a chest of drawers. The other worker follows, panting and grunting while carrying the bottom. They pause with concerned faces.

"Sorry for the damage to the wall, *signoras*," the worker holding the bottom of the dresser says. "We'll be back to fix it later."

He must assume I live here.

"Thank you. I appreciate it," I say.

We watch them as they make their way down the stairs, scarcely fitting through the tiny staircase. When they are out of sight, Angelina and I step into the first bedroom, the one we haven't been in yet.

Right away, we notice what the workers were referring to.

"Oh no."

I walk over to the wall to assess the damage. It's apparent right away that moving a dresser didn't cause this. These walls of sturdy stone and brick may have weakened over the years, but whatever went through it didn't just happen now. The wall appears caved in, as if someone threw something heavy through it or cut through it. With my hand, I follow the crack below the partial hole straight down to the bricks at the base. The wall attached to the bricks crumbles and falls, piling on the wood floor below. I push and pull at the top brick, loosening it from its position.

Angelina squats beside me, and together we pull out brick after brick as larger pieces of the wall fall away with ease, as if it's done this before. Soon we're peering into an open space behind the wall.

We look at each other, our mouths open as goosebumps gather on my arms.

"What is this?" I say.

Angelina stares at me, and her eyes confirm that we're thinking along the same lines. Someone has purposely concealed whatever is behind this wall.

"What are you doing?" Angelina says as I make my way head-first into the small space.

"I see something," I say. "Can you see it?" I move out of the way so she can poke her head through.

She pulls herself out. "Is that a shelf?"

"I think so," I say, climbing back in. This time, I'm able to squeeze myself all the way inside. My lungs fill fast with dust, making me cough. I hear Angelina ask if I'm okay, and I assure her I'm fine. But right away I can tell I won't be able to stay in here for long. I scan what is visible from the scant amount of light coming from the small bedroom window.

The object we thought was a shelf is a partition. And there's something inside of it. A container. I pull the container, about the size of a shoebox, away from the partition. Right away I'm filled with nostalgia and déjà vu, remembering not so long ago when I found the box in Poppy's study. The one he told me about just before he passed away. The box that started it all.

As soon as I get out of that dark, dingy space, I'm coughing and covered in a coating of white dust, holding the box in front of me.

"What have we here?" Angelina says of the box, which in the light appears to be an antique jewelry box. She stares at me wide-eyed and then runs to the door to check that the hallway is clear. We sit on the floor and place the box between us as we slowly lift the lid.

I don't know what I was expecting, but it wasn't a dainty, thin, white sock folded in half. Or a barrette with a little sapphire stones. A few odd trinkets are tucked beneath them. Angelina and I glance up at the same time, and I wonder if she's thinking what I'm thinking about these tucked-away items, most likely belonging to one or more young girls.

CHAPTER 22

ELLA

Something curls in the pit of my stomach as I pick up the sapphire barrette. The steel clasp is cold, and something about it feels clinical, sterile, and reminds me of death. There is only one reason a young man keeps this barrette and the other items in such a secretive place behind a stone wall. And now I know I'm standing in Luca's room. In Luca's secret world.

My thoughts revolve around the girl who owned this beautiful barrette. Perhaps she saved it, thinking about the day she would wear it for a special occasion. I can't help but reflect on the life she lived and the person she could have become had she not met Luca. She wouldn't have known Luca was dangerous. While he pretended to be charming and made her laugh or blush, she remained unaware that her days were numbered. That he had her right where he wanted her.

A sitting duck. An easy mark.

Had Luca ever crossed paths with a young woman who'd made it difficult for him to carry out his plan? Had Gianna been the only one to outsmart him? I'm sure it angered him to discover that she was alive and living her best possible life despite what he had done to her, and that he hadn't left her still buried in the dirty, musty earth. What does it do to the mind of a narcissistic psychopath to realize that your best plan has come undone? It makes me wonder if someone like Luca can be defeated and if their plan can unravel. Or if he himself can come unglued.

Angelina nudges me. "Snap out of it and tell me what you're thinking."

Voices echo from the front door and through the house, and we pause to listen, but they eventually fade away. Likely the movers on the lower level.

"I'm thinking about the girl who wore this." I place the barrette inside the box and pass it to Angelina.

"What was in your other hand?"

I unfurl my fist to reveal a ruby earring.

Angelina takes it. "It's a beautiful ruby," she says, flipping it over to the post on the back. The ruby is about an inch in diameter, with a string of diamonds encircling it. "I think it's real."

I inspect it. "I think Nonna owned something like this once. Maybe not exact but something similar. I used to play in her jewelry box all the time when I was a little girl, and I swear she had a ruby like this."

"With diamonds around it?"

"Yes, or cubic zirconia. At least I think I remember correctly that it was Nonna's. Where else would I have seen this before?" I glance at Angelina. "I need to go back in there one more time to make sure I didn't miss something else."

Angelina gives me a look. "Ella, we really shouldn't stay up here much longer. The workers might see us again and get suspicious. Don't push your luck. They might see the box and accuse us of stealing."

I promise her I'll be quick. This time, I remember to turn on the flashlight of my phone and hold it up to the open space.

I climb inside and sweep the light back and forth into the dark space. Something catches my eye and takes my breath away. With my camera, I zoom in on a large envelope or a folder that is tucked further back into the wall.

I reach, and I can barely grasp it in my hand as I bring it out into the bedroom. Inside the dust-filled folder are several newspaper clippings. The headlines tell a grim story: "Local Girl Missing from Scilla Neighborhood," "Two Young Girls Missing," "Body Found Near Marina," among several others.

Our eyes lock, and we know exactly what we have found.

"This was it. His hiding place," I say. "It's probably not the only hiding place of Luca's, but this," I grab the newspaper clippings in my hand, "this is huge." The hairs on the back of my neck rise and prickle at what this means—that the items in this box more than likely belonged to the girls in the articles.

"They're speaking to us from the grave," Angelina says. "Like they've led us here. Who knows how long they've tried to tell us, and now we're finally listening?"

I used to brush off comments like this, but I know better now. Angelina has a connection to a spiritual side that I have little understanding of.

"This kind of thing doesn't stop, you know," she continues. "Someone like Luca doesn't just one day decide to stop. He has undoubtedly continued to feed his dark appetite."

She's right. Luca was cunning enough to live a double life under our noses. It's what he's always done and is still doing.

She shakes her head. "There is much more that we could never possibly know."

"But we can still make a difference," I say. "We can use this as evidence." I hope I'm right. With advances in science, technology, and forensic criminology, there is so much that can be done with DNA today.

"Maybe Emma can help," Angelina says. "Isn't this her field of study?"

"Yes. She's still learning, but she's a natural. I'm sure she would love to help with whatever she can. We still have to go to the police with this, though."

"Absolutely," Angelina says. "Luca is a sick man, and he won't stop until someone stops him."

I take one last look through Luca's hiding spot, and when I'm confident that I've left nothing behind, I throw the fallen, crumbled pieces of the wall into the now larger hole we created. We clean up as much as possible, and then we slide a slightly smaller dresser from an adjacent wall in front of the hiding spot. Except for a few cracks, the dresser almost covers it.

Angelina puts the jewelry box in her oversized purse and clutches it tightly against her body. I tuck the folder inside my jacket, holding it in place with my arms. We quickly descend the stairs, hoping to avoid the movers.

As we're about to exit the house, I hear an unusual noise that makes me freeze.

"Did you hear that?" I ask Angelina.

"Hear what?"

"Wait. Just listen." A few seconds pass, or maybe a minute, with no noise. Maybe I imagined it. "I swear I heard something. Like a big bang, but from a distance. I can't describe it."

"Maybe it came from outside," Angelina says.

"No, it didn't sound like it came from out there."

"Well, we've been through the house, and there's nothing we didn't see."

"You're right," I say. As we reach the front door, I hear it again. "There it is. Did you hear it?"

"Yes. That man out there slammed his car door so hard, I could almost feel it. Jeez, what's his problem?"

But that's not the sound I heard. What I heard sounded like it came from inside the house, but where? It's a small house, and Angelina is right. We've been in all the rooms. It's more likely that it probably came from the Russos' house next door, and I've let my imagination get the best of me.

As we slip out the front door, I look for the man who slammed his car door, but I don't see him. Instead, I catch the eye of the old woman greeter in the Russos' front yard. She looks as if she's trying to get our attention, but I point at a fictional item in the street, pretending to be showing Angelina something.

Angelina is right with me, pretending to see what I'm referring to on the road. We blend into the crowd of people with our treasures, walking in stride with the others who are scavenging the estate sale, looking for treasures of their own.

CHAPTER 23

ELLA

My body stiffens as we put distance between us and Poppy's house. It feels like the jaws of a vice are locking and gripping my insides, likely a mixture of nervous excitement and dread from what we've found. Add to that a guilty conscience for going behind Nico's back. I replay Nico's words to me last night and the words I didn't say. He was right. I am obsessed with finding Luca. It's like I'm addicted, and Luca is my drug.

Doing this without Nico's support feels wrong. It fills me with uncertainty and makes me feel like I'm dangling in the air, about to fall at any moment. Nico and I were about to plan a wedding, and now I don't know if he will ever again want anything to do with me. We've gotten through difficult situations before, and I thought we would get through this. I had hoped he'd come around and realize he was overreacting.

Nico and I shared everything. Deep fears and parts of ourselves we never shared with anyone before. Secrets we would never share with anyone else. We'd have deep conversations that sometimes went well into the night or the next morning. It's a closeness I can't describe with words. And it's Nico I want to call first to share what Angelina and I discovered in Poppy's house just now.

Instead, I slide up the screen on my phone to make sure I've disabled my location with him and my mother, and I notice there are no texts or missed calls from either of them, and nothing from Vinny either. They're probably busy. Vinny is teaching a cooking class at the villa this afternoon, and my mother is taking Nonna and Aunt Lena into the shopping village of Tropea. Nico will be busy at work throughout the day. If there was ever a time to go back to Poppy's neighborhood, this is it.

But we're not finished yet. I didn't come this far to not go to the infamous Perri-family-owned marina. There have to be more answers at the marina, but will I recognize what I need to know, or will I be too late?

My phone vibrates in my pocket. I jump, thinking it's Nico, but it's only Miles from the hospital, who is in a group text with Chase and Anastasia.

"You can cut the tension with a knife around here. Ella, where are you?"

I respond, telling him I'm spending the day with Angelina and staying away from the hospital like I was told. He says he's surprised that I listened. Anastasia emphasizes his reply and adds that I need to come back to the hospital. She says Jonella didn't show up today, and something strange is going on at the hospital. I reply that I'm out of town, but I promise to check back as soon as possible.

"I wonder what's going on at the hospital?" Angelina says, scratching her arm, which she often does when she's anxious.

"I don't know. Maybe it's just awkward because of the accusations against me and the investigation," I say. I still can't believe I got suspended. "But it's also unusual for Jonella not to show up."

"Maybe she's sick today." Angelina pats my back, and when I don't respond, she says, "It will be okay. Everything will work out. The truth will come out."

On our way to the beach, hoping to find the marina, we decide to stop at the gastronomia to get something to eat, but the sign on the door says *chiuso*, closed. On the wall next to the door, we notice several postings, mostly advertisements, except for one picture of a young woman with long, dark hair and a cheerful smile.

"This is the woman we saw on the news," Angelina says, excited.

"Are you sure?"

"I'll never forget it," she says. "Remember? The reporter was standing in front of that bar, or café as you call it, and we realized it was near the gastronomia your Poppy went to." Angelina removes the picture from behind an advertisement. "And look what it says right here." She points to the caption above the photo. Confident in my abilities to read and speak Italian now, I read it aloud: "Have you seen this woman? Bria Mirando, twenty-seven years old. Last seen at Tamara's Bar."

"That shouldn't be far from here," Angelina says.

Before we head to Tamara's, I put the picture of Bria right in front of all the advertisements. Her smiling face watches us as we go.

* * *

Tamara's Bar is a small, simple building of stucco and stone. A wooden sign with daily specials hangs on the wall to the right of the entry. Dried herbs adorn both sides of the doorway, and a sign above says "Tamara's Piccolo," and I agree—Tamara's is a small coffee bar. People gather at the three round tables on a crowded patio for coffee and sweet breads.

Before going inside or even walking up to the door, we stand at the corner across the street from it. I imagine Bria entering the café, possibly standing where we are standing, or perhaps on the sidewalk next to Tamara's. I look at the post office and stores across the street. Had she come from one of those buildings? Was she alone at the time?

At the lamppost in front of Tamara's, I see a picture of the same young, beautiful woman with a smile and one word above her: *Smarrito*. Missing. It takes my breath away. Angelina and I step in for a closer look. Bria's name is below her picture along with a phone number to call with information.

Angelina's hand goes to her mouth.

"What do you think happened to her?" I say. "Does this kind of thing happen often around here?"

"Oh, no, hardly ever. This is very unusual for this part of town nowadays, especially ever since they fixed it all up." Angelina sighs. "But, a long time ago, this wasn't unusual at all."

When we step inside Tamara's, I'm transported back to an older, simpler time when people easily found satisfaction in life. I feel it. I can tell that the old bones of this bar are still here. A framed picture of Tamara's grand opening years ago on the wall by the counter confirms this.

The old man at the counter must have seen me looking at the photograph. "That's the original picture of this place back around 1901. Bet you can't tell, but that's a sketch, not a photograph," he says, pleased.

"A sketch?" I am amazed and impressed at the details and shading of this sketch. It looks exactly like an old, black-and-white photograph.

"Yep," he says. "Not much has changed. Some fresh paint, a little redecorating, and we added a few other things like those tables and chairs," he says. "But other than that, it's just like it was back then."

"I love it," I say.

Angelina smiles and adds, "This young lady's grandfather used to come here all the time when he was a boy."

"Is that so?" the old man says. "What's his name?"

"Franco Perri," I say. "Salvatore Franco Perri."

The old man coughs. "Perri, did you say? I used to know a Perri fellow, but he was much older."

"Perhaps it was my great-grandfather?"

"Perhaps," he says. The bells on the door ring as someone enters, drawing his attention away from us. "Excuse me," he says, and he walks around us to greet the police officer who entered. It's strange how they glance at us as they talk.

I whisper to Angelina that we should probably get going if we want to find the marina, and she agrees, keeping her eyes on the policeman. I give one last look around Tamara's, wondering if Bria came in to purchase some pastries or if she sat at a table. And if she sat at a table, did she sit by herself or with someone? I'm sure these are questions the police have already asked.

The police officer hands the old man a business card and then leaves.

Before we leave, I go back to the counter where the old man stands again.

"Excuse me," I say. "I was just noticing the signs around here of the missing woman."

"So very sad," he says.

"Yes," I say. "The news reported that she was last seen here. Were you working that day when she was here?"

He rolls his eyes. "Yes, my wife and I were both here," he says, huffing. "They sat right there." He points to a table behind us. "I think—"

"They? You mean 'she'?"

"No, she wasn't by herself," he says. "She was with an older man. I'm not sure if it was her husband or maybe her father, but she wasn't alone that day."

"And it was a man she was with," Angelina confirms.

"Yes," he nods.

"Did you see her leave?" I ask.

"Are you gonna order something or ask me questions all day?" he says.

"Sorry, yes, we will order something," I say.

"No, I didn't see her leave," he says, annoyed. "I must have gone in the back when she left. I told the police I didn't see her leave, so I don't know if she left with the man or by herself." After a pause, he softens a little and adds, "I sure do hope they find her, but the more time goes by . . ." He shakes his head and doesn't finish his thought.

We thank the man for his time and tell him we will return soon to have coffee and a bite to eat.

CHAPTER 24

ELLA

We leave Tamara's Bar behind, but Bria remains on my mind. I think about her smiling picture posted on buildings and lampposts, the old man at the deli who saw her, and the police officer who stopped by while we were there. Was the man she was with at Tamara's the same man who shot and nearly killed her sister and then set their house on fire? Was Tamara abducted, or did she escape the fire and now is hiding, too afraid to speak and draw attention to herself?

I recall Poppy mentioning in his diary how his father and Luca would take a shortcut from their backyard to the marina. At the far edge of the bergamot plantation was a passageway to a neighborhood. They would cut across a few of their neighbors' backyards and get to the marina pretty easily. I would love to follow in their footsteps, but since we're already on the streets leading to the beach, Angelina and I walk the usual route.

A text buzzes on my phone. I jump, thinking it's Nico, but it's not. It's a number I don't recognize.

Don't stop. You're very close. Someone's life depends on you.

I show Angelina, and she is just as baffled as I am.

"Is this a trick?" Angelina says loudly. "Are they talking about Bria?"

We stop walking and scan our surroundings.

"We're being watched again," I say.

"Or messed with," she says.

"No. We're being watched. I feel it now."

Someone could watch from any of the windows of the houses that line the street. I glance up at the taller buildings, thinking whoever is watching could have a higher and better view from someplace we'd never suspect. The thought makes my legs wobbly.

We get to the end of the street, and I feel a difference in the air and in our surroundings the closer we get to Chianalea di Scilla, the picturesque fishing village in the historic center of Scilla. The beauty, the enchantment, the lure of the sea. The salty sweetness in the warm breeze pulls us in. We can easily get lost in its magic. I can see on Angelina's face that she has already become lost in this small village—in awe, like me. I point out Castello Ruffolo to Angelina. The majestic, ancient castle juts out right above the fishing village. I remember the first time I felt its magic.

It's like being inside a postcard picture. We walk along the narrow cobbled path, both sides flanked by rows of houses and local shops packed in tightly. Attached to the old stone walls are peculiar items: a bicycle with a basket in front holding a plant, its long, trailing vines spilling over the sides; a mask hangs on one wall, and paintings and various sculptures adorn others. We can hear ocean waves gently lapping against the backs of the houses, a repetitive, splashing rhythm that makes you dizzy and beckons you towards it. I sense we're getting closer to the beach as the splashes grow louder and the air is saltier. A breeze sweeps through, and we're almost at the water's edge.

"Look." Angelina points towards rows of boats bobbing in the water, many of them a striking light-blue like the sea. Some boats have been tied to a dock. Just past the rows of boats are several buildings that look like they are growing straight out of the ocean, and just before those buildings is what I think must be the marina.

"Angelina," I say, "I think that's it."

Angelina's eyes widen.

We slip off our shoes and trudge through the sand toward the building.

"I don't see a sign or a name, but it must be it. It was the only one on this part of the coast. It has to be the one."

The building itself is old and weathered, but someone must have recently added a stone path leading to the entrance, as well as a few landscape beds.

Angelina and I walk the path to the front door and step inside, noticing the recently remodeled interior. But even the fresh paint and new fixtures can't hide the fishy smell I would expect in a marina. Three young men stand behind the counter, each wearing black T-shirts and jeans, their lush, black hair flipped back, which reminds me of Nico. One young man writes something on a notepad, another seems to check items inside an open box, and the third speaks with an older man near the register. They must be brothers. Maybe they are all sons of the old man.

The man with the notepad glances up. "Can I help you?" he says in a heavy Italian accent.

I feel surprised at first. I haven't thought of what I was going to say yet.

Angelina steps ahead of me. "Yes, thank you, young man. I was wondering if you could tell me how to go about taking one of your boats out on the water."

He looks at Angelina and then at me. "Are you looking for a boat for you and your daughter?" he asks.

"Um, yes," she says. "Is that possible?"

"What kind of boat are you interested in? A sailboat, a fishing boat, or a motorboat? And how long will you plan to have it?"

"I was thinking—we were thinking—of a fishing boat for next week sometime. Just for a day."

The man looks at Angelina strangely. "You two are going fishing?"

"Of course we are," she says, not skipping a beat. "But we'll need to rent fishing gear. Do you have fishing supplies? We're not from around here."

The man makes a funny face.

Soon the older man who was near the register joins us. He furrows his brow and appears annoyed, but he refrains from saying anything. He just stands and waits.

The younger man says. "Papá, it's okay." He waves his hand as if to say, *"Go back to what you were doing. We're good here."*

But the older man doesn't budge, and neither does his brow.

I face the old man and smile. "We were walking through the village and along the shore, and we spotted your marina. My grandfather grew up in Scilla. His father used to own a marina years ago in this area."

The old man continues to stare at me, unmoved and silent.

"I wondered if this is the same marina he owned all those years ago."

The young man smiles apologetically at me. "Papá," he says, "are you going to say anything?"

The old man clears his throat and, in a thick Italian accent I can hardly decipher, he grumbles, "I thought you said you weren't from around here, so what are you doing here now?"

"My grandfather passed away two years ago, and I've always wanted to see the beautiful town he was from," I say. "He spoke of it often, and I know he missed being here every day. He moved to America when he was young, and that's where he raised his family. I came here to see where his life began."

"That's very nice," the young man says, smiling. He turns toward his father. "Isn't that nice, Papá?"

The old man grunts. "This is a family-run business, and it has always been in my family's name. It couldn't have belonged to your grandfather or great-grandfather or whoever." He turns around and heads back to the counter.

His grumpy attitude irritates me immensely, and I realize I don't have time for his demeanor any longer.

"Salvatore Perri," I say.

He turns around.

"Most people called him Sal. His wife was Isabella. They had two boys, Franco and Luca."

A look of shock and disbelief freezes on his face. He can't even hide it. He points his crooked finger at us. "No," he says. "No. I have never heard of them. We're closed." He looks at the young man with the notepad. "Massimo, put out the closed sign and lock up."

The other two young men from behind the counter pop their heads up and exchange concerned glances with Massimo.

"Get going!" the old man yells, and Massimo ushers us out the front door.

Before he locks up, he apologizes for his father's behavior and tells us to come back in one hour.

CHAPTER 25

ELLA

We walk away from the marina, silent and confused. The sign saying *chiuso* still sways on the door. The window blinds on the front two windows snap shut. We pass empty boats and walk beside the calm, blue sea as befuddled faces disperse from the marina back to where they came from.

"That old man knows your family," Angelina says. "Did you see his face when you said their names?"

"I thought he was going to throw something at me. He's hiding something."

"He either didn't like the thought that someone else owned the marina before him, or those names meant something to him," Angelina says.

"And why would it matter unless he's hiding something?"

"Massimo must be his son or grandson," Angelina says. "Maybe the other two young men are Massimo's brothers."

"Why do you think Massimo wants us to come back?"

"Maybe he feels bad and wants to apologize for the old man's behavior."

While we wait for the right time to return to the marina, Angelina and I decide to go back to Poppy's neighborhood to see if we can find the shortcut from the back of the bergamot plantation to the marina.

Instead of the meager stalks remaining of the plantation at the back of Poppy's yard, I imagine the lush, hardy, green bergamot trees standing in rows emitting a strong citrus scent into the air. It must have been beautiful.

"Your great-grandfather must have made a good living between the plantation and the marina," Angelina says. "What do you know about the plantation?"

"Well, according to Poppy's diary, my great-grandparents first used bergamot for cooking—spices, pastries, and sometimes in salad dressings," I say. "My great-grandmother, Isabella, sprinkled it over their salads because she loved its delicate flavor. Later, my great-grandfather discovered bergamot was perfect for fragrances and in medicines for its calming effect. Sometimes he would add it to my great-grandmother's headache medicine to help her rest. His business flourished because of this discovery, and the word spread like crazy."

Angelina says, "I recall using a blend of oil with bergamot. I'd dab a little on my wrist. What I love is the pungent smell of it. So relaxing. Sometimes I add it to my tea. Before my time, people used it for fevers. I understand why it became such a profitable venture for your family."

At the end of the yard, past the plantation, I can see Poppy's and Gianna's houses, with only a few feet of space between them. I see a small sitting area at the back of Poppy's house taken over by weeds. There's a tall pole with a light at the top, almost like a streetlight in the middle of the yard. I think how peculiar it is to have an enormous light in such a small area. But, then again, my great-grandfather was particular about safety.

According to his diary, when Poppy was a young boy, he'd stop at Gianna's house every day. But on one particular day, he'd found it empty. Her whole family had disappeared in the middle of the night.

"What's that creepy thing?" Angelina says, pointing to a small structure on the property behind the house.

"It *is* creepy." I remember thinking the same thing when I saw it from the bedroom window upstairs. The dark grains in the wooden door appeared warped or damaged, and I remember how they stood out against the lighter grains. I also noticed a lock hanging open above the metal doorknob. "Probably just a tool shed."

Angelina convinces me to go closer to the shed. "I need to see it," she says, and I agree.

The windows are dark, and condensation gathers at the corners. There's a moldy, mildewy, sulfuric odor coming from it that makes me sneeze. I look around, afraid the sound might have drawn someone's attention.

"I want to open the door," I say.

"Not a chance," Angelina says. "I don't do dark, abandoned, creepy buildings anymore."

"I thought you wanted to see it."

"I wanted to see it, not go in it," she says.

"I think we should," I say, reaching for the door. "Just a peek. I won't go all the way in."

Angelina gives me a disapproving look.

I remove the unlatched lock from its holster and swing the door wide open. A gush of dank air escapes, making me want to vomit. I hold my breath and step into the doorway, allowing the daylight to illuminate the space inside. It's just a small room with an old desk and some garden tools, as I'd expect. Light entering from the back of the shed outlines another door.

"Get out here right now!" Angelina yells. "Hurry!"

I spin around and see her waving her arms at me, urging me to come towards her. When I do, she's very panicky. She has a crazed look in her eyes, and she fans herself with her hands.

"Put the lock back the way you found it and let's get away from it."

I know Angelina has seen something or sensed something bad. Her eyes fill as we move away from the shed.

"What's the matter?" I ask.

"I don't know," she says. "Just a horrible feeling. Like someone was in that shed with you." Angelina brushes her wet cheeks with her hand. "Your great-grandfather was a terrible man. I'm getting a sense that some of his evil carried into the next generation and the one after that."

Another text comes in: "*She's not in there.*"

I show Angelina the text. "'Her' who? Why aren't they saying her name? Text them back. Hurry."

I nervously look back and forth between Angelina and the phone.

And then I text back: "*Who are you talking about? Who is this?*"

But, of course, there's no reply.

Angelina and I run to the back of the bergamot plantation, hoping to find the shortcut to the marina and get as far as possible from that shed.

A branch snaps behind us and stills my heart.

Angelina's eyes are wide. "Let's go," she mouths, and we tread as lightly as possible on top of the grass, crouching low, hoping to be camouflaged among the trees.

* * *

As the distance between us and the house increases, the knot in my stomach loosens. When we are far past the plantation, we emerge into another open space. Angelina and I race through the opening and soon find ourselves in a neighborhood. It's surprising to find it here in the middle of nowhere. It's small and private, maybe ten to fifteen houses at most. The houses are modest and older, and I imagine, from the look of them, they mostly comprise long-time residents.

We walk quietly side by side, afraid to speak, stopping only when we come to a dead end and have to change our direction.

Carefully we scan each house, peering as far back between them as our sight allows, but note nothing unusual in any of them.

Soon, we come to another dead end, but this one is different. We notice a path off to one side of this dead end, and it appears to have been used often—a timeworn path, a natural feature etched into the earth. We look at each other wide-eyed, and we know this must be the path that will connect us to the marina.

Despite feeling uncertain and apprehensive, we persist because we have no other choice. We do not know what we might encounter or what awaits us on the other side, but soon the sun brightens and the path ends at a clearing. And maybe fifty to a hundred yards away is a building that sits on the sand, surrounded by more sand and a hint of shimmery blue.

"The marina," I whisper.

Angelina nods.

This is how they got to the marina—my great-grandfather, Sal, Poppy, and Luca.

"This is the way they went."

"Makes sense," Angelina says. "It's easier than walking around through the streets and probably faster."

"And private. More secretive," I add. I check my watch. It's approaching one hour since we left the marina. "We should go now and meet Massimo."

"Do you think the old man is gone?" Angelina is hesitant.

"We'll wait a few more minutes if that makes you feel better."

"I just don't want anyone to see us coming from this way," she says. "I can't imagine how the old man would react to that. Do you think *they* know about this path?"

"I don't know."

"Let's just go," she decides. "It's time."

As we get closer to the marina, we see four white chairs low to the ground at the center of a white stone platform facing the building. Between each chair is a small square side table. Abandoned landscape beds surround the platform. At one time, it was probably a beautiful little haven where people could sit and relax after a long day of work.

I notice something moving in one of the back windows. I pull Angelina's hand and we stop, frozen in the sand. The silhouette of someone comes closer to the window and stops moving as well. We seem to watch each other. I contemplate running back the way we came, but would we even make it without getting caught?

The back door swings open, and Massimo steps through the doorway. We are relieved to see that it's only him. We continue to walk toward the marina as Massimo approaches us, showing with his hand that we should sit on the chairs. When we gather on the stone platform, he kindly invites us to sit down. After we sit, he sits in a chair across from us.

In a thick accent, Massimo apologizes for his father's rude behavior. "He has a lot of pride, and he is very protective of his family and his marina." He glances over his shoulder. "We have to be fast. You don't look like you're from around here. Tell me why you are really here at the marina."

I explain to Massimo that the marina once belonged to my great-grandfather, Sal, and that he and his youngest son, along with several other men, used to work here every day. "Why would your father say that no one else owned the marina before him?"

"Because no one did," he says.

"That's simply not accurate," I say. "I know for a fact that this is the marina my grandfather wrote about in his diary. There are no other marinas on this side of Scilla."

He ponders this for a few seconds. "There must be some mistake. Some confusion."

"I saw your father's face when I said my family's names. He knows them somehow. He knows who they are. What is his connection?"

Massimo looks over his shoulder and leans in close to us. In a voice just above a whisper he says, "Listen, you are right. He knows them. Everyone around here not only knows who your great-grandfather was, but they're still afraid of him. Even long after his death. Words cannot explain the power that man had; his connections to both the good and bad extend far past this small community. We don't speak of him. We don't even utter the name of his youngest son—he is like the devil himself."

"Luca," I say, and he looks away, disgusted.

I knew of my great-grandfather and Luca's criminal connections and that many people feared him. But I didn't realize almost everyone feared him.

"I know why you are here," he says, "and you cannot stay much longer."

"Why did you agree to meet with us?" I say.

He checks his watch. "Come," he says, turning toward the door to the marina. "We don't have a lot of time."

"Wait—you said you know why we're here."

"Come," he says again.

We follow Massimo to the back door. He steps aside to let us in and then closes and locks the door behind him. I'm uncomfortably aware of our vulnerability, having stepped into a locked building with a man we've only just met. Someone with potential ties to the bad side of my family.

Massimo flips on the lights, which brightly illuminate the room. A small, well-stocked bar with four tall chairs is on one side. Across from the bar is a two-seat leather sofa and a club chair, each with its own glass side table. Several unique bottles of whiskey are on a narrow counter against the wall behind the sofa. I never knew there were so many variations. Massimo grabs three shot glasses from behind the bar and sets them on top of the bar counter. He pours whiskey into each and brings them to the table.

Immediately, I recognize a dark-framed black-and-white photograph on the counter. I walk over to it and pick it up. "Do you mind if I look?"

He shakes his head, but I can tell it makes him uncomfortable.

The photograph shows Poppy and Luca as young boys standing in front of their father, with two other men flanking him. One man appears to be a younger version of Massimo's father.

"Is this your father?" I ask, pointing to him.

Massimo seems hesitant. Reluctantly, he answers, "That's my grandfather."

Angelina, who has been oddly quiet, scrunches her nose and furrows her brow. "So they knew each other. Even though you said they didn't."

"I never said they didn't know each other. My father did."

"That's fair," she says. "How?"

"You don't know any of this?" he says, surprised.

"I know next to nothing about my great-grandfather," I say. "I only know what he was like and how he treated his sons. I know he was a criminal, and I know a lot of bad things about his son, my uncle, Luca."

"When my father was a young child, the 'Ndrangheta killed his father and abducted his mother. Sadly, they never found her, but they found my father hiding in a closet in one of the bedrooms."

"Who found him?" I say.

"Your great-grandfather, Sal Perri. Secretly, he raised him as one of his own without ever telling anyone. He didn't bring him to his home with his family. Instead, he kept him here and let him stay in the loft above the marina," he says, pointing up to the ceiling. "He took him under his wing and taught him how to work at the marina. He was a little younger than your uncle, but they became very close.

"At first, my father thought Sal was a strong, upstanding citizen who would love and protect him. But he quickly learned that Sal and his son, Luca, were using him for their benefit. They wanted someone who would work at the marina, charm the customers, and make a big profit for them while they did who-knows-what at night."

"So, did your father have any connections to the criminal side of things?"

"Yes—by association, he was. Anyone who worked the marina at night was essentially working for the other business. Makes it seem like he might as well have done the crimes, if you catch my drift. He covered for them all the time. To this day, he remains remorseful—accepting their payment to keep silent as they engaged in their unethical activities. You saw how he froze when you mentioned their names. That's why."

Something still doesn't sit right with me. "Can I ask you something?"

"Yes, of course," he says.

"You said earlier that you've heard my uncle Luca's name mentioned several times."

"Yes."

"And you said your father still feels bad about hiding things for my grandfather."

Massimo stares at me blankly.

"You said that in the present tense."

"I was thinking the same thing," Angelina says.

"Is your father still in contact with my uncle? Have you seen him recently?"

Massimo's eyes widen. "Well, I—I thought, I mean, I assumed you were also in contact with your uncle and had seen him recently. He comes here so often it angers my father. Your great-grandfather sold this marina to my father, and now Luca wants it back."

I can't believe what I'm hearing. I pull up a photo of Luca on my phone, taken two years ago before I went to Italy. "This is Luca. Is this the man you say comes to the marina often?"

"Yes," he says.

"When was he here last?"

"This morning," he says.

My stomach churns. "Why was the marina sold to your father?"

"That's a long story," he says, "but your uncle comes here almost every day. And sometimes, especially recently, she comes too, but for completely different reasons."

"She?" Who else is coming here with Luca? Is there someone else in the family betraying us? Hiding him?

"Is it an older woman? Do the names Lena or Sienna sound familiar?"

"No, not older," he says. "She is very much younger, like yourself."

"Younger? Do they seem like they're together—like a couple? Are they coming here together?"

"Oh no," he says seriously. "He does not know that she's been watching him."

"Who is this woman? Do you know her?" Angelina says.

"I've never seen her before today, but my father says she's been here before," he says. "She has long hair like yours, but lighter. A bright smile. Pretty like you." He removes an envelope from a pocket inside his coat jacket. "She asked me to give this to you."

I suddenly feel nauseous, like I've walked into some kind of trap. Like someone played a trick on me.

"How did this woman know I was coming here?"

I look to Angelina for some insight, intuition, a premonition, anything. She raises her eyebrows. She doesn't know either.

"I know nothing else except for early this morning when she walked into the marina. Luckily, my father was not here. Maybe she knew he wouldn't be here, or it was just luck. She told me that a young woman would arrive shortly and ask some questions related to her grandfather. She described you perfectly. I knew you were the one she was talking about, and when you mentioned your family members' names, it confirmed it. She asked me to give this to you. That other people's lives depended on it, especially one. I'm giving this to you now because I couldn't with my father around."

I turn over the sealed envelope in my hand. Massimo places his hand on top of the envelope. "Do not open it here. I was told explicitly to say that and to make sure you walked out of here without opening it. So that's what I'm doing. I'm giving it to you, and I will make sure you do not open it until after I've closed the door and said goodbye."

Angelina and I exchange glances.

"Okay," I say. "I won't open it until after we leave. Is there anything else you want to tell us? Anything you think we should know before we go? Can we trust this woman?"

"No, there is nothing else," Massimo says. "But be careful. The girl who gave this to me said you have a dangerous journey ahead of you."

Massimo stands, and without another word, he walks us to the door. We thank him for his time, and he only nods and closes the door. The deadbolt clicks into place.

We walk along the shore and away from the marina under a dimly lit sky. The sun is pushed far behind the dark clouds rolling in.

CHAPTER 26

ELLA

O nce we are long past the marina and it is no longer protruding from the shoreline, it feels like I can breathe again. We decide to go back to Tamara's Bar to escape the potential storm brewing above us and around us.

A pang of guilt hits me when I see it: the bistro where Nico and I shared our first dance and where I first felt our connection. It was an incredibly powerful moment, the electricity that passed between us when we touched. It is the first link in the chain that connects us. If Nico knew I was here, he would be so angry with me. He should be here with me. But he may never speak to me again. Maybe he'll want our time apart to become permanent. I can't fathom the idea.

Angelina and I sit at a table with white linens beside a tall terra-cotta flower pot brimming with red flowers. A server comes to the table, placing menus before us and filling our glasses with water. She tells us she'll be right back.

Angelina watches as I carefully tear open the envelope that Massimo gave us. It contains a note and a black-and-white photograph. Immediately, I recognize Poppy and Uncle Luca as boys, maybe around fourteen or fifteen years old. They are sitting on the water's edge with friends around them: the Russo sisters, two other boys, and two other girls I don't recognize.

"It looks like they're at the marina, doesn't it?" Angelina says. "Look behind them. Those are the same kinds of boats we just saw at the marina. Can you see them? Right there and there." She points to the boats peeking from behind.

"You're right," I say, also noting and pointing out an edge of what might be the marina itself.

I empty the contents of the envelope onto the table. It's an old newspaper folded in half and a note written on white paper. Before I unfold the paper, the word *Luca* jumps from the note. I put the note between us, and we read it silently:

> *I think Luca has the missing woman, and her life could be in danger. The police won't help—many of them still work for him. He keeps moving. He found the tracking device I put on his car, and now I can't keep track of where he is anymore. I think he kept her in the Montepulciano house first, but he has moved her again. She must be in one of his other houses or the storage unit. I'm afraid I can no longer help you. I need to step back. I'm afraid he knows what I've been doing. Be safe, Ella.*

"'Be safe, Ella,'" I read aloud.

Angelina and I look up at each other after we finish reading the note.

"They know me. Who would know me and want to help? Who else has been trying to find Luca?" I say.

We pause as our server returns, and we order two meatball sandwiches and minestrone soup.

"Could it be one of your aunts?" Angelina says after our server leaves.

"No, they would have just texted me or called me. They wouldn't have left an unsigned note. Besides, Massimo said it was a young lady. It's someone else Luca knows—someone he trusts."

"What about their nieces or nephews?" Angelina says. "Does Lena or Sienna have any nieces or nephews who might be involved?"

"I really don't think so. Sienna is afraid of Luca. She doesn't want him to know where she is."

But Angelina has a point about Aunt Lena. She's been acting so strange ever since I picked up her and Nonna from the airport. The odd things she's said. Her somewhat distant behavior. Could she or one of her nieces or nephews be helping Luca again like Marco did? Who is writing these notes trying to warn me?

Angelina picks up the newspaper, opens it, and reads the headline: "'Local Girl's Body Washes Up on Shore.'" In smaller letters: "'Killer Still At Large.'" The picture above the article shows an arrow pointing to the spot on the shore where someone discovered a body. In the background is the same familiar scene—the boats lined up along the shore, the walkway from the water through the sand to the front door. And the building the farthest back is unmistakably the marina. A second photograph to the right of the article is a school picture of the victim with her name in the caption: Julia Bernardi.

I hold the photograph of Poppy, Luca, and their friends next to the picture of Julia Bernardi. "That's her," I say, pointing to one of the girls I couldn't identify in the photograph. "They all knew each other."

"If these girls knew your Poppy and Luca, then they probably also knew your great-grandfather," Angelina says. "I'll bet Luca and his father had something to do with her disappearance."

"I wonder if Massimo's father knew anything about this, or maybe he was involved," I say. "Maybe they were all involved, except for Poppy."

Our server returns with our sandwiches and soup and sets them on the table.

"So, what do we do now? Take all of this to the police?" I say.

"Is there anyone in the police department you can trust?" Angelina says. "They might have to place you under protective custody for a while, at least until they find Luca."

"They would have to put my whole family into protective custody. It's not realistic. And I'm not taking any chances, especially when the note explicitly says not to go to the police."

"What's unrealistic," she says, "is *not* going to the police. You have a lot of evidence now."

"It's all circumstantial. There's nothing directly tying Luca to any of this. No witnesses. Nothing."

"What if there's DNA on those trinkets we found? Or on that folder?"

I'm so overwhelmed I can't think straight enough to know what to do next.

We spend the next hour analyzing our visit with Massimo, the information in the note, who might have written it, and why they are choosing to stay anonymous. We talk about the newspaper article and question the connection between Julia Bernardi and my family. Was it just a coincidence that Julia was friends with Poppy and Luca? But why would our informant enclose the article and the picture together unless it was meant to show a connection? It's because someone wants us to make a connection. They want us to pay attention.

"If we can't get help from the police, are we supposed to find Bria ourselves before it's too late?" I say. "I can't imagine what she's already been through."

"I don't know, Ella, but we can't do this alone," Angelina says. "Is there anyone else we can tell? Someone who can help us?"

I know she means Nico and my family. I'm afraid I can't tell Nico right now. Other than Angelina, the only person I can trust right now is my mother. I'm just not sure about anyone else.

CHAPTER 27

ELLA

A cool breeze sweeps past the bistro, and a low, rolling thunder grumbles in the distance. Our stomachs are full from sandwiches and soup, but, since we still have more to talk about, we order sweet tea and pastries, which our server brings to us right away.

I take out my phone and, in the notes section, I tap everything that comes to mind about the houses that my grandfather and Luca have inhabited. There's the house here in Scilla, the one Poppy and Luca grew up in. Then there's Luca and Sienna's house in Montepulciano with the hidden hallway and secret rooms. According to the note left in the door, this was the house where Luca initially held the missing woman, who we now believe to be Bria. The author of the note claims that Luca has moved her somewhere else. This is the same house that Luca's father, Sal, gifted to him when he was a young man. Sal used it to carry out his own secret life. Of course, there's the house in New York, where Luca lived with Aunt Lena. Those are the houses I'm aware of where Luca has lived. Luca's father, my great-grandfather, Sal, had his own set of houses.

"Angelina," I say, "do you remember when I visited Giovanni, the architect? Giovanni told me Luca lived in a different house before he lived in Montepulciano. Luca asked Giovanni to design the Montepulciano house while he was still living somewhere else. Do you remember which one it was?"

"It's the old, abandoned one where someone attacked me," she says. "I remember how awful it felt to be in that house."

"I think so too," I say. "What if Luca has Bria in a house that we know nothing about?"

"I think it's got to be a house we're familiar with. The person who wrote the note would have said it's a house we've never been to, don't you think?"

"Not necessarily. How could they know what we know or don't know?"

Angelina gives me a strange look.

"Why are you looking at me like that?" I say.

"I was going to ask you the same thing," she says.

Sometimes my face reveals my thoughts. "It's my deep-thinking face," I laugh. "I keep thinking about what the old woman said when we were at the estate sale—that there was a man who was interested in buying the house."

"I don't remember. Did she say the person who wanted to buy it was a man?"

"Yes, she referred to the person as 'he.'"

"Would Luca want to live in plain sight?" Angelina says. "Where the locals could recognize him?"

"Luca probably thinks this is the last place anyone would ever look for him. He hasn't been back here since he was a child. I think he might be the one buying the house. It's the perfect place for him. And Luca doesn't know I've found it, so he'll have no idea that I've caught him. It makes perfect sense to me. He'd be living where people either loved his family or feared them. If someone in the neighborhood finds out he's back, they'll welcome him. And if they don't, it's because they're too scared to breathe a word about it to anyone."

Angelina scratches her head. "And if Luca is still controlling the police, he'll be protected."

"And I'm guessing he has more than one hiding spot in that house. If I know Luca, the thought of his house being demolished and exposing all of those hiding spots—all the secrets that can tie him to his crimes—terrifies him."

"He won't allow his trophies to be destroyed," Angelina says. "There's no way he'll give those up. Although he may have to relocate them to a better hiding place, he can never eliminate them."

A drop of rain splashes on the note. "I think we should go back to the house. If no one is there, we'll go inside again and look around. We're already here. We might as well, right?"

"I'm right with you, dear," Angelina says.

I carefully return the note, the article, and the picture into the envelope before sliding them into my bag. Under the floral centerpiece, I tuck money for the tea and pastries, plus a little extra. We stand and hurry away from the bistro as raindrops dance on our heads.

* * *

We race through the rain back the way we came, only to duck inside a store to buy an umbrella. When I pop it open, I'm thankful for its ample coverage and stability as we push it against the forceful wind.

A few minutes later, we're dipping beneath the eave of a shop door. The rain gathers and spills over the eave like a waterfall. I give an apologetic look to the unhappy employee who stares at us from inside the store, probably unhappy that we're blocking their door. When the rain turns to a sprinkle, we continue on our way. As I close the umbrella and shake off the excess rain, a peculiar feeling falls over me.

I notice that the friendly eyes of the townspeople now appear suspicious and questioning. Their stares linger on us as we pass. Side conversations on street corners and glances over shoulders.

A looming, foreboding sensation clings to us as if we're being followed. I tell Angelina, and she feels it too. I'm afraid someone will get to the house before we do or that someone is watching us, ready to alert Luca that we're on our way. I have doubts about the person who wrote the note, and I fear that they're not who they claim to be. Doubts crowd my mind. Maybe the note really is a trap. Maybe Massimo is in on it, too.

Angelina and I whisper to each other while we walk, comparing what we're seeing and feeling. The intense feeling of someone watching me is reminiscent of the first time I was in Italy, walking alone on Via Rosa. I was looking for Nina but found Maria instead.

Nina. Could she know something that might help us? How would I find her?

We reach Poppy's street and see his and Gianna's houses again. A light shines through the window at the top of Poppy's house. It must be the attic light. Does that mean someone is there? I point it out to Angelina.

A text comes in from Nico saying he wants to talk today if possible. I mark it unread so I'll remember to text him back. But now I have to concentrate. I have to be aware of what's happening around me. I cannot afford to be surprised.

As we approach the house, I notice a sheer, white curtain billowing in and out with the breeze. The window is open. Angelina sees it too. We try to remember if it was like that when we were here a few hours ago. Maybe someone opened it to get some air flow.

An idea occurs to me, so I wave down a young boy riding his bike and offer him twenty euros to go up to the house and ring the doorbell. I can tell by the way Angelina is biting her thumbnail that this makes her very nervous. The boy agrees to ring the bell, and I instruct him that, if someone answers, he will pretend to be looking for someone and then realize he has the wrong house.

Angelina and I do our best to blend in with the overgrown shrubs. The boy firmly knocks on the door, and I'm so nervous I can't stand it. We wait thirty seconds to a minute. The boy glances back at us as if awaiting further instructions. Extending my finger, I signal for him to wait. I motion for him to knock again, and he does, but no one comes to the door. Out on the street, very few cars are present, and the spot right outside the house is empty, showing that it is highly likely that no one is home. I thank the boy and pay him, and then Angelina and I make our way to the door.

Surprisingly, the doorknob turns, and we find ourselves inside the middle of the entryway. It is quiet, dark, and cool inside. And empty. They must have moved out all the furnishings to prepare for the new owner. We move through the small kitchen, opening the empty cupboards, and then we return to the empty living room.

The staircase leading to the bedrooms is off the living room. We carefully climb the creaky stairs, trying not to make a lot of noise. The doors to each of the three bedrooms are closed. I already know that the first room on the right is Luca's room, where we uncovered the letters and small objects hidden within the wall. We'd left the dresser in front of the hole we'd made. It is the only piece of furniture that remains in the room.

We check the other two bedrooms, intending to go back to Luca's room after. Both bedrooms are empty. In the bedroom farthest from the stairs, Angelina finds what we believe to be the entrance to the attic. "Usually, in old homes like this one, you'll find the attic door in one bedroom. Often it's the owners' bedroom." The attic door is about half the height of a regular door, and it sticks when we try to open it. When we finally can push it in, a gust of dank, hot air pushes out, instantly making us cough and gag.

We climb up a small, dingy, dark stairway with cobwebs strewn across. At the top, we turn around to see the attic spread across the length of the house to an open window at the other end. A rocking chair faces it. It immediately gives me the creeps.

Angelina pauses and closes her eyes as if she is summoning something. "I'm not getting very good feelings from this room. I sense sadness, loneliness, longing for a different life."

"Luca?"

"No, definitely not from Luca."

"Be careful where you step," I say, noting that the floor-boards are weak and feel as though we might fall through with each step to the window. We probably didn't have to go to the window. It's easy to see everything from this vantage point, but something tells me to go there and sit in that chair.

Angelina warns me not to sit down, fearing I might absorb the feelings of whoever sat there. I love her sweet ways and how tuned in she is to her intuition and the future, but I do not share the same fears that she does.

I sit in the chair as soon as I reach it. Strangely enough, there is an odd feeling I get, but I don't think it's because of any lost emotions from the past. I think it's because, when I sit in this chair, the slight angle of the room and the house itself provide the perfect view of the Russos' house and all the windows on its right-hand side.

"Do you think this is where Luca or his father used to sit and watch Gianna?" I say. "Look—it's perfectly lined up."

"Well, knowing what I know about your great-grandfa-ther, Sal, I'd say he had it built precisely for that reason. And I'll bet he shared that with Luca. Maybe that's how Luca's obsession with Gianna started. Makes me wonder if that's all it took. Just a simple, distorted sharing between father and son, and Luca was hooked."

"You sound pretty confident about that," I say.

"Because I am," she says. "This house has a lot of secrets, and not just from Sal and Luca."

I make a mental note to circle back to this conversation because she is just too sure of herself.

We decide to leave the attic and go back to Luca's room. We hardly make it to the room when we hear something downstairs. Footsteps in a hurry. Someone is opening drawers and cupboards. The path of the footsteps suddenly shifts, and it sounds as if they're on the staircase coming up.

Angelina and I face each other, momentarily frozen in fear. We slip into Luca's room and slide back the dresser as carefully as we can. The hole in the wall is our only possibility of not getting caught. The opening is just enough for me to climb through. With Angelina, it is even harder. I pull her through, taking another part of the wall with us, and then we slide the dresser back in front, but not enough to make a perfect seal. I hope and pray it's enough to keep us hidden.

I hear whomever it is coming toward the dresser for something, and I hope to God it's not to move it.

CHAPTER 28

MONA

My head hurts from thinking about all the questions I keep asking myself. *When will this terrible nightmare end? What could have been done differently?* I should have paid attention to the way my stomach felt when I first saw him enter the coffee bar. Or how the hairs rose on the back of my neck while he stood behind me as I talked with the baker. He kept his distance, but I felt his eyes.

It sickens me that I put myself directly in harm's way. So many red flags, and I ignored them all. He seemed familiar, and he claimed to have a wife who I supposedly knew. Something about him told me he was safe. How wrong I was. How could I have been so stupid? So careless? Getting into that car was the worst thing I could have ever done.

A commotion on the floor above me, or possibly the one above that, pulls me from these thoughts. My heart sinks. Is he back already? It seems like a lot of noise for one person. I pray that, if it's him, he has come alone. But then I think, *What if he's abducted someone else like he did with me?* I hear people speaking—no, they're yelling, arguing.

I have to get out of here.

I sit on the cold floor against the wall and rest my head in my hands. The noise above me fades. I wait, half-expecting to hear Lorenzo's footfall on the stairs, but it doesn't come. Whatever happened upstairs is not coming down here.

It must be a bright, sunny day outside because streams of sunlight filter in through the cracks of a boarded-up window. It's enough to cast a dim light, illuminating a chair in the center of the room next to a small table with various tools and cutting devices. My eyes catch sight of a small cot and the door. Having my sight back and my hands no longer bound gives me a slight sense of confidence.

I devise a plan to steal one of those sharp objects from the tray on the table. But I think it's strange that Lorenzo would leave them where I can see them and take them. Is he getting tired? Sloppy? Or is he considering my offer to be with him? I'm anxious and worried that the reason Lorenzo left those sharp utensils there is to see what I will do. What if he's testing me to find out if I am trustworthy? What if there's a hidden camera, and he's watching to see if I'll take something or if I'll sit quietly and behave? And since I have a terrible track record of making reasonable decisions, I don't know if I can trust myself to make the right one now.

And then a terrible thought occurs. If he were to release me, I could easily identify him because I know who he is and what he looks like. He won't let me go no matter how much I pretend to like him.

I have to get out of here somehow. I envision different escape strategies and contemplate the specifics of how I could retaliate against Lorenzo when he's nearby and taunting me. I imagine myself sliding a knife into the waistband of my underwear. I'll pretend to fall or faint. While on the ground, as he attempts to lift me, I'll grab the concealed knife from my underwear and swiftly jab him in the neck, or maybe his eye. But it will have to be fast, and it will have to be powerful. My heart races while I replay these thoughts over and over in my mind.

I hold the knife at different angles and practice, shoving and slicing it into an imaginary person, throwing all my weight behind the knife. I remember what my professor said in class when we practiced our safety drills: "*Your mind will not go where it hasn't gone before. If you can picture what you want to do before you do it, you'll be successful at whatever it is you want to do.*" I have to be strong and confident and, above all, I must be accurate, because I will not get a second chance. If I fail at this or show any sign of weakness, he will easily overtake me, and then it's just a matter of time. I will die right here in this horrible room.

These thoughts lie with me through the rest of the day until the last streams of sunlight fade away. I breathe easily for a moment, knowing that even if I do fail, at least I did something to help myself.

* * *

I awaken, startled but unsure if the loud bang I heard was real or part of a dream. And if it was real, it might have been an explosion or a gunshot. Whatever it is, it jolts me like an electric shock because I know that, if that sound has anything to do with Lorenzo coming down to this disgusting, dank basement to do God-knows-what, I will have to follow through on my plan. And it has to work.

I hear the noise again but much quieter: footsteps above me and the familiar drag of something light sliding across the middle top of the ceiling, and then the hinges scream open. A most hideous screeching that makes my ears ring and my body shiver. Footsteps descend slowly down the stairs.

The lump in my throat grows larger as the damp, musty basement smell and the smell of fear itself pierce my nose. I try to calm my body and pretend I'm asleep, but my heart races. I remove the knife from the waistband of my underwear. The handle is warm from my skin, but the blade is cold. In my mind, I rehearse the movements I must make and the strength I must call upon. I picture the place on Lorenzo's neck where the knife must penetrate to make it all worthwhile.

From the other side of the door, a key slides into a lock and then a twist and a click. The doorknob turns, and the screeching hinges release the door, but no other sounds follow. Is he standing there to see how terrified he can make me feel? I will myself to hold still and not let down any part of my guard. *Stay vigilant. Be aware. Get ready.*

"We have to go," he says, breathless, as if he's been running. How strange that he hadn't run down the stairs. Maybe he's nervous. His voice sounds eerily calm and doesn't match his breathing.

"Where?" I stir briefly before sitting up, pretending he woke me.

"Come on, stand up. Let's go."

"I can't stand," I say, feigning weakness.

"Now."

His voice is firm, but I don't budge. I want him to come to me so I can surprise him with my attack.

"Please help me up," I say, making my voice sound frail. "I can't stand up."

"I don't have time for this," he says, and he flies from the door to where I'm sitting, bringing with him a stench so strong it's as if he hasn't washed in days. His breath is heavy with whiskey.

It happens fast. He wraps his arms around me and pulls me up to standing. It is the moment I've been waiting for. As soon as I get to my feet, adrenaline pumps through my blood, and my heart pounds out of my chest. His hand squeezes my left arm, and he faces away as if he's ready to lead me out. I feel like I might pass out, but I'm still breathing. Every little breath I take keeps me going. The motions and sensations of my body feel as if it is not mine.

I take the knife and raise it high. Then, with everything I've got, I thrust the knife into his neck, just below his ear. It doesn't go as deep as I thought it would, but it stops him in his tracks. He lets go of my arm and brings his hand up, but before he can cover his wound, I yank out the knife and stab him again, this time more successfully. He drops to the floor, screaming in agony as blood spills through his fingers.

My heart feels like it might explode as I run past him to the door. I throw it open and sprint up the stairs two at a time. When I get to the top, I'm confused at the tunnel-like hallways that run in two different directions. I decide to go to the left, anything to keep running and putting distance between us. The sounds become muffled, like when I am underwater.

I'm going as fast as I can, but it feels like I'm moving in slow motion through quicksand. Like a bad dream. But I think I hear his voice groaning, still behind me, still in the room. The muffled, watery sounds break with his scream. I want to look back to see how close he is, but I have to keep running.

At the end of the tunnel, the light from the bright sun shines its way through the opening.

But suddenly my world goes dark.

CHAPTER 29

ELLA

The back of the dresser budges as we watch in horror. Each drawer is recklessly and urgently opening and closing on the other side. Someone is frantic and looking for something important. The movement comes to a sudden halt as someone retrieves the object from one of the drawers.

But then the dresser moves like it's being shimmied away from the wall. I pull Angelina back as far as the confined space allows into a small cove, a groove far enough away to keep us hidden. We crouch low and hold our breath as someone attempts to pull the dresser away from the wall. I want to fade into the floor and disappear.

A dark, obscured face pokes in, looks around, and takes my breath away. I look at Angelina, who has her hand cupped at her mouth. He can't see us, but we can see him, and we know who it is. I catch glimpses of the man I used to know when I was a child, lost in the hardened features of the face I no longer recognize. His dark soul is etched into his expression lines, revealing evil, rage, and hate.

Black eyes bulge from their worn, leathery sockets. Frantic eyes searching for something. And I know what it is because I found it and took it: the box of trinkets. His trophies. His security.

"No," he says to himself. And then a louder, "No!" He thrusts his hand in, and then his arm, the exact amount he expects to feel the box. It's obvious he's done this several times before, probably each time he added a treasure to it or just to admire what he had.

I fully expect him to crawl inside, but he slams the dresser to the floor and screams, "No! You bitch! No!"

I know I'm the bitch he's referring to, and it makes my skin crawl to hear his voice sound so evil. Angelina and I look at each other with horror-filled faces. Her hand still covers her mouth, her eyes are watery.

This is not how I want to confront him. I want him to least expect it when it happens. But now I know where he is, and I won't let him out of my sight.

Luca runs heavy-footed down the hall, and it sounds like he's bursting into each bedroom. I can't keep track of where he's going—maybe up to the attic? Then it sounds like he's running down the stairs to the living room and kitchen. He's tearing through the house in a rage, and finally I hear the front door slam.

"Go," I say to Angelina. She looks back at me as if I'm crazy, but I have to know where he's going. "We have to follow him. Please go," I say with a slight push against her back.

I know she must be as scared as I am, and she would probably stay crouched against this wall for the rest of the day if she could, just to make sure he never sees us. But we can't take any chances, and she knows this. Angelina finally moves. She takes a second more, but she moves forward, pausing at the opening but then squeezing out of the space.

I follow and run to the window. I don't see Luca, but what I see is that the door to the shed is wide open.

"He's in the shed," I say.

Angelina frantically punches the keypad on her phone.

"What are you doing?" I ask, keeping my eyes on the shed.

"I'm calling us a cab," she says. "We have to get out of here. I'll have the cab pick us up on the next street. We'll have to run."

"I'm calling the police," I say.

"No, don't do that. The note says not to involve the police."

"It's different now," I say, dialing the emergency number. "We know where he is. They can catch him."

My heart beats so fast that I feel as though my chest might explode. I can barely get the words out, but once I get through to the police, I tell the dispatcher where we are and who is in the shed. I explain how dangerous Luca is and that he might have taken Bria. She reassures me that the police are on the way.

"Ella, what if the officers who show up are the ones helping Luca?" Angelina says. "What then?"

"Oh my God, you're right," I say. I'm so confused, and I can't think straight anymore. "Maybe I shouldn't have done that. We have to get out of here."

We don't waste any time running down the hall and descending the stairs. Every time we pass a window that views the shed, I watch for any sign of Luca leaving the shed.

The front door is wide open, but I also notice another door off the kitchen. We run to it, hoping to sneak out the side, but we find it locked. Rushing to the front door, we glance outside. Once we feel it might be okay, we slip out fast and over to the side of the house as far as possible. Listening. Waiting. Then we run to the bergamot plantation, where we know we can hide better.

I don't know whether Luca has come out of the shed or how close the police are to the house. But I know I've given all the details to the emergency receptionist, so when the police arrive, I'm hoping they will go straight to the shed. I'm counting on it. There is nothing more I can do now.

We wait, hoping the police will arrive quietly and not give themselves away with their lights and sirens. Luca does not need any opportunity to get away. Unless, of course, the police are here to help him and not us. Then we will hear the sirens warning him to run.

I send a group text to my mother and aunts telling them what is happening and suggesting that some of them go to the

Montepulciano house in case Luca hides there, and others should remain where they are and be ready to help or to confront.

I also send a text to Nico, knowing that I'm risking everything good in our relationship for the sake of honesty. This is happening and I can't deny it. And I hope he can forgive me, but there's no stopping this now.

Angelina and I tread lightly through the back entrance to the plantation toward the marina, watching in all directions, over our shoulders, everywhere as paranoia slithers through us. What I've learned about Luca is that he's got connections—smaller than what he used to have and seemingly innocent—but they are everywhere. For all I know, those connections could be right here, ready for us.

And then, just as we emerge from the path behind the houses to the open sand, I see someone standing on the patio of the marina. The blur from the heat slightly distorts the person's appearance, but I can tell by their physique it's a woman. And she's poking around the marina. She peers through the back windows and searches for something, and then I assume she goes to the front of the building because I can no longer see her. We move closer while staying near the edge of the property, in case we need to hide. As we reach the patio, I don't expect her to come around to the back so quickly. But all at once, she's there at the same moment we are, each of us stepping closer.

We stare each other down. Angelina is by my side. I'm dumbfounded at who it is. But, then again, I should have known.

Under my breath, I scarcely say her name: "Jamie."

CHAPTER 30

ELLA

"Hello, Ella," Jamie says with very little expression.

I glance at Angelina. "Is this for real?" I step forward toward Jamie, but Angelina grabs my hand and stops me.

"It could be a trap, Ella," Angelina says. "I don't like this."

But the rage surging inside of me is too much to bear. I shake off Angelina's hand and walk towards Jamie, who is now facing me. My feet press hard with anger into the hot sand. I feel my hands and my jaw clenching as pent-up emotion from such betrayal rises through my body.

She seems hesitant as I come closer, her body shifting as if she's unsure whether to meet me halfway or turn around and leave. But she doesn't do either. She remains in place, waiting for me to get to her.

I sense Angelina close behind me, mumbling something under her breath, probably a prayer or a spell of some sort. The air is so hot and dense I could touch it. It encroaches upon my skin and stays with me like a weighted blanket as I draw nearer to the traitor.

Jamie is fumbling with something in her pocket or her hand. Maybe it's nervous energy, as she often fidgets when she's anxious. Or maybe she's pulling something out—a weapon to protect herself—because I'm sure that the image of what she's seeing of me is giving her the feeling that she should protect herself.

I stop, allowing several feet between us.

Her face is uncertain. Her lip twitches.

"I should have known," I say.

She opens her mouth, but I don't let her talk.

"It wasn't enough that you pretended throughout our entire friendship that you gave a damn. Everything we went through together . . . Jack . . . Poppy . . . You were my best friend in the entire world. You always pulled me through. I shared the deepest, darkest parts of my soul with you."

She opens her mouth.

"Don't talk," I say. My legs tremble, so I pace back and forth. It's hard to look at her, to see the face of someone I loved and would do anything for, but I force myself. "You were there," I continue, "but not for me. When you betrayed me, you took one of the most sacred parts of my life: *you*. You were part of me. I couldn't imagine my life without you. And now I—I can't imagine it with you.

"Why would you do something like that? It's something I'll never understand. To you, blood is thicker than water. Even if it's the worst kind of blood. But not for me. You didn't have to be my blood relative to love you like one. And now it makes me sick to know we *are* related by blood thanks to Sienna. You only think about yourself," I say, feeling a bit jittery and unstable. I refuse to give her the courtesy of hearing what she has to say. It's clear that everything she does is for Luca.

"Ella—" Jamie keeps trying to speak, but I don't want to hear her voice.

"I'll tell you when to talk," I say, pointing my finger at her. "I should have known. You never left his side. Once again, you've been following me and telling Luca where I am and where I'm going. You're the one. It's always been you. Luca's success evading justice all this time is because you've been helping him."

Jamie shakes her head and reaches out her arm like she wants to touch me, but I shake my head right back and wave her off.

"You know, you're now an accessory to a crime. Did you realize that? A kidnapping—a young woman, the one we've seen on TV, the face posted in every public space there is. But of course you already knew that, and you don't care because, whatever your Grandpa Luca wants, and no matter how dark and evil he is, his little granddaughter, his protégé, will be right there for him, paving the way. Clearing the path so it's easy for him to get away with murder.

"Well, you know what? Now it's too late to save Bria, because once again you are in the way. Go ahead—text Luca and warn him I'm here if you haven't done that already. He's probably long gone from that disgusting shed. If Bria's dead, then I guess that makes you a murderer, too."

My mouth is erupting with everything I've imagined saying for so long. But if the words are finally out, why do I feel empty inside?

"I'm so tired, Jamie. I've given up so much only to be constantly sabotaged by you. You make me sick."

Angelina gives my hand a reassuring squeeze.

"You're wrong," Jamie blurts, "about why I'm here. You're so wrong."

I throw up my hands. "And how is that?" I say.

"I'm not here for Luca," she says. "I'm here for you."

"It never stops with you—the lies. It never stops," I say sharply. "You can never undo what you've done. Can't you just be honest for once?"

"You've been getting anonymous notes, right? Warnings? Hints?" she says. "Texts from an unknown number? That was me. The note at the door in Montepulciano—I put it there. How else would I know all this?"

"Because you're still working with Luca, and you're both messing with my mind," I say, disgusted.

"Ella, just think about it," she says.

"Who threw the boulder at the windshield?"

"I didn't know about that," she says. "I left as soon as I put the note in the door. Luca must have thrown it, which means I just missed him. It would have been catastrophic if he had seen me there."

"You expect me to believe you?" I say. "Now?"

"I know I have been an awful friend," Jamie says. "I can never express how truly sorry I am for hurting you, El."

"What you're saying makes no sense," I say. "You say you're not working with Luca, but you know where he is and what he's doing."

"Yes, I have seen Luca, but not for the reasons you think," she says.

I cross my arms.

"I'm on your side, Ella. This time I'm on your side. I've had a lot of time to reflect, and I've spent thousands of dollars on therapy. I can't believe I betrayed you like that." Her eyes fill and her nose reddens. "I allowed myself to be manipulated. I knew very little about Luca's overarching plan for us—that he had strategically placed me into your life so we would grow up together, become close, and stay connected. He wanted to make it easier for him to know what you were doing and what you might know about his secrets."

She steps forward, but I step back.

"Please believe me when I say that our friendship was real. Everything I said or did, everything we went through, those were genuine moments we shared. My feelings for you were—*are*—real."

I shake my head and look away. I don't want to hear this. It's taken a lot to get over the loss of our friendship.

"Ella, please look at me. When we came to Italy two years ago, Luca asked me to look after you, and I really believed he was trying to protect you. At first, I believed everything he said because he sounded so sincere. But I started questioning his motives after a while, especially when he integrated me into his private affairs. I should have said something then. It was a game for him. I should have told you when I realized it, I know. But by then it was too late. You had already discovered our connection and wouldn't listen to me."

"Girls, look." Angelina points to the hills behind us as a train of several police cars climb slowly down, one behind the other.

"We have to go," I say.

"We'll take my car," Jamie yells. "I'm parked on a side street. Come on, I know where he's going."

Angelina and I exchange fast glances and then follow Jamie the way we came through the back entrance to the marina. As she said, her car is parked on the side road. Jamie could be part of Luca's plan to catch us and bring us to him. But there is something about the way she spoke just now that makes me believe her a little.

While we're driving, I ask Jamie why she showed up at the marina, and she said it's because she was checking to see if Luca had come by. She had also hoped to find us before he did.

She weaves through the narrow roads like a maniac, climbing the high cliffs of the countryside. I hold my breath as our car comes within inches of several parked cars, homes and businesses, and pedestrians. One slight shift in the wrong direction would be disastrous. I ask where she's taking us, and she replies that it's somewhere we haven't been before, and it's the only place left for Luca to go.

"I hope we're not too late to save Bria," I say, "and catch Luca."

Jamie doesn't reply. Her eyes are trained hard on the road before us.

* * *

We careen around a bend, and Jamie speeds up to accommodate the steep climb. A text arrives for her, and she pushes play so we can all hear it:

"Text from Nina: '*He's driving on the SS16 highway. She's in the trunk.*'"

"Is that the Nina I think it is?" I say. "Who's in the trunk?"

"We think Luca's got Bria in the trunk and Mona at one of his houses."

"Mona? Who's Mona?"

Jamie points to her glove box. "In there," she says.

I open the glove box, remove the file folder, and open it. It's a file on a young woman who went missing around the same time as Bria, but her case didn't get as much media attention, probably because, according to her file, she's poor.

"I didn't know two women were missing," I say to Angelina.

"Bria's sister was shot and almost died in that house fire," Jamie says. "Luca is responsible for everything. He has Bria." Jamie's hands are locked on the wheel, her elbows bent. She sees something. "That's his car," she motions with a quick tilt of her head.

I follow her intense gaze and see the black, shiny car. Black like his heart. "We have to get to him before he leaves Scilla. Once he's out there, it will be much harder."

"I thought you knew where he was going," Angelina says doubtfully.

"I think I know where he'll go, but you know Luca—he's always got another move. If I'm wrong and we lose him, we'll never find him."

We emerge from the tiny roads of Scilla's fishing village to several open roads extending from the main road, like a sea monster's arms reaching out. We cannot let him out there. He can't win this time.

Luca's car whizzes past us as Jamie desperately tries to keep up. Two police cars race by. Angelina mentions that there were at least two to three other police cars that stayed back at the house. Maybe they are the ones working for Luca.

Buildings outside the window whip by in a blur. I hold my breath and check my seat belt as we fly in and out of small gaps between cars that blare their horns at us. Angelina mumbles a prayer in the back seat behind me, likely regretting her decision to come here at all. But Luca seems to evade us, gaining far more distance from the rest, leaving us all in his dust. Jamie punches the gas hard, throwing us back in our seats. Sirens scream from the police cars as they, too, speed up.

It happens so fast my brain can't keep up with it. Luca makes a last-minute U-turn at an opening we don't see coming and quickly merges into traffic, going in the opposite direction. We miss the turn, but in the back window, I see a black car like Luca's flip over like a piece of wind-driven cardboard. It flies into another car, pulling it into the median, while oncoming traffic swerves to avoid the inevitable crash.

"Oh my God!" Angelina says. "Did you see that?"

We immediately take the next exit, which quickly becomes blocked off. But despite the accident causing a traffic stop, we can make it through. A siren warns people to move to either side while a police car pulls through. We drive as far as space allows and then Jamie slams fast through an opening to the shoulder of the road, where we illegally drive a little further. She stops the car. We get out fast and run toward the accident.

It is a terrible sight of chaos, confusion, and injuries. We push through until an officer stops us and tells us that no one is allowed closer to the scene. I frantically explain that the man driving the flipped car had a kidnapped girl with him. He tells us he can't imagine anyone surviving in that car. I beg him to check, and he radios to another officer. The officer informs us they are currently checking the car for survivors and instructs us to stay where we are or risk being arrested. After that, he turns and goes to assist the others.

I notice the look on Jamie's face. Watery eyes replace determination and anger. I should expect this. Luca is her grandfather, after all, and I suppose she must love him. But are her emotions revealing regret or worry?

Two ambulances pull in as far as they can go. An irate driver of the first ambulance slams his horn and turns on his sirens. Jamie, Angelina, and I move our car back into the traffic on the road. Jamie suggests she wait in the car while Angelina and I walk up ahead, but Angelina says she's too tired to join me and waits with Jamie. If I know Angelina, the real reason she stayed behind is because she doesn't trust Jamie to be alone.

I feel the same. Jamie still can't be trusted. For all we know, she could make a phone call alerting someone connected to Luca. This could all be a diversion so that we'll trust her again while she continues to help Luca.

Jamie is quiet as I step out of the car. She just stares out the window while I walk to the spot where we were stopped.

I don't know how much time has elapsed, but it seems like hours. I text Angelina to check on things in the car. She says Jamie's been quiet the whole time. Emergency technicians tend to the passengers and drivers of the four cars affected by the crash while an officer directs traffic toward an exit. One ambulance leaves the scene, and, as it drives away, the officer I spoke to earlier approaches me.

"You said you knew the person driving that car," he says more than asks while pointing to the car.

"Yes, is he—"

"Gone. There's no one in that car."

A sickness fills my stomach. "Is he in the ambulance?"

He shakes his head. "No. Our emergency workers checked all of the vehicles as soon as they got there. I spoke with each of them. No one tended to anyone in that vehicle."

"I thought you said no one could have survived in that car. It didn't just drive itself, so where is the driver?"

"That's what I thought when we first arrived. The entire passenger side and part of the driver's side were damaged. The driver must have climbed out through the window. He probably felt dazed and wandered off. The driver likely sustained severe injuries. I can't imagine he'll get very far. We've got officers searching everywhere. "

"No one saw him get out of the car? He's a criminal, and he's getting away!"

"We've got a team searching now," he says. "How do you know he's a criminal?"

"Because he has killed someone and almost tried to kill me. He's abducted several women."

He steps aside and turns back toward the wreckage like he's not processing what I'm saying. "I'm sending someone over to take your statement."

And then something within nudges me. A tap on my brain or maybe my heart.

"Wait!" I yell.

He comes back.

"What about the trunk? Have you opened the trunk?"

He eyes me strangely.

"Please, please, please—you have to do it now!"

"What?" he says.

Another officer approaches, as if to console me, like I've lost my mind or something. He puts his arm around me, but I move away.

"No, I'm serious. Please, just listen to me." I point to the car and yell, "Someone's inside that trunk!"

And I hope and pray she's alive.

CHAPTER 31

ELLA

The officers turn toward the horrific scene of the accident. The car that Luca was driving is flipped over and mangled on one side. One officer runs to the rescue team surrounding the car as Angelina and Jamie come to my side and then a third officer approaches. We watch as a conversation ensues at the car and then the rescue workers attend to the lock on the trunk while it remains tipped on its side. I assume they're not righting the vehicle to prevent further injury to anyone potentially in the trunk.

Officers are rerouting traffic around orange cones, outlining the area. Tow trucks have towed away the other two cars involved in the accident. Two ambulances have departed for the hospital, and one is standing by, possibly to claim another crash victim. Everyone else has left, leaving only the officers and ambulance crew, along with Angelina, Jamie, and me. And the only reason we're here is because of my claim that there is a body in the trunk.

While our eyes are locked on the car, we witness the trunk release and pop open. The rescue workers open the trunk the rest of the way, look at each other, and move in close against the car. Their arms reach inside the trunk. Angelina makes the sign of the cross and prays as Jamie takes my hand and squeezes. One officer who is standing with us rushes to the vehicle to offer support.

We watch side by side, hardly moving, barely breathing, while the rescue workers carefully pull a petite, limp body from the trunk. They gently fold her into their arms and place her on a stretcher. The rescue team evaluates her, covers her little body with a blanket, straps her to the stretcher, and carries her into the ambulance.

"Do you think it's Bria? Is she alive?" Angelina says. "She must be . . . otherwise they wouldn't have put her in the ambulance, right?"

Jamie and I glance at each other and don't answer. The doors of the ambulance close, and we can no longer see them. Another tow truck arrives and parks next to Luca's half-demolished car. One officer leaves to talk to the driver of the tow truck while two other officers remain at the car, writing notes, taking pictures, and probably gathering evidence. The police officer who was standing with us earlier returns and asks if we can come with her to the police station for further questioning.

"How is she?" I say, ignoring her question. "The girl in the trunk—is she okay?"

The officer pauses when she looks at me, as if she's unsure how to answer. "She's alive, but we know nothing else. She could have internal injuries."

"Which hospital are they taking her to?" I ask.

"Arcispedale Santa Maria Nuova," she says, and my heart stops. It's the hospital where I am completing my fellowship. Angelina's eyes flash up at me. We both know that I'm not allowed on the premises, but there's no way we're not going. We have to know if that girl in the trunk is Bria. If it's Bria and she's alive, she might have information about Luca that can lead us to him.

"Would it be okay to talk at the hospital?" I ask. But the officer informs us that, since we're not family, they won't allow us to see the patient. "I don't need to see her. I just want to be there to make sure she's okay."

"What's your connection to this girl?" the officer says. "How did you know she was in the trunk?"

"I don't have a connection with the girl, but the man driving the car is my uncle, and, as I have said before, he is dangerous."

"I'm sorry," the officer says, "but if you're not family, they won't tell you anything. The hospital will take care of her, and it's *my* job to catch the guy who did this to her. Are you going to help us with that or not?"

"Of course I will," I say. "But Luca, my uncle, could be any-where. And you have a team looking for him right now." I look at the officer and Jamie. "Can you give us a minute?" Then I motion for Angelina to come closer. Jamie and the officer glance at me, annoyed, as Angelina and I move away to talk in private.

Angelina and I agree that, since we don't trust Jamie, we cannot leave her alone. We decide Angelina will say she's going back to the villa, but she'll actually be going to the hospital. Jamie and I will go to the police station together, which is probably where she will prefer to be, anyway. Luca is her grandfather, and she will want to know what is happening with him, whether it's to help him or to help us. Angelina promises to keep me informed of anything she finds out at the hospital.

My hands are shaky, and I feel jittery as soon as Jamie starts the car. I think my mind and my body are feeling the true weight of everything. I feel like I might collapse. The air in the car is heavy, and the awkward silence might be telling me something. I crack open the window as we drive to the station. Eventually, when I feel a little more collected, I consider asking Jamie what she thinks about all of this.

I clear my throat. "So, what are the odds of Luca getting out of that car?"

Jamie keeps her eyes forward, saying nothing.

"How could he find the strength to climb out the window after that crash? And no one saw him. How is that possible?"

After a minute, Jamie glances at me and says, "I'm really not surprised."

"You're not?"

"Luca has always been physically active and fit—more fit than you and I, and we're much younger." She swerves into the right lane. "I'm sure you don't know this, but he used to practice."

"Practice what—escaping from crashed cars?"

"Well, yes," she says, "and other things."

"How do you know this?" I say.

"My mother told me," she says.

I have to remind myself that Jamie's mother, Cecelia, is Luca and Sienna's daughter. It was Cecelia and Luca who tried to brainwash Jamie against me.

"What other things did he do?" I say.

"I don't know any specifics," she says. "Only that he used to practice getting himself out of various predicaments."

This should not surprise me, and yet I continue to be surprised to learn something about Luca I never knew. I wonder if Luca, being older and injured, could still get himself out of an accident as serious as this one or if someone helped him escape. I don't know how he slipped away with no one seeing him.

"Did someone help Luca get out of that car?" I say. "Was someone there, Jamie? Just tell me. You must know. Did one of his police officers help him escape?"

"I don't know," she says. "But if I had to guess, I'd say someone must have helped him. There is always someone on call, ready to provide whatever he needs."

"Where is he, Jamie? Where would he go from the accident? Where would he hide? You must have an idea."

"I think I might know where he's headed," she says, staring at the road. "That's where we're going."

"Hold on," I say. "If you know where he might be, why didn't you tell the police when we were with them? Why did you say we would meet them at the hospital after we go to the police station?" I say.

But Jamie keeps her mouth closed, her eyes on the road, and steps on the gas.

"Stop the car."

"Trust me, Ella," she says.

"I don't trust you," I say.

"Right now, this is all on a hunch," Jamie says. "A big hunch, but still just a hunch. When I'm certain I know where Luca is, I will tell the police right away."

"This is bullshit." I yank my phone from my pocket and tap the emergency number.

"What are you doing?" Jamie says. "Don't do that!" She swats at my phone and it falls between the seats. "Don't call yet, Ella. This could all backfire right in front of us. Trust me."

"Trust you?" I repeat as I reach between the seats and feel for my phone with my fingers. Someone on the other end picks up and says, "This is the Emergency Department. Who am I speaking with? Hello?"

"False alarm!" Jamie yells. "I'm so sorry! Fat fingers!"

But I think we got disconnected, because I no longer hear the voice on the other end. There's a burning in my chest and my stomach is in knots. I will never know if Jamie is still colluding with Luca. Maybe she really is helping him, and this is part of an elaborate plan to bring me to him—throw me right into the fire.

Panic sets in, making me wary. I reach over, grab the steering wheel, and yank it down. It jerks fast to the right, and now we're driving on the shoulder of the road.

She attempts to pull it back, but I'm stronger than her. We drive onto the grassy area, and Jamie slams on the brakes, thrusting us forward. She throws the car into park and faces me with crazed eyes.

"What the hell are you doing?" she says as I throw open my door and jump out of the car. I'm standing on the grass with my legs wide, arms out, prepared to defend myself.

"If we don't call the police and agree to meet them wherever you think he might be, I won't get back in that car. I don't give one shit about whether Luca is there. Or if he's prepared for us or surprised to see us. There's no way I will get back in that car with you." I pace back and forth, giving my demands. I realize I am simply not safe, and I will not feel safe unless the police are here. "So, if you need to go to this place to confirm Luca's whereabouts, then go. But I won't be going with you."

"Ella . . ." Jamie's tone softens. Her eyes fall slightly. "I would never do anything to cause you harm. I told you I'm here to help you find Luca. I'm trying to do the right thing."

"But why? Why now? Why not a hundred other times before?" The lump in my throat hinders my voice. My authentic voice.

Jamie is quiet. She's thinking or planning. Maybe she's figuring out what to say. Which parts to make up. "We don't have a lot of time," she says. "I know you don't believe me, and you have every right not to believe me. I understand—I have proven that you can't trust me. But Ella," she swallows before she continues, "I promise you I am on your side this time."

"You shouldn't have left my side," I say, my voice cracking. *Don't fall apart.* "I never thought otherwise."

"Ella, please believe me. I've had a lot of time to think and reflect on what happened between us. I was wrong," she says. "I was so wrong. The things I believed and the people I thought loved me—it was all a lie. But Luca, my *grandfather,* used me to get to you—like he's God—putting us together, orchestrating our entire relationship and our lives for his selfish gain. I see that now. And . . . I don't regret that we became so close. Our friendship was genuine."

"I don't know, Jamie," I say.

"I get it," she says. "I understand why you doubt me. I want your forgiveness, but I don't expect it. What we had might be gone forever, and I'll never forgive myself for that. But I understand."

I feel an urgency to turn around and run for my life, but there's something inside me, a small shred of hope or wishful thinking, that tells me she might mean what she's saying.

Something in her voice. Something in the way she's speaking to me.

"Then prove it," I say. "Do this one thing for me. Call that police officer who told us to meet her at the hospital." I hand her the officer's card.

"I have her card," she says.

She taps in the number on the car's display screen. The police officer, Martina Ferraro, announces her name after she picks up. Jamie explains what's happening and gives her our location and the location where she predicts Luca might be. We're directed to stay where we are and wait for them.

About twenty minutes later, Officer Ferraro pulls up in an unmarked car. Officer Ferraro follows Jamie and me as we speed off to Luca's supposed location.

CHAPTER 32

ELLA

Angelina texts me and confirms that the woman in the trunk of Luca's car is Bria. She has three broken ribs, a broken collarbone, and a broken arm. They had to put her in a coma to reduce the swelling on her brain and to allow her body to relax and heal. Angelina also found out that some of Bria's injuries are not accident-related. The police are guarding Bria's room for her protection and for when or if she can eventually speak. From what Angelina is telling me, it's not looking good for Bria.

Another text from Angelina immediately follows. She saw Dr. Girofolo. Thankfully, he doesn't know who she is. He was talking closely with a young woman fitting Jonella's description. I wonder what they're talking about, and why so secretively. I update her briefly on what has happened since she left the scene of the accident and inform her we're on our way to a house where we think Luca might be. She agrees to keep an eye on Bria as well as Dr. Girofolo and Jonella, and she will wait for me at the hospital.

We turn off of the main road, which is lined with beautiful, well-maintained, historic homes, into an unusual neighborhood. I'd never expect to find a neighborhood like this, behind these houses, almost as if it doesn't belong here at all. A neighborhood that could have had such potential. Perhaps in its prime it was larger than life and not as its current state, a lost soul. Abandoned in every sense.

The further we drive, the darker it gets. We maneuver around the broken roads with cracks that rise in the earth. We pass tipped-over street signs and boarded-up houses, with shutters hanging by a thread. Some houses have caved-in rooftops. I'm surprised to see an occasional car in a driveway. Being here makes my heart weep and my hands feel clammy. It feels like we're invading something private. Something we should not be looking at.

Jamie pulls into a spot in front of an old house. Most of the paint on the white, two-story house is chipped and peeling. Some areas around the door and steps show signs of darkening and weathering. A large window overlooks the porch, which is mostly covered by overgrown shrubs. The other front windows are barely holding on. Jamie puts the car in park and gets out. She holds the door so it won't slam and doesn't let it close completely. I do the same and follow behind her. Officer Ferraro is a few steps behind us. A smaller house at the back peeks from behind, like an old carriage house. Maybe at one time it was a guest house.

Officer Ferraro unsnaps her holster and heads toward the back of the house, to the area Jamie had described to her earlier. While following closely behind, Jamie and I exchange glances at each other's concealed weapons—hers in her ankle holster and mine in my crossbody. In the backseat of the patrol car, Jamie had covertly lifted her pant leg to reveal a gun at her ankle. She handed me a gun from her bag that was heavier than I expected. It reminded me of when I'd found Poppy's revolver hidden in his secret box two years ago. It took Luca breaking into my house in New York to make me consider owning a gun for the first time. After a few lessons, my aim is excellent, although I've never had to use it in an actual situation.

Treading lightly, we follow Jamie and make our way around the back of the main house to the carriage house. A dim light filters through a window.

My pulse races. My senses are on high alert. This is it. This could be the end. All truth converging into this moment.

Officer Ferraro readies the gun in her hands and motions with her head for us to step aside. With the gun held in one hand, she reaches for the doorknob with the other, turns it, and pushes it open. She enters the house while we wait in silence. It's quiet, as if nature is holding its breath.

Moments later, the officer steps outside. "All clear," she says. "No one's in there. But you should come and look at something."

I glance at Jamie, but I can't gather anything suspicious from her reaction. She looks as surprised as I am.

We stand at the threshold of the entryway. To the left is a living room and to the right a dining room. White sheets cover all the furniture. A narrow staircase rises between the two rooms. At the back of the house, there is a filthy kitchen with a table and four chairs in the center. It looks like someone stood up and left one chair pulled away from the table.

Bloodied tissues and a bloody towel are in a garbage can next to the table. But the most interesting piece of evidence is a pen, resting on a bloodstained, torn piece of lined journal paper. A Montegrappa pen like the one I'd gotten for Luca as a Christmas gift a few years ago. Luca has an extensive luxury pen collection, and that year he'd told Lena that the only thing he wanted for Christmas was this Montegrappa pen. Lena didn't want me to spend that kind of money on a pen, but Luca had always done so much for me, and when it went on sale, I bought it for him. I even paid extra to have it monogrammed.

I reach for the pen, but Officer Ferraro stops me and tells me not to touch anything because this is now a crime scene. So I get as close as possible to the pen and immediately I see the over curve at the bottom of the *L* and the under curve at the end.

"That's Luca's pen," I say. "I gave it to him. I'm sure of it."

Officer Ferraro and Jamie look at me with surprised faces. That he brought *this* pen *here* to write a note next to his bloody mess is more than ironic. It's like a sick joke. It's evil.

"You should read the note," Officer Ferraro says. "But don't touch it."

Out loud, I read the note with the crooked letters all different sizes scratched across the lines:

You can't outsmart me.
You've taken my freedom, my family.
Now I'm taking something of yours that you love.
You won't win. Just give up.

My stomach drops as soon as I read it. "This note was meant for me," I say, looking at Jamie.

Immediately, I think of everyone I hold dear to my heart: my mom, my sister and brother, Nico, Angelina. *This is deeper than a threat.*

"Oh my God, would he really do this? Will he harm my family?" *What if we're too late?*

Officer Ferraro calls for backup. I give her the names and contact information of each of my family members, as well as Nico's and Angelina's. She assures me that additional officers are currently en route to each of their homes and to the hospital.

I text them all to let them know an officer will arrive shortly and tell them to text me right away. Officer Ferraro believes Luca stopped at the carriage house right after the accident so he could clean up his injuries before he went on the run again. She asks Jamie if she has any idea where Luca might go next. Jamie tells her she thought we would have found him here, as she is the only one who knows about this place.

Officer Ferraro says, "Whoever was here has lost a lot of blood. He won't get very far without medical attention. He's going to need it eventually."

"If Luca wrote the note knowing you would see it, Ella, then he also knows I brought you here," Jamie says. "And it's a terrible thing for Luca to realize that I am helping you, because all this time he thinks I've been helping *him*. That's how I've been able to keep close tabs on him. It's why, until this point, I've known so much."

She must have been telling me the truth.

Texts come in simultaneously from everyone except for my mother. They are all frantic and want answers I can't give them.

Nico's response is brief: *"El, please tell me you're okay."* It hurts my heart and melts it at the same time. He called me El. He still cares. Of course he cares. He's always cared; he's just not okay with what I'm doing.

My shaky fingers send off another text to my mom, telling her to text me back right away. As the minutes tick by without a response, panic rises to my chest. I call her and it goes right to her voicemail.

Angelina sends another text informing me that Bria is resting and two police officers remain outside her room. I tell her to be careful because Luca could show up at the hospital. Surely, by now, someone has alerted him that the police have found Bria in the trunk of his car. It wouldn't surprise me if one or two police officers were at the accident scene on Luca's behalf. I fear that the police sitting outside Bria's room might not be there to help her but to silence her. I'm sure she has information Luca would kill to keep hidden. Information about what he's been up to and where he's been these last few months. Maybe he's hiding other girls in other places.

I tell Angelina to be on alert but do whatever she can to stay close. Angelina says so far no family has come for Bria, so she will keep pretending to be her aunt until someone shows up, and more than likely someone will.

I call my mother again and it goes straight to voicemail. I hear the fear in my voice when I leave a brief message telling her to call me back as soon as possible. Only when it's absolutely necessary, I'll call Vinny and Nonna to check on my mother. I'm holding off because their extreme reactions could make things worse. Texting or calling Nico might be my only option of finding out where my mother is without creating more chaos. But, then again, the police will go to the villa eventually, so it really doesn't matter if I wait or call him now.

Before I decide to call Nico, Angelina texts me again, saying that she tried to get a hold of Vinny to let him know the police will arrive shortly to check on things, but he didn't answer, so she had to leave him a message. Angelina says she has a bad feeling about this and wants to go home now.

When the investigation team arrives, Officer Ferraro tells us we need to leave. Jamie and I sit close beside each other in the back seat of the police car as we leave the carriage house and drive to the police station. Everything that could be said out loud stays in our heads, and I wonder what is inside Jamie's.

I keep checking for a text from my mom, but there's still no reply.

Jamie straightens and leans to the middle. "I just thought of something," she says. "Maybe you should call Gianna."

"Why Gianna?" I say. "He doesn't know where she is, right?"

"I'm not sure what he knows anymore, but it wasn't long ago that he was close to finding out where she might be living. That's another reason I tried to reach out to you anonymously, and why I came to the marina, knowing you would be there and I could tell you in person what I know."

Officer Ferraro says, "Do you think Gianna could be in danger?"

Jamie looks at me with regret. "I think she might be."

"Why didn't you say something before?"

"I was sure Luca was at the carriage house," she says. "I was almost one-hundred-percent sure that would be there."

"Almost," I say, calling Gianna.

It's happening again. A race to Gianna. Will we get to her before Luca?

"I don't think he would harm her," Jamie says.

"That's not convincing at all, Jamie," I say, listening to Gianna's phone ring without going to voicemail. Could she be on the phone with someone? I dial again and the same thing happens.

I give Officer Ferraro Gianna's address, and she sends it to an officer who will check on her. Everyone I know is in danger. Who will Luca try to hurt to get back at me?

I send a text to Nico:

> *"I'm sorry to do this, but you are my only hope. After the police leave your apartment, could you please go to the villa to check on Vinny and my mother?* Then I send another: *"I will never ask for another thing. Please help me."*

Nico responds right away:

> *"The police were here. They think I should find a safe place to go. I'm on my way to the villa."*

I'd hoped for a little more, but he responded right away, and he *is* helping me. I suppose that's all I need at the moment. Right now, I'm desperately trying to keep it together and not think about the terrible things going through my head.

Neither my mother nor Gianna have responded to me. Losing them is not an option.

He won't win. I won't allow it.

* * *

We arrive with Officer Ferraro at the Comando Stazione Carabinieri, a police station in Scilla. When we get inside, it is clamorous and much busier than usual. Several people are sitting in chairs in the small reception area, others are in separate work rooms in private meetings. Two guards stand beside two handcuffed suspects in the hallway. I do a double take as one of the older suspects reminds me of Luca. But, on second glance, the scowl on his dirty face is even worse than Luca's.

Officer Ferraro leads us to her office in the back, where it is slightly quieter. She closes the door, stares at us for a moment, and then gets started with her questioning. She wants to know everything regarding my connection to Luca and what I know about him. I tell her that Luca is guilty of kidnapping, harassment, stalking, and murder and that he may be a serial killer. I explain that Gianna might have been his first victim, that she had been in hiding for decades, and how I found her.

When I tell the officer about the sapphire barrette and other trinkets Angelina and I found in Luca's childhood home, Jamie jerks her head at me, and the look in her eyes is telling: she doesn't like what she's hearing. Not one bit.

"Where are these trinkets?" Jamie asks coldly.

"They're with Angelina," I say.

"And where is she?"

"She went back to the villa," I lie.

Jamie squints her eyes as if she's examining each word I say.

Officer Ferraro's fingers jump across the keys of her laptop, keeping up with our conversation. She stops typing and glances up. "Are the items you found in the house similar to the ones in the storage unit?"

"You know about that?" I say.

"It is in the report you recently filed."

"Yes, the items are similar." Women's accessories—hats, scarves, necklaces, pins—similar to what we found in Luca's house, only several more. The items were neatly packed in small shoe boxes. "While you're looking, do you see a report from Sienna Russo filed against Luca?"

She searches on her computer for a few seconds. "No, I don't see anything like that."

"Are you sure?" I say.

Jamie looks at me. She doesn't know that Sienna made a police report when she found out about Luca's storage unit and some of the illegal activities he was involved in.

"Positive. I'd be able to find it, and it's not here."

When it's Jamie's turn to talk about her relationship with Luca, her connection to me, and our friendship, I examine her tone of voice and body language closely. I also notice Officer Ferraro's expression and the way she sits back in her chair and crosses her arms like she's judging us.

I show the officer pictures I'd taken of the anonymous notes, and we discuss the note that was left in the old carriage house. She does a quick search of Luca's name and pulls up a decades-old article about the body that washed up on the shore of the marina and the speculation about the Perri men.

She faces her computer screen towards us, and at the top of the article is a picture of the young girl they found, Julia Bernardi. My heart stops for a second when I see her picture, and I have to go in for a closer look to make sure I'm seeing it correctly. I've read the article before and seen the pictures, but not how I see it now. I never paid attention to the decorative barrette holding back her beautiful, dark hair. Although it's a black-and-white photo, there's no mistaking it. It has to be the same barrette I found in Luca's childhood home. *Julia Bernardi's barrette. A connection to Luca.*

"I'm not gonna lie," Officer Ferraro says. "The Perris have deep connections in this town. They are not the kind of family you take down easily. If you have all the items you say you have, we will do everything we can to find this Luca Perri."

"Can you perform a DNA test on the items?" I ask.

"If we feel it's necessary," she says.

A loud knock comes at the door and then an older officer steps in, asking if he can be of any help. Officer Ferraro tells him we're just about finished, but she would like his help to assemble a team of investigators and police.

The older officer approaches the computer and glimpses the screen. "I remember that story," he says, pointing at the headline. "It was one of the first cold cases they assigned to me about twenty years ago. Are they reopening the case?"

Officer Ferraro introduces us to Jimmy Boxxo, a retired detective who currently helps with cold cases in Calabria. "This is Ella Perri and her friend, Jamie," she says to Jimmy Boxxo.

Jimmy squints his eyes like he's thinking. "Perri," he says. "Any relation to the Perri boys—Franco and Luca?"

"Franco was my grandfather, and Luca is my great-uncle," I say.

"Hmm. Interesting," he says. "They faced wrongful accusations in a few missing girls' cases. It's a shame we never caught the person responsible. They questioned a few boys—Franco, Luca, and a couple of others—but since there was no concrete evidence connecting them to the cases, they released them. But you know what I think?" He strokes his chin and pauses for effect. "I think someone got away with murder. And now I'm wondering what brings you to this little police station in Scilla digging up old articles about the past?"

Officer Ferraro replies, "Miss Perri thinks her Uncle Luca is involved in some trouble again. She thinks he was the one driving the car they found the Bria Gallo girl in."

"And what makes you think after all this time it's your uncle who's responsible? Isn't he an old man now?" Jimmy says. "Don't get me wrong. You're probably right. I've been leery of him for years." Jimmy hovers close to Officer Ferraro's desk.

Officer Ferraro minimizes the window on her computer screen and holds some notes she'd written on paper to her chest like playing cards. "We need to get back to what we were doing, Jimmy. If you could assemble that team, I'd appreciate it."

I can tell by the way Jimmy grins and nods as he turns to exit the room that he's not okay with being dismissed like that.

Jimmy pauses at the door and says, "You all have a good day now."

"Something's not right about that guy," I whisper to Jamie.

"I agree," Jamie says.

Officer Ferraro appears fidgety and uneasy as we return to our discussion. A few minutes later, there is another knock at the door. She gets up from her desk chair to see who it is and then excuses herself for a moment.

My phone lights up and vibrates. A call from Nico.

CHAPTER 33

ELLA

"El," Nico says, and the weight of his breathless voice reveals that something dreadful has occurred.

"What's wrong?" I say. There's a long pause. "Nico?"

"I'm at the villa," he says, panting. "There's been an accident—a fire."

My heart sinks to my stomach, and I feel the blood drain out of me.

Jamie gets in front of me and studies my face.

I shake my head.

"Is everyone—"

"I don't know," he says. "The fire trucks and police were already here. No one can tell me anything."

"We're on our way," I say.

Nico agrees to stay with me on the phone until I get to the villa. I open the door just as Officer Ferraro is about to re-enter the room. I tell her we're leaving because there's a fire at the villa where my family is staying and I have to get to them. Officer Ferraro informs me that the reason she left our meeting was because the officers she had sent to the villa had just informed her about the fire. She suggests we'll get there faster if we ride there with her.

It's an eternity until we get there. Even with the flashing lights and sirens, we can't get to the villa fast enough.

"Don't worry, Ella," Nico reassures softly over the phone. "Everything will be okay."

"It has to be, Nico. It has to."

*　*　*

High in the sky, billowing black smoke fills the air, which is easily seen as we approach the neighborhood where the villa sits.

I'm nauseous, and my body is trembling out of control. Jamie puts her arm around me.

We park as closely as we can. Two fire trucks flank the villa, and several firefighters aim hoses at the fire, striving to win the fight against the blazing flames that are engulfing half of the villa.

Officer Ferraro directs us to stay in the car as she steps out and radios someone.

"Nico?" I say into the phone.

"I see you," he says. "I'll come to you."

Not even a full minute later, Nico is speaking with Officer Ferraro outside our car. *What is she saying? Does she know something she's not telling me?* She opens the back door to the police car, and Jamie and I step out. Nico embraces me and holds on for a long time before letting me go. My body slackens against his chest as a flood of emotion releases and I can't stop the tears from coming.

He pulls back and cups the back of my head in his hands, and pushes the tears off of my cheeks with his thumbs. His chocolaty eyes flood as they peer into mine. "El, it's okay. I'm here and I'm not going anywhere. The officer said everyone got out of the house. Emergency technicians are tending to them now. They're alive—your mom, Vinny, Nonna, Lena—they're all alive."

My knees give out, and Nico steadies me. Jamie is standing next to me with her hand over her mouth. Nico acknowledges her with a brief, stiff nod.

A cab pulls in beside us, and the back door flies open before it even comes to a full stop. Angelina bursts from the car, screaming and crying in Italian. Nico and I run to her and tell her that Vinny and everyone in the villa are safely out and they're okay, but she doesn't believe us.

"No, no, no!" she says.

Does she know something?

Angelina is inconsolable, trying to break away from us so she can run to the fire. I can only imagine her emotions at watching the fire destroy the beautiful home that she and Vinny built together. They saved every penny they had and put it all towards the villa after they were married. It was their dream to own a villa and share it with others. She took such pride in every part and put her own special touches throughout. Thank God everyone is safe, but I can't imagine the loss she feels right now.

When Angelina calms down, Jamie steps away and starts talking to Officer Ferraro. I see Jamie talking and waving her arms as if she's angry. Officer Ferraro puts a hand on her hip and appears to be annoyed with her, but then she shakes her head and starts talking into her radio. I wish I could hear what she's saying. While we're trying to keep Angelina calm, I keep an eye on Jamie and the officer. A couple minutes later, they approach us.

"I have some information," the officer says. "The two older women, Lena and Olivia, and the man—"

"My husband, Vinny!" Angelina blurts.

"And your husband, Vinny," Officer Ferraro confirms, "are all being treated for smoke inhalation."

"What about the other woman?" I say, nervously. "Younger— late forties. It's my mother. Her name is Gabriella."

Officer Ferraro speaks into the radio and asks for confirmation about my mother. I hear someone on the other end say that she appears to be fine. "They are all being taken to the hospital,

206 🔒 MOMENT OF TRUTH

and they expect them to be okay. I was trying to get as much information as possible, which is why I didn't tell you sooner. But your friend here insisted that I tell you what I know now." Officer Ferraro looks at Jamie, annoyed.

"Thank you for telling us," I say. "Olivia is my grandmother, and Lena is my great-aunt. I'm so grateful that they are all okay. Thank you so much for telling us."

Officer Ferraro smiles briefly.

"I would like to ride with my mother, and Angelina would like to ride with her husband if that's okay."

Officer Ferraro says, "I'll find out and let you know. Hold on." Stepping aside, she engages in conversation with someone on her radio. While speaking, she's nodding her head. A few minutes later, she tells us we can ride along, and she will take us to the ambulances right now.

Angelina's worried face relaxes a bit once she hears she can be with Vinny.

I face Nico and Jamie.

"Yes, go," Nico says. "We'll meet you there."

If only Nico could come with me. I struggle to leave him behind after the intense moment we shared.

Angelina and I hold hands on our way to the ambulance. I glance back at Nico, fearing that the distance I put between us before will return.

As we approach the ambulance, smoke and a few resistant flames cling to the right side of the villa. Although the fire is almost under control, I can't deny the deep sadness I feel.

Another officer approaches and takes me to one ambulance while Officer Ferraro leads Angelina to the other.

The emergency technicians assist me as I climb into the vehicle. My heart sinks when I see my mother lying on the slightly reclined stretcher. Her hair is a mess and her face is dirty, but other than that, she looks okay. When she sees me, she removes the oxygen mask, opens her arms, and I fly into them. Our cries are silent; only our shaking shoulders reveal our overwhelming relief.

On the way to the hospital, she tells me the story of the terror that occurred at the villa. Her lower lip quivers as she recalls the details of how Luca broke into the villa, waving a gun around. He tossed long zip ties at my mother and ordered her to tie everyone to the kitchen chairs. When she refused, he held the gun against Nonna's head and threatened to shoot her.

My mother's eyes fill with tears. "Then he tied me to a chair," she says. "I tried to reason with him, and I begged him not to harm any of us, but—" She puts the oxygen mask back on her face for a few seconds.

I place my hand on her arm. "It's okay, Mom."

She removes the oxygen again. "His eyes were vacant, like the person I once knew and loved had disappeared. I can't believe he tied up Lena, his wife, his confidant, the one who stood by him and helped to hide him. What had she done to deserve that? I knew when I saw those empty eyes that it was too late for any reasoning. He was already too far gone.

"Luca told us he was going to set the villa on fire. His intention, as he stated, was to begin the fire in the two front rooms initially, so that we could all witness its burning and watch it to spread. You should have seen the grin on his face—pure evil—as if he took pleasure in our terror, fully aware that the fire would soon engulf us.

"And right before he struck the match, he admitted taking Julia Bernardi decades ago, as well as the other missing girls. He said he'd followed in his father's footsteps, and it was his father who helped him cover it up. His *father!* He confessed to abducting Bria and mentioned another woman named Mona, whom he planned to 'take care of next.'"

My mother's voice is weak and trails off as she cries. I wrap my arms around her, horrified at what she experienced and deeply grateful that she is unharmed.

"Do you know who called the fire department?" I ask, and she shakes her head no.

"Rest, Mom," I say. "You were so brave. Everything will be okay."

The technicians lower her stretcher and check her vitals as my mother closes her eyes.

Unfortunately for Luca, the fire didn't spread as quickly as he probably expected, and the first responders rescued my family just as it was reaching them in the kitchen.

I am overwhelmed with emotion and filled with rage at the details my mother shared of Luca's terror on my precious family—Nonna, my sweet Nonna.

How could he do this to them?

CHAPTER 34

ELLA

By the time we arrive at Arcispedale Santa Maria Nuova hospital, my mother has drifted off to sleep, exhausted from her ordeal. The hospital staff whisks us from the ambulance to the lobby and to an examining room right away. Before the door closes, I think I see Jonella pass by our room, but when I get to the door, she is nowhere to be seen.

Officer Ferraro enters my mother's room, followed by Nico and Jamie. When I see Nico, I want to run to him. But I hold back, questioning the realness of his recent concern for me. Was it just in the moment, or did he mean what he said about being there for me? As soon as our eyes lock, he rushes to me and wraps me in his arms. *It was real.*

Jamie seems hesitant and awkward standing next to Nico. I reach for her and pull her into a hug. My mother smiles when she sees Nico, but she does a double take when she sees Jamie before she closes her eyes again.

The doctor on call tonight tells us they should be able to release my mother within the next couple of hours. Vinny, Nonna, and Lena will spend the night because the smoke has had a significant impact on their breathing, so they will give them oxygen and monitor them through the night. If all is well, they will release them tomorrow. Officer Ferraro has agreed to stay with them, which reassures me a little.

While Nico and Jamie are in the room with my mother, I check with the nurses at the information desk to see how the other three are doing. Thankfully, they are in satisfactory condition. I picture Angelina with her chair pulled close to Vinny's bed. She's probably got her head resting on her fist, watching Vinny's breathing.

As I return to my mother's room, Jonella is speaking with Dr. Girofolo a few feet away. She pretends not to see me, but I don't let her avoid eye contact. When Dr. Girofolo walks away, Jonella fidgets with her cell phone.

"Jonella!" I say.

Her eyes dart everywhere before landing on me. She acts surprised to see me.

I wave her over.

"You're not supposed to be here," she says, crossing her arms.

"My mother was in an accident," I say.

"Oh dear, I hope she is all right," Jonella says with concern.

"She will be," I say. "You're here later than usual. Putting in some overtime?"

She lets out a fake laugh. "I guess you could say that. I'm working closely with Dr. Girofolo on a presentation. He asked me to give it to the fellows at the end of the week." She keeps glancing at her phone.

"Is that so?" I reply, trying to hide my anger, and I do everything I can to keep my face neutral and my feelings hidden. Before I was suspended, Dr. Girofolo was preparing *me* to give that presentation.

"Yes," she says. "We work very well together." She jumps when her cell phone lights up with an incoming call. I swear I see the initials LP flash on the screen. Jonella fumbles with the phone, attempting to silence it, and then she slips it into her pocket.

"You can answer that," I say. "I don't mind."

"It's not important," she says nervously. The phone lights up in her pocket as another call comes through. "Excuse me, I have to take this call. Good to see you." She rushes down the hall as she puts the phone to her ear.

What are the chances that those initials LP belong to Luca Perri? But why would Luca call Jonella?

Because Luca has connections everywhere.

When I get back to my mother's room, I tell Nico and Jamie about my interaction with Jonella and the phone calls from an LP. They both think it's more than a coincidence, and they believe it can only be Luca, which I know in my heart to be true. It had to be one of Luca's dirty cops who planted the notes at the hospital. Knowing Luca, he placed Jonella into the same fellowship program as me to keep eyes on me. Who knows what he told her to make her loathe me so much. They have to be working together. In addition to having Jonella keep tabs on everything I was doing at the hospital, Luca also wanted to ruin my fellowship opportunity. And it worked.

After my mother is released, she, Nico, and I find Angelina sitting beside Vinny in his room, just as I'd imagined her to be. Angelina gets up right away and comes into the hallway so we don't wake Vinny. The frizzed edges of her hair fall wildly around her worried and tired face. She smiles through heavy-lidded, bloodshot eyes and gives us a sleepy hug when she sees us. She informs us that Vinny is doing well and anticipates his release tomorrow.

I then tell her about my uncomfortable run-in with Jonella and the LP caller.

Angelina rolls her eyes and says, "We know that's Luca, and he most certainly has been working with Jonella this whole time. They're getting close to getting him, El. I can feel it all coming together."

"We have a lot of evidence now and eyewitnesses, but we still don't have Luca," I say.

"Did you hear about Bria?" Angelina says, glancing over her shoulder before continuing. "There are three police officers outside her door in case the person who did this to her returns to finish what he started. And that's not all," she continues. "Bria has awakened from her coma. She is weak and frail, but she mumbled a name: Luca."

Hearing this excites me, not because of what Bria went through but because she now connected Luca to her, and I'll bet Luca wasn't counting on that.

"Strangely, though, they said Bria also said the name Lorenzo."

"Lorenzo?" I say, confused. "The only person I know named Lorenzo is Gianna's husband. She must have been confused."

"Well, that's what she said," Angelina says.

"How were you able to get that information," I ask.

"Well, since no family has come to claim Bria, I have acted as her family member," Angelina says.

"And she didn't ask you who you were?" I ask.

"I think she was relieved to see anyone other than Luca's horrible face, and she must have just gone with it. She knew I wanted to help her, and I told her I would protect her. Everyone assumed I was a family member. And when the police questioned Bria, I was there."

"That's incredible," I say.

"But that's not even the most incredible thing," Angelina says. "When Bria was a little more alert, she told the police that someone else was being held captive in Luca's old house . . . and she said *old house*. She said it was another young woman."

"Mona must have been at the house when we were there," I say. "How could we not have known?"

Then I recall the noise I heard in the distance when Angelina and I were leaving Poppy's and Luca's old home. *An old house.* I remember it was unsettling to hear the noise but not know what it was or where it was coming from. I also remember what my mother said about Luca confessing before he set the villa on fire.

He'd said something about a woman named Mona. And he was going to take care of her next.

"Angelina! Did she say the woman's—"

"Mona," Angelina blurts. "She said Mona."

I glance at my mother and Nico. "Oh my God. We have to go."

With no time to spare, I find Officer Ferraro and tell her what Luca told my mother before he set fire to the villa, and then I give her the address to Poppy's and Luca's childhood home. She immediately makes a call and sends officers to the Perri family home on Via Gratta to search for Mona.

I feel the adrenaline pumping through me and want to go with them to the house to witness Mona's rescue and Luca's capture myself. Will they find Luca there? Will they get to Mona in time?

When we get to Nico's car, he insists that my mother, Jamie, and I stay at his apartment tonight. We agree to stay on the condition that we go to Via Gratta first.

CHAPTER 35

ELLA

The police take the highway to Via Gratta, and my mom, Nico, Jamie, and I follow the same back roads that Angelina and I had taken when we had first gone to Luca and Poppy's old home. Very few streetlights and porch lights are on this late at night. Everything is black—the sky, the roads, everything around us is dark. Even the brightest lights of our car are barely enough to illuminate the path ahead, which means we have to go slower than if we were to drive in the daytime.

The roads appear so different at night and, if it weren't for our GPS confirming our location, I'd start to question whether we're going the right way.

While we're driving, all I can think about is getting to the house and finding Mona. And praying that she is still alive. And fearing what will happen if we run into Luca while we're there.

"Ella, I have an idea," Jamie says. "When we get close, go around to the marina and park. I think we should come in through the back."

"But won't the police have the entire area surrounded?" my mother asks.

"Yes," she says, "but we won't be taking any path they will take."

"How will we get there, then?" I ask.

"Do you remember a long time ago when Sophia had given you all of Nina's letters to Poppy, and Nina mentioned or alluded to something about a secret passage?"

I had to think about this. When I first came to Italy two years ago, I'd stayed at Angelina and Vinny's villa, and that's where I met Marco and Sophia. They were very odd and for good reason. I didn't know it at the time, but Marco was Luca's nephew on Aunt Lena's side. Luca took Marco under his wing when Marco was young and, in the process, he exposed him to his illegal business and his involvement in crime.

Luca created a monster in Marco, who thought he was helping his uncle by stalking and manipulating the person who was trying to take Luca down: me. Meanwhile, Marco ended up in possession of some important letters from one of Poppy's oldest and dearest friends, Nina. These letters from Poppy to Nina revealed incriminating information about Luca, about his lies and deceit that had begun as a teenager, and they were the evidence I'd needed at the time to prove Luca had been lying and betraying all of us.

Sophia, Marco's fiancé, caught on to what Marco was doing when she found the letters he'd hidden. Thankfully, she had a change of heart and handed the letters over to me. Nina was Poppy's confidant and guide during a troublesome time in his life when he was serving in the war and being blamed for Gianna's disappearance. These letters further proved Poppy's innocence. Unfortunately, Poppy never found out if Gianna was alive before he passed, but he believed she was.

"Yes, I remember all of that vividly," I say.

"Didn't Angelina say something a while back about secret tunnels?" my mother asks. "Are they talking about the same thing?"

"Yes," Jamie confirms. "These are the tunnels that Luca used and still uses to this day. His father was the one who revealed them to Luca. It became their little playground, for lack of a better description. It makes me sick and I can't believe I supported him and looked up to him."

"Me too, Jamie," I say. We were both conned by Luca in unique ways. I'm glad Jamie sees that now.

"But other people are free to use the tunnels, too, aren't they?" Nico asks.

"Well," Jamie explains, "there are the public tunnels, which aren't used all that much anymore, and then there are the private tunnels off of those that only a handful of people know about."

"The layers of Luca just get worse and worse," my mother says.

Jamie shows us where to park, and we follow her along the shoreline and through the sand to an area where the beach meets the town. She takes us down a set of stairs to cobbled roads that stretch to the left and to the right and straight ahead. We turn left and dip under a walkway with a low ceiling. It's very dark and smells of old rusted metal. Stone walls flank either side of us, and it feels like we're walking in a tunnel.

"This is the area no one goes to anymore," Jamie's whispered voice echoes through the tunnel.

About ten minutes into our walk, Jamie turns to us and tells us to stay quiet. Up ahead I can hear rummaging noises. As we walk, it feels as if we're descending lower although there are no stairs. Jamie stops walking right away, and we almost bump into each other.

"The door is open," she says.

"What does that mean?" I say.

"It's the door leading to another secret tunnel to Luca's old house," Jamie says.

"What?" I say, staring into the faces of my equally surprised mother and Nico. "I was here with Angelina, but there was nothing in the house that appeared to lead to anything like this."

"With Luca, everything is a facade," Jamie says.

As we're about to enter through the door, an officer blocks our way. She is coming from the other side, and she's angry and wants to know why we're there and how we know about this tunnel. Jamie does the explaining and tells the officer that the man who lived there is her grandfather. She asks if they've caught him, but they're not saying.

"The girl who was here—is she okay? Did you find her?" Jamie asks.

But, of course, the officer explains she can't divulge any information like this and tells us to get out of there or she will arrest us. She stands firm with her arms crossed, not budging until we turn around and walk away.

"Now what do we do?" I ask Jamie.

"Unfortunately, there isn't anything we can do except wait to hear something on the news," she says.

"Does Luca still try to contact you?" I ask.

"Not anymore," she says. "Not since he learned that I've been helping you."

"What a waste to come all this way for nothing," my mother says.

"It's not a waste," Jamie says. "This is a good sign. Things are finally happening. Everything, including this secret passage, has now become exposed. There are less and less places for *Nonnino*—Luca—to hide."

CHAPTER 36

MONA

'm awake. And still alive. But my eyes, my head, and every bone in my body are heavy like they're covered in wet cement. I force my eyes open and strain to see through my blurred vision. There's a pulsing light, dimmed by shadows. The nagging pain at my side reminds me of my reality. Am I back in that room again, or has he moved me somewhere else? I'm surprised he hasn't killed me by now. I wish he had. Better to be dead and away from him than alive and with him.

Disgust and defeat overwhelm me—how close I'd come to being free. I saw the light ahead, and I knew I only had a few more steps to go. The fresh air coming in from the back door made my eyes water. I knew I was close. Despite my best efforts, I was not strong enough or not smart enough to escape him. He is unbeatable. How could he run like that after losing all that blood and nearly passing out? He outsmarted me and outran me, and now I'll never be free of him.

I blink a few more times as warm tears spill from the corners of my eyes into my hair. I think I might see the silhouettes of someone in the room—actually two people. Who has he brought with him? My chest tightens and tears trickle to my ears. The people are talking just above a whisper. Maybe they're trying to figure out what to do with me. Maybe these are the people who "take care of loose ends" like me.

My back feels cushioned, like I'm lying on a bed or a cot, but I'm covered. Maybe they'll wrap me in the mattress and discard me like trash. It doesn't even matter, though. I can't take it anymore—I've reached my breaking point. I couldn't get away right now even if I tried and I can't move a muscle. It feels like someone drugged me.

I force a scream and it escapes my lips, much quieter than it sounded in my head, but someone hears it and turns towards me. Both of them are coming closer. My mouth completely dries up and tears flood my eyes, making it difficult for me to see anything. They're talking to me. A soft voice is saying something.

"It's okay," one of them says, blotting my eyes and cheeks with a warm cloth.

"She's waking up," another voice says, and two others rush over. Now I think there are four of them standing over me, backlit by a soft, glowing light.

The first voice speaks again, gentle and soothing. "You're safe," she says.

But I'm afraid to open my eyes again. Afraid to trust this kindness. Maybe it's only a dream.

Someone's warm hand takes mine and holds it between both of their hands. Another puts a warm, wet washcloth on my forehead and pats it over my face, my cheeks, my hairline.

"Try to open your eyes," the first voice says.

I'm terrified, but I try slowly to blink my eyes. Small glimpses at first and then longer until they are completely open. Two women dressed in similar clothes are on either side of me. One of them continues holding my hand while the other appears to be monitoring the beeping and flashing screens next to my bed. And it really is a bed—a soft, comfortable bed with clean sheets and a fluffy pillow.

And the best sight of all is standing at the foot of my bed. They're both crying and hugging each other and, when the nurses move aside, my parents rush in and cover me with hugs and kisses. It's almost too much to bear at once, but I sink into it and relish in their love. I never thought I'd see my parents again.

But then fear jolts through me and my body jerks. One nurse puts her hand on my arm. "You are safe. You've been rescued. Do you remember any of that?"

"Where is he?" I say.

"They're looking for him now."

"No!" I shout. "I'm not safe! He'll be here—he'll come back for me."

"No one is going to let that happen," she says, pointing to the door where three armed policemen are standing. "We will not let anyone other than a family member with the proper identification through those doors. You are safe here."

I want to trust them, but I'm petrified. I don't trust that I'm fully safe. Not while he's out there.

After a few minutes, a female and a male police officer enter the room and I recognize them right away, but at first, I can't place them. I can picture myself running toward the light and feeling the cool air. I remember feeling weak, and I knew if I didn't get out of there then, I never would. When I got to the half-opened door, I pushed it all the way open as two officers ran toward me. I must have fainted just as they got to me, but I *had* made it out. And theirs were the first faces I saw when I had finally escaped.

Now, in the hospital room, they introduce themselves to me as Officer Agosto and his partner, Officer Larisa. They ask me if I feel strong enough to speak with them. My parents emphatically say no, telling me they want me to rest, but I assure them I'm okay and I want to talk to the officers.

"Before we get started," Officer Agosto says, "we would like you to identify the man who did this to you. Would it be okay to show you a photograph?"

Although I never want to see his face again, I want him to pay for what he did to me and anyone else. He is a dangerous man, and if he is still out there he needs to be caught before he hurts someone else. So, reluctantly, I agree to take a look at the photograph.

Officer Larisa holds the photograph in front of me and tells me to look when I'm ready. At first, I can't look, but I make myself. As soon as I see his face, horrible and rage-filled, and I see his dark, piercing eyes, I want to throw up. My body trembles and I have to look away because it feels like I'm right back in that house with him.

"Yes," I say, looking away. "It's him. Please get it away from me."

"His name is Luca Perri," Officer Agosto says. "Have you ever seen him before? Do you know him?"

I shake my head no.

"Thank you," Officer Larisa says. "We know that was difficult for you, and we appreciate your cooperation. We are doing everything we can to get this man."

During the rest of our discussion, the officers tell me about a girl named Bria who they had to rescue from the trunk of Luca's car. They said Luca had become weak from the stabbing and loss of blood. I must have been running so fast that I put enough space between us and he couldn't catch up to me. He also knew authorities were closing in on him and he had to get rid of Bria first before coming back for me.

According to what Bria shared with the police and what police have pieced together, they believe that Luca's original intent was to throw me in the trunk with Bria and dispose of us both at the same time. But when I stabbed him, it thwarted his plan. They think Luca assumed the door I ran out of had been locked. But it wasn't. Authorities who were guarding Bria's room alerted Officer Agosto and Officer Larisa to my location. I don't know how they could have known where I was unless Bria somehow knew.

"We'll stay with you until you're released," Officer Larisa says. "We'll be right outside your room if you remember anything else or if you need anything."

"It will always be one of us or both of us outside your door," Officer Agosto says. "We will protect you. You have nothing to fear."

"Thank you. I appreciate everything you're doing," I say. "If he knows I'm here and alive, he will find me. Please do everything you can to get him before he does. I beg you."

The officers reassure me they are the closest they have ever been to finding Luca. There is significant evidence against him now, including eyewitnesses and officers staking out each of Luca's houses. There is nowhere else for Luca to go. It's just a matter of time. In the meantime, they tell me I'll be safe at the hospital. I pray they are right about that.

CHAPTER 37

ELLA

We keep the television on and check the news channels for any information, but we probably won't hear anything until the morning. After a couple of hours, when my mother and Jamie have gone to bed, Nico asks me to sit with him on the *loggia* off of the living room. Whimsically strung bistro lights adorn the roof and outer wall of the *loggia*. He brings with him two glasses and a bottle of red wine.

"I thought it might help you relax after everything that happened today."

"Good idea," I say.

A cool, refreshing breeze of nighttime air swirls around us. We clink our glasses together and sit side by side in comfortable silence. It's a dark night, almost completely black except for the bistro lights giving a warm ambiance.

I still feel a bit unsettled by the lack of closure I had hoped for today, but I will admit there is a shift in our atmosphere. Something has changed, and—I daresay—I'm hopeful that things just might head in the right direction for my family.

Or maybe it's me who's shifting. Maybe I'm letting things go and trying less to manage the events that have happened to my family. I'm realizing that no matter how hard I've tried to control the outcome with Luca, it's always been an uphill battle because he is always a few steps ahead. And if Luca's revenge on me and my family was to kill us for exposing his sins, wouldn't he have done that by now? He's had countless opportunities and near misses, which now seems unlikely for someone with such precision and accuracy. Someone with severe obsessive and compulsive thoughts that control his actions.

If it weren't for whoever called the fire department, Luca might have succeeded in kidnapping, arson, and murder at the villa. It's peculiar to me that the fire department and police arrived just in time. It makes me wonder if Luca might have been the one to call.

Regardless, I think things are changing because *now* Luca is the closest he's ever been to being caught. As the police have said he might even be dead already because of his injuries. If Luca is still alive, this time there is a wealth of evidence against him, including DNA and wanted pictures. All we're waiting for is Luca himself. Maybe that's why I'm a little more at ease than I normally would be.

I wonder what Nico is thinking. I have so much I want to say right now while we have this opportunity alone. But I still doubt myself and the feelings I have about our relationship at this moment. Can we get through this or has too much happened between us? Should it be this hard or is it *me* making it harder than it is? Where do I begin?

When I look at Nico, he seems pensive. He's been staring at the bistro lights with a serious expression. Is he thinking the same thing I'm thinking? Will he tell me he still believes we should be apart? At the same time, we face each other and begin speaking.

"You go first," I say.

"Ella," he says. His voice is smooth like honey. He places his hand on mine. "I am deeply sorry for everything that has happened to you and your family. I regret not being there for you—supporting you more. If only I had listened to you. While

I was concerned about you, I couldn't help but think about how these things were affecting our relationship and myself as well. But that's not fair. You were right about Luca, and no one knows that better than you. I guess what I'm trying to say is that I'm sorry. I should have never told you we needed space. And—"

"Nico, it's okay," I say, placing the palm of my hand on his cheek. "I forgive you. But this is not all on you. You were right. I got a bit obsessed with Luca. Maybe the time apart has given you perspective, and for that, I'm grateful."

Nico's mouth opens and faint signs of a smile appear on his lips.

"If you think that someday you will want to move forward with our relationship, I just want you to know that I'll be ready. But there's no rush. Take as much time as you need." It's difficult to get these words out, but I have to let be whatever is meant to be, and I have to respect his feelings.

"No, Ella," he says. "If there's anything I've learned over these last few weeks, it's that I don't need more time or more space from you. And I'm not good when I'm without you. The only thing I want is *you*."

My heart melts.

He takes my hand. "And I want you to know that if you need to see this through with Luca until you have closure, then I'll be by your side. You don't have to hide things from me anymore. We will wait until Luca is caught to get married if it's important to you. We have our whole lives ahead of us."

Knowing how Nico felt about my involvement with Luca, I'm stunned to hear him say this so sincerely. I honestly started doubting we would ever get married. I want to pinch myself to make sure it's real.

"Nico, are you sure about this?"

"I've never been more sure about anything in my entire life," he says.

"Then we're not waiting," I say. "We're not putting off our marriage or our happiness until we get the closure we want with

Luca." I can't believe it's my voice saying these words, but I mean them. I haven't been fair about this. "Luca is on the verge of being caught. It's going to happen. It's just a matter of time, and I feel strangely comfortable with that. I've had such tunnel vision that I didn't notice how I've stopped living, and that's exactly what Luca wants me to do. He wants me to stop living my life, and I'm not doing that anymore."

Nico's face lights up. "What exactly are you saying?"

"Nico, let's get married. Soon. Like . . . next weekend."

"Next weekend? Are you serious?" he says.

"I almost lost my family tonight. Life is too short to wait around for things to happen. I don't need a fairytale wedding with hundreds of people I hardly ever see. I'm not interested in an extravagant dress, an overpriced venue, and the headache of all those plans. I just need my family, your family, you and me."

"Are you sure about this, El?" Nico says.

"I've never been more sure," I say.

During the next hour, we finish the bottle of wine and make plans for our wedding on the beach. It will be simple, beautiful, and perfect. I'm so excited that the next thing I do before going to bed is wake my mother up and tell her everything.

CHAPTER 38

ELLA

One week later

I t's the morning of my wedding day, and I'm staring into the mirror as Emma wraps the curling iron around a few strands of my hair and gently pulls out a soft, wavy curl. In a few hours, I will marry my best friend in the backyard of my cousin Emma's house, right on her private beach. A safe beach. Emma's house is the perfect location, as it is where my mother and I first laid eyes on the mysterious Gianna, who at one time we only knew on the pages of Poppy's diary. It's where we met Grace, Gianna's other daughter and my mother's twin sister, and Grace's daughter, Emma. Gianna's sister, Sienna, also joined us on that magical day. A whole family I never knew existed on Poppy's side. Marrying Nico on Emma's beach in front of the most important people in my life couldn't be more perfect for us.

My insides are squealing with joy to start this chapter of my life with Nico. I feel relaxed and, finally, a sense of contentment. But I'd be lying if I said I wasn't a little nervous. It's impossible to not have *some* thoughts about Luca, even though this past week has been uneventful as far as he's concerned. It's unrealistic to think I could dismiss him completely when he's been a nagging thought in my mind for the last two years.

I keep thinking about the tunnel Jamie brought us to. Luca's private tunnel, which connected to the once well-traveled passage between the beach side of Scilla and the fishing village of Chianalea. It was all over the news the next day about Luca being the prime suspect in the abduction of both Bria and Mona, with his picture plastered on the screens of every news channel. One article mentioned his "houses of horror" and referred to his secret tunnel as his "alley of death." Another article stated Luca is the crucial link connecting the decades-old cold cases of the girls who were eventually discovered near the marina to the recently found women.

And it identified four police officers and retired police officers who had allegedly been working under Luca since long before when his father was in charge. It was Jimmy Boxxo, the retired officer we'd met when we were talking with Officer Ferraro, who helped crack the case. He'd come back to his department to help with a few cold cases. Jimmy was also working undercover and following leads on some of the crooked police officers, and he offered proof of their involvement.

Right after the emotional reunion between Bria and Mona and their families, both women asked to speak with me. They thanked me for not giving up on exposing Luca and said that my determination to collect evidence and keep pressure on the police led to their freedom. They also thanked Jamie for doing the right thing, even though Luca was her grandfather. Eventually, both women will testify against Luca, and authorities will keep them in protective custody until Luca has been officially caught.

Luca is cunning and elusive, and nothing about him surprises me anymore. But this can no longer be my problem. I have done everything in my power and more to get this man captured, and now—especially today—I have to put my trust in the police. Thankfully, the officers who truly work hard at their job protecting people and keeping law and order are the ones searching for Luca. So I have to have faith in that now.

This is my day, and I won't let Luca or thoughts of Luca creep in and take it away from me.

Things are changing. Good things are happening. Dr. Girofolo met with me immediately following the press release on Luca. All of the fellows except for Jonella were there. Dr. Girofolo offered a formal apology on behalf of himself and the hospital regarding their erroneous claims that I was harassing Jonella. He presented paperwork for me to sign, which renounced the accusations against me and stated my readmittance into the fellowship program.

Although it still leaves me with a sour taste in my mouth, I have accepted their apology and plan to return to my position as a fellow. Everyone seemed genuinely happy for me that the investigation was over and that I was returning. When I asked Miles where Jonella was, he said they were told that she was transferred to another hospital. Nonna, Aunt Lena, and Vinny were released from the hospital a few days ago, and they have been staying at my Aunt Grace's house. Gianna and Sienna met us at Emma's yesterday and helped us set up everything inside and outside of the house for the wedding. Last night, my mother and I stayed over at Emma's, while Nico stayed at our apartment, ensuring we had separate spaces to prepare and truly see each other for the first time before walking down the aisle.

While Emma finishes my hair, there's a knock on my door, and I jump slightly. My mother peeks and then she steps in and closes the door.

"I have something for you," she says, holding something behind her back.

Emma leaves to give us some time alone.

I get up from the chair and face my mother. How lucky I am to have her.

She puts a small, white gift bag on the table, smiles at me, and says, "Before you walk down that aisle, I want you to know how incredibly proud I am to have you as my daughter and as my friend. I am so proud of everything you have done—all the obstacles you've pushed through, and especially what you did for Poppy. We have all sacrificed a lot, but none more than you. Because of you, we are all here together, celebrating your wedding with all the members of our family. And it's because of your unwavering dedication and determination." We both blink away tears, and she hugs me. "I love you so much," she says.

Then she takes the gift bag and hands it to me.

I remove the sparkly white tissue paper on top, and inside the bag are two small boxes and a book. I remove the first box and open it.

"The necklace," I say. "You fixed it . . . for me?"

This is not just any necklace. It's *the* necklace that confirmed Gianna was alive when I first discovered there was a Gianna. I had discovered that, long before I was born, Gianna and Poppy were in love and expecting a baby—my mother—right before Poppy was deployed to fight in World War II. Poppy had this necklace made for Gianna to wear while he was away. I've always loved the beautifully scripted gold "F & G Forever," which I later learned stood for Franco and Gianna Forever. Gianna wore that necklace every day, including the day Luca attacked her and left her for dead in the woods behind the vineyard.

My mother was only a baby when Luca left her on the doorstep of his childhood home, knowing his mother would keep the baby and raise her as her own. In the attack, the *G* from the necklace had broken off and fallen into the baby carriage. My mother always wore the necklace with the *G*, and as a child I'd assumed it stood for *her* name, Gabriella. But I was wrong; it was for Gianna.

My mother wipes a tear from her cheek. "I had it restored to its original design and added Gianna's, Poppy's, and your birthstones to it," she says, pointing to each stone.

I struggle to hold back tears. "I don't know what to say. I'm so touched. Will you help me put it on?" My mother clasps the necklace at the back of my neck, and when I see it in the mirror, lying against my skin, it takes my breath away.

In the second box is a small antique framed photo of Poppy about the size of a half dollar. It has a clip on the back.

"You can attach this to your flowers so he'll be with you as you walk down the aisle," she says. She takes it and fastens it to the ribbon on the underside of my flowers so, as I hold my flowers and walk down the aisle, his picture will face me.

"Look what you've done to my makeup," I say, laughing and crying and blotting my face with a tissue. "I don't know if I can take anymore," I say.

I reach into the bag for the last item, the book. I open it and my heart melts again. It's a book of all of Poppy's recipes, even the secret ones. When I was a teenager, Poppy had given me a box of recipes. My mother took each one and had them formatted and printed into a book.

"Oh, Mom," my voice catches. I put my hand to my mouth and swallow the rising sob. "This is so special. *You* are so special to me."

We hug once more, holding on to each other tightly, and a few minutes after she leaves, Emma steps in, reminding me it's time to get going. I glance at the clock, take a deep breath, and open the door.

CHAPTER 39

ELLA

'm standing with my mother at the edge of Emma's patio. A warm breeze from the Tyrrhenian Sea caresses the hem of my dress, whirls around us, and beckons us to walk down the stony path toward the pergola. Neat rows of crisp white chairs face the pergola and the sea before us. My family and Nico's family sit and whisper while they wait. Four undercover police officers, Agosto, Larisa, Ferraro, and Paulo, position themselves near the house, the patio, and the pergola, and I feel safe knowing they are there. I left my purse on the patio, tucked behind a pillow on the sofa. Inside my purse is Jamie's gun, which I only have as an extra precaution.

Sheer white fabric gently falls at each of the four corners of the pergola, waving in the breeze, and floral vines cling to its legs. It's a beautiful sunny day except for an occasional rumble of thunder and a few gray clouds in the west.

When the first few notes of the piano play, my mother and I glance at each other, smile, and begin our walk.

My mother and I walk down the aisle arm in arm. The smiles on the faces of my entire family as they stand facing us, the peaceful feeling in this moment, are all surreal to me. As we walk, I catch glimpses of Nico in the pergola, but his face is mostly hidden. To the right is another pergola, which Emma rented for the dinner. A white wooden table extends from one end of the pergola to the other, surrounded by white chairs. An exquisite floral arrangement stretches the length of the table.

About two-thirds of the way down, I see Nico waiting for me. He's wearing sand-colored khakis and a white linen shirt. His hair bounces in the wind. The moment his eyes meet mine, his hand flies to his mouth for a second and then up to his wet eyes. His reaction makes me even more emotional, and we're both crying as I finish my procession.

Nico takes my hand. "You are stunning," he says, and I melt into his chocolate-brown eyes.

"You are too," I reply.

My mother places her hands on us, and we face her. I'm surprised to see her standing where our deacon should be standing.

"I hope you like this surprise," she whispers. "Instead of Emma's deacon, I'd like to be the one to marry you." She must have read my confused reaction because then she says, "I became ordained online. It was pretty simple."

Nico and I glance at each other and almost laugh, but then we tell her we're ready to get started.

We have a sweet and simple ceremony, take pictures, then gather at the table for dinner. The music plays, and Nico takes my hand and leads me to the dance floor. We dance close, forehead to forehead, holding each other. Then everyone else, even Angelina, Vinny, Nonna, and Aunt Lena are dancing. I dance until my feet hurt and I have to step away for a minute to take a break.

But my sister, Liv, and my brother, Sal, drag me back to the dance floor because our favorite song is playing, and the three of us hold on to each other in a circle like we used to when we were little. We dance the next three songs together. It brings tears to my eyes. I didn't realize how much I missed them and need them. It makes me so happy that they traveled to Italy for me.

My mother approaches us and gives us a group hug. "I got a lot of great pictures of the three of you," she says, pulling up the photos on her phone. We crowd together over her shoulder as she swipes through them. She has incredible shots of everyone candid and posed throughout the night and several of the three of us being our usual crazy selves, making faces and dancing funny. "Wait, go back to the last one," I say, pointing. "That one."

I take the phone from my mother's hands and zoom in. It's a picture of Sal and me laughing and pointing at Liv when she fell. But behind us, where other people are dancing, I see something else—no, *someone* else. I can't get a complete picture because they're blocked by other people dancing.

"What is it?" Liv says.

"It's nothing," I say, walking away. *But it's not nothing.* "Send me those pictures, please. I'll be right back."

I can't believe it. It can't be. He was here—*is* here somewhere.

He actually had the balls to come here. How did he know? How had he stayed under the radar until now, of all days? He couldn't have been more than a few feet behind us when my mother took the picture.

I text the officers right away and see three of them fly to the west side of the house, undoubtedly searching for Luca.

Nico must have noticed something wasn't right, and he immediately comes to me as I'm standing outside of the dance floor, studying the empty spaces in and around our family. I show him the photo, and anger flashes in his eyes. Nico examines each photo my mom sent to confirm it's Luca and to see if he shows up in any other photos.

I ask Officer Ferraro if we should clear the area, but she tells me it's better to keep everything normal as if we do not know of Luca's presence. The officers have the area covered and they're ready. She asks to see the pictures and, while she's examining them, I see movement near the edge of the pergola closest to the sea.

It's hard to tell what it is because the bistro lights cast strange shadows on the sand. If Luca is by the beach, then who are the officers pursuing near the house?

Our band singer approaches and asks Nico for his opinion on something. He gives me an uncomfortable look, but for the sake of keeping things normal, he says he'll only be a few seconds, and then he goes. When I no longer see him, I slip away as well.

Staying out of the lights, I use the darkness to hide myself as much as possible until I can get to my purse on the patio. I put the strap over my head and across my body, keeping my right hand on top of the purse. I cautiously look around to get my bearings, slip off my shoes, and move closer to the edge of the pergola, where I saw and continue to see movement. As I approach, I see footprints in the sand leading to the beach. It could be anyone's footprints, but since the movement has now stopped near the pergola, I follow them.

My stomach flips as I realize how vulnerable I am, but there's no turning back now. I can only hope that the officers are also heading this way and that Luca has come alone. The wind picks up and thunder growls in the distance. The restless sea wildly rushes around my ankles.

And as a shaking thunder rolls, I sense a looming presence behind me.

CHAPTER 40

ELLA

"Looking for me?" says a deep-toned, gravelly voice.

My fingers move to the latch on my purse. My skin crawls and prickles.

"Don't do anything you might regret. We *are* by the water, after all."

My pulse races. I stop and slowly turn around. "You won't get away with this," I say.

"Oh, Ella," he says sarcastically. "What was the name your Poppy used to call you? Ella-my-Bella, or something stupid like that? I used to hate it when he called you that."

"I could scream, and they will be on you in minutes."

"It's such a shame that it has to end like this . . . on your wedding day," he says.

"I will kill you if I have to, Luca." I hear my voice trembling, and he probably does, too.

He tuts his tongue. "I would hate for another body to wash up on the shore."

I quickly pull the gun from my purse and aim it at him at the same time he aims his at me. "Did you think I would come here unprepared?" he says.

"Don't make me shoot you," I say. *Death is too easy.*

"What if I shoot first?"

"Then we'll both die right here in this sea," I say.

"No," he says, stepping closer. "Only you will die today."

He could shoot and kill me right now, so why hasn't he?

"Do not come any closer," I warn.

But he takes another step, and in the glint of the moon I notice bruising and swelling on the right side of his neck, and I see an occasional grimace on his face.

"Now, turn around and walk into the water like a good girl," he says. "You have taken my life, and I am about to take yours."

"What happened to you, Luca? How did you become this— this evil person? You must have pretended to be a devoted uncle the whole time. Did you ever love us?" *Where are the police?*

"You did this, Ella," he says. "You brought this on. Now walk."

His cold-hearted voice is flat and robotic. My toes grip the sand and my hands remain wrapped tightly around the gun, my finger positioned on the trigger. I'm just about ready to shoot and end this madness once and for all.

But then I recall a conversation I had with a patient while I was in my residency in the States. He was an inmate, a psychopath who required heart surgery, and I was part of his cardiology team. He'd said that to disarm a narcissistic psychopath, you have to think like one.

I need to keep Luca talking and make him think he's in control until the absolute last minute.

Instead of seeking immediate justice by killing him, the police could apprehend him and sentence him to life in prison for what he has done to us. And if a narcissist spends the rest of his life in a jail cell, constantly reminded that he's not in control, maybe that is the justice we want.

Luca loses his footing and fires his gun, and the bullet whizzes past my head. It shocks me, and I lose my balance and almost fall into the water. Luca swings at me but misses and becomes more unsteady. He falls towards me, and with all my might, I thrust my fist right into that bruised area on his neck. He releases an animalistic moan and winces in pain, and then he drops his gun into the surf. My toes grip the sand harder as the water rushes to my knees and I steady the gun in my hands.

It's come down to this one moment.

I'm face to face with Luca, now my nemesis, and I have the opportunity to end him..

Luca cups his hand at his neck and attempts to stand, but he's swaying as the waves rush in. A painful grimace replaces his glare.

I could easily shoot him now and he would die right here in the sea, the same sea where at least two of his victims' bodies floated to the shore by the marina.

But I can't shoot him. Not because I don't want him to die, but because I want him to live every day in pain for what he's done to us.

"I never wanted it to come to this, Luca," I say, my voice cracking.

Behind Luca, I think I see the officers finally approaching on the sand. A few others follow behind them. I try to keep Luca engaged with me as the officers close in.

Luca looks into my eyes and, although his are empty, his face softens slightly. "You were my favorite," he says.

In a flash, I catch a glimpse of the man I thought he was.

"You were mine," I say, recalling how he'd stepped in without hesitation to help my mother when my father died in the accident. I was just a little girl. Aside from Poppy, Nonna, and my mother, Luca was my favorite person.

"If only you hadn't meddled," he says. His eyes remain fixed on me as he reaches his left hand into the water and waves it around. And I'm watching him—watching that left hand.

"If only you were who I thought you were," I say.

"You could have pulled the trigger by now," he says, as if he's testing me.

"That wouldn't be enough," I say as two officers encroach upon Luca.

When they try to hold him down, Luca passively submits. I'm surprised that he's giving up so easily. But Luca's left hand leaves the water. He rams his head into the officer directly behind him, making him flinch in pain. Luca swiftly pulls a second gun from his jacket and fires at the wounded officer.

The other officer shoots at Luca. Luca cries out in surprise, letting go of his gun and falling into the water. The officer lunges at Luca, and for a few seconds, I can't tell what's going on.

Over the radio, a third officer announces, "Officer down! We need backup! Officer down!" He joins the officer as they wrestle with Luca. But together, they're stronger than Luca and they pull him out of the water, yank his arms back, and restrain him with handcuffs.

He's been shot, but he's not dead. I'm sure if he wasn't in pain he'd put up more of a fight, but Luca stops struggling. His face contorts as he likely realizes what's happening to him and there is nothing he can do about it. There's no one coming to get him out of this predicament.

He glances at me one last time with a dead stare. Then he hangs his head low as the police walk him up the beach and out of our lives for good.

Nico rushes to me and lifts me from the water. He puts me back down and kisses my head, my cheeks, my nose, my lips. "Thank God you're all right," he says. "Thank you, God."

I am overwhelmed with emotion, yet also at peace.

Our worried and frightened family stands by the pergola at the water's edge as Nico and I walk out of the sea. My mother runs toward us and embraces us. I hear someone clapping and then the rest join in a loud applause until we reach them at the center. When their applause dies down, they look at me with hesitance and anticipation, probably wondering what to do next or how I'll handle this on our wedding day of all days.

I don't think they expect my response, judging by their surprised faces as the sirens from the ambulance blares in the distance.

"Let's party!" I yell.

The uncertainty falls from their faces and an enthusiastic applause erupts once more.

Poppy is with us today, celebrating right beside us. He is proud of his family. He is proud of me. I sense his presence everywhere, but this time, it's different—this time, it's not shadowed by darkness.

EPILOGUE

Our wedding was the most incredible moment of our lives. After Luca was carted off to jail, I changed into dry clothes and we danced and talked and clung to each other long into the night. Maybe we were afraid to let go, to leave each other and go our separate ways. Perhaps we were afraid because we're so used to feeling afraid. We all wanted that feeling of happiness and relief to go on forever. I'm thankful to have had brief, private moments with each family member before they left for the night.

Gianna and her husband, Lorenzo, were the first to approach Nico and me. Speaking of Lorenzo, we later found out that Luca sometimes went by the name Lorenzo, among other aliases. When questioned, he told the police he was hoping to turn their attention away from him and towards Lorenzo, which was why he used that name with Mona.

Gianna's warm embrace and the admiration in her eyes filled me with love. "I can't tell you how proud I am of you, Ella," she said. "Because of you, we can live freely. We can breathe easily. We won't be looking over our shoulders anymore, waiting for something terrible to happen. No more hiding. I don't know how to live without hiding. Your determination and devotion to your Poppy, your belief in family, and the truth are what have lifted this heavy veil we've been wearing and freed us. Who would have thought that the granddaughter I never knew existed would be the one to save us all? I hope you feel a great sense of pride in what you have done."

Gianna's heartfelt words filled me with joy and peace. Then she took both of my hands and gazed into my eyes once more before she said goodbye for the night.

Angelina, Vinny, and Grace approached us next with worried, tired smiles. Angelina cupped my face in her hands. "You are a blessing to all of us," she says. Pulling my head close, she whispered, "But especially to me." She hugged me tight and said, "Make sure you keep wearing that Italian horn necklace." She looked at Nico. "I bought one for you, too, but I'll give it to you after the villa is repaired, when you and Ella come for dinner. I know you keep one in your car, but you should have one to wear too. Does that sound good?"

Nico laughed and he told her he was looking forward to it.

Nico's parents and his sister came to us next. They seemed genuinely happy for us, but I also noticed a bit of worry, and I can't blame them. They don't know my family very well yet, and, although they were well aware of what had been happening with Luca, I think what happened at the wedding still scares them. I have to give them credit for being supportive and understanding through it all.

Next came my sister, Liv, and my brother, Sal, with Nonna and Aunt Lena trailing slightly behind. "You are amazing," Liv said. "I am so proud of you."

"We all are Ella," Sal added. "We have to be better about staying in touch, especially now that you're living in Italy. And congrats on your return to the hospital. I knew they would welcome you back after they confirmed your innocence. It was just a matter of time."

On their way out, they promised to come and see me before they went back to the States. Then they stepped back to allow Nonna and Aunt Lena in.

Aunt Lena looked up at me with her chubby little face and I pulled her in close. I whispered, "I'm sorry I doubted you, Aunt Lena."

"Oh no, no," she said. "You had reason to doubt before, so why wouldn't you now?" She let me go and said, "I have to confess something I did. Remember when you couldn't find me at the airport? Well, I was talking on the phone to Luca. I'm so sorry I didn't tell you. I knew where he was because I told him I'd help him one last time. That was a lie, of course. I had no intention of helping him again. I finally came to my senses and saw him for what he was. And I'm pretty sure he was aware of that, which made him even more dangerous.

"I should also tell you it was me who made those phone calls and hung up. I wanted to tell you that I had turned against Luca so many times, but I lost my nerve each time. The thought of everything backfiring and the threat of Luca killing us scared me so much. I'm so sorry I made you worry more than necessary." She looked down at her feet. "I hope you can forgive me."

I'll admit it was shocking to hear Aunt Lena confess those things to me. I knew something wasn't right at the airport. But Aunt Lena was trying to do the right thing this time. It was maddening to think about all the chances she had to warn us, particularly when Luca's secrets were starting to surface. But I'd decided that there was no more looking back. No more regrets. If I wanted to move forward then I had to forgive, because my family is just too precious to me. "Of course I forgive you, Aunt Lena," I said. "We're all moving forward together now."

"Thank you, dear," she said, stepping aside for Nonna.

Just Nonna's presence alone makes my heart smile. "My little Nonna," I said.

"My beautiful granddaughter," she replied. "Remember when Poppy used to call you Ella-my-Bella?"

"Yes," I agreed, recalling Luca's mocking comment just before his capture.

"So much has happened since Poppy passed," she said. "So many surprises and too much pain. But, Ella," she pointed her crooked finger at me, "Poppy was wise to share his secret with you out of all of us." She brushed my cheek with her palm. "I know it was an immense sacrifice for you with terrible consequences, but Poppy knew if anyone could reveal Luca's secrets, find justice, and see it through to the end, you could do it. And you did. We no longer have this dark cloud above us." She kissed my forehead. "I have never felt more proud of you." She looked at Nico and took both of our hands. "I know you will build a beautiful life together."

Nonna means the world to me. I recall her sadness when we discovered that Gianna was not only real but alive. She'd known about Poppy's first love, and I think she worried sometimes that he still loved her. I know she worried about my love for her once I knew she wasn't my biological grandmother. I think I'd convinced her then that none of that mattered because, to me, she was my true grandmother.

Across the patio, Jamie was talking with both Emma and Sienna, the last three guests remaining. Since everything that happened with Luca, Sienna had distanced herself from me. I saw it in her eyes. She couldn't hold eye contact with me. Emma believes it's because Sienna really loved Luca and, although he betrayed all of us, including Sienna, she can't deal with the thought of him being out of her life for good. Emma also thinks I am now a constant reminder of Luca's demise. In addition, she believes Sienna's peculiar behavior may have indicated that she was involved with helping Luca at some point.

Perhaps Sienna was torn between helping Luca and doing what was right. Now it makes sense why Sienna's police report against Luca wasn't in the database. Could it be that in her own twisted way she was jealous of the obsessive love Luca had for Gianna and, in turn, she became obsessed with Luca? I guess we'll never know for sure.

I'd been unsure about including Jamie at my wedding, but she proved that her involvement in Luca's affairs this time wasn't for Luca but for my family and me. It took a lot to convince me of that, but her motives seemed sincere this time, and she risked her life trying to help us.

Before the wedding, I asked her why she appeared upset when I told her I had found the jewelry box in the wall behind the dresser. Judging her reaction, I assumed she knew about the jewelry box and was upset that I had found it, but I was wrong. Jamie said when I told her about the jewelry box, that's when she realized that the rumors she had recently heard about her grandfather were true. Knowing that made her angry, but she couldn't say anything about it then.

I took a leap of faith and decided to be friends with Jamie again. Not everything was driven purely by Luca. There was a time when Jamie and I were very close and our friendship was genuine. There was nothing better than having her in my life. If there's one thing I've learned, it's that we are all flawed, and that everyone deserves a second chance. Life is a gift, and we all deserve to make the most of this precious gift.

When Sienna and Jamie left and Emma and my mother went to bed, Nico and I returned to the patio. We were not yet ready to end that day. Nico lit a fire, and we sat side by side on the sofa, recounting everything that had happened from the moment my mother and I stepped off of the patio to the near catastrophe with Luca and our last moments with our beautiful family. The rolling waves relaxed us and it felt like we were the only ones on the beach.

I pondered the day when our beloved Poppy left this world and the hole in my heart that resulted. How Poppy's words sparked new life into my sad heart when he whispered, "Ella, there's a box. Find it." But then he quickly warned me, "Watch who you trust."

The wheels of his last words set into motion a series of events that followed over the next two years, and it wasn't anything I would have expected. But I knew those moments had to happen, and now that I was on the other side, I wouldn't take any of it back. I couldn't. Because the pain and suffering we endured gave us Gianna, Sienna, Aunt Grace, Emma, Angelina, Vinny, and, of course, Nico. We wouldn't have known about any of them.

As Nonna always said, "There are no coincidences in life. You are where you are meant to be. Everything happens for a reason." And Poppy always reminded me to be happy because life is too short. Our family has experienced a lot, and it has forever changed us. But we are also stronger than ever before. In the process, we saved at least two lives, probably more. And we've brought a long overdue justice to the little fishing village in Scilla. We have accomplished a lot.

* * *

To mark our one-month anniversary, I asked Nico to join me on the veranda, just like we did on Emma's patio on our wedding night. We recalled what people had said throughout the night that made us laugh or cry. We expressed how happy we felt and how blessed we were.

But there was one more gift I still had to give.

Nico's black locks blew back in the breeze, and I told him to wait right there on the sofa because I had something to give him.

"I thought we weren't doing that," he'd said.

"It's not what you think! Don't worry, I'll be right back."

I went to the kitchen pantry, grabbed a small gift bag I'd hidden on a shelf, and brought it to the sofa. The wind whooshed in as the fire sparked and crackled in the logs, releasing the perfect scent you can only get from a real bonfire. Like our wedding night, I wanted this moment to last forever.

My heart drummed wildly in my chest with excitement as I handed the bag to Nico. He gave me a suspicious look and quickly removed the tissue paper from the bag. He reached inside and pulled out a box. Pausing for a moment, he put the box on his knees and opened it. A puzzled expression crossed his face as he held the tiny knitted white baby booties. Then his head snapped up.

"What?" he said. "Is this real?"

I nodded.

"We're going to have a baby?"

"Yes," I said, hardly breathing.

We sat in awe on the sofa under a soft blanket beneath a star-lit sky. The memories of our beautiful day and especially the moment we just shared remind me that life is precious, even fragile. I snuggled into Nico as he clutched the booties in his hand and we stared into the fire and watched the flames dance in the wind.

As the liquid gold cascaded towards the sky, I drifted into a warm and cozy trance. A tendril of smoke escaped the fire, spiraling skyward as a glowing ember chased after it. I watched the ember fade into the night and relished in that one moment beneath the stars with Nico. I placed my hand on my stomach and smiled, pondering things I'd never given thought to before . . . like having a baby.

Perhaps if we have a boy, we'll name him Franco for my Poppy.

ACKNOWLEDGMENTS

I would like to thank several people for helping me bring this book to life. My husband, Jimmy, who has my books on display in his office, which often piques the interest of new readers. He spreads the word about my books by sending mass text messages, encouraging people to check them out and support me. Both my daughter, Sarah, and my son, Michael, are incredibly supportive of my writing, offering encouragement, a listening ear for my ideas, and valuable feedback at every stage.

My parents, Yolanda and Dennis Parnell, affectionately nicknamed my "managers" or "agents," are always the first to read my stories. They frequently recommend my books, and they are always searching for venues and chances to display them. Corrine and Gary Baccaro, my in-laws, enthusiastically spread the word about my books and can't wait for the next one to be released.

I'm also grateful to my editor and friend, Megan Basinger, whose sharp eyes and expertise helped refine this story and elevate it to a new level. I appreciate her straightforwardness, encouragement, and advice. It is just what I needed.

My beta readers serving as the VIP team during this pivotal stage were essential contributors to this process. I am grateful for their time, insightful feedback, and enthusiasm for this book.

My cousin Gary, who felt that the Ella Perri Mysteries required a final book to reach its full potential, was the driving force behind the existence of this novel. This novel was born from one particular idea he had about Luca and I loved it so much, I started writing it immediately. His inspiration and encouragement also led me to take a risk and try a new publishing platform.

My heartfelt thanks goes out to all my readers, whether you are discovering my books for the first time or have been a loyal supporter since the start. I am forever grateful to you.

And finally, *a special thank you* to the following people who, along with others, generously supported me throughout my Kickstarter campaign. I hope you all enjoy this book!

Gary & Corrine Baccaro
Linda Blum
Ally D
Dave Fedrau
Kim Hagenbach
Laura Jones
Tammy Lisi
Cindy Maiorani
Karen Moscato
Al Murphy
Dennis & Yolanda Parnell
Amanda Ross
Sierra Wanzer

ABOUT THE AUTHOR

K RISSY is an Award-Winning Finalist of the 2023 Page Turner Awards for Best Mystery/Cozy Mystery and the 2022 Wishing Shelf Book Awards in Adult Fiction. In 2022, the Page Turner Awards shortlisted her debut mystery novel, Buried Secrets, for Best Cover.

Krissy was born and raised in Upstate New York in the charming town of Fairport, where she has taught for over 25 years. She and her husband live in Fairport, New York, and Venice, Florida.

Krissy remembers her love of reading as a young child and how she couldn't get enough of great books such as The Chronicles of Narnia, Lord of the Rings, and The Hobbit. Her love of mystery was first revealed within the pages of From The Mixed-Up Files of Mrs. Basil E. Frankweiler by E.L. Konigsburg and Nancy Drew's mystery series. She mostly reads mystery, suspense, and thriller novels but also enjoys fantasy and historical fiction. Some of her favorite suspense/thriller authors are Janelle Brown, Karin Slaughter, Lisa Jewel, and Mary Kubica.

Krissy is a proud member of Sisters in Crime, Mystery Writers of America, and several online writing communities.

Krissy is currently teaching writing and reading to 5th-grade students and thoroughly enjoys sharing her love of writing and reading with her students.. When the school day ends, the writing begins, and there is never enough time for that. Krissy resides in upstate New York, not far from Skaneateles, where the Ella Perri Mysteries began.

BOOKS BY KRISSY BACCARO

ELLA PERRI MYSTERY SERIES
Buried Secrets
One Last Secret
Lies That Bind
Moment of Truth

SHORT FICTION
Luca
Psychological Thrillers Box Set

ANTHOLOGIES
Once Upon a Story
The Rearview Mirror

Dear Readers,

Thank you for reading *Moment of Truth*, the final book in the Ella Perri Mysteries series. If you enjoyed it, please consider leaving a brief review on Amazon or a post on my Facebook page. I love hearing from my readers.

To learn more about my upcoming book and to receive free mysteries and thrillers, visit my website and subscribe to my mailing list. You may unsubscribe at any time.

With gratitude,

Krissy Baccaro
https://krissybaccaro.com/books/